# New Beginnings: We Are On Our Own

## New Beginnings M/M Series Part One

### Kashel Char

WE ARE ON OUR OWN

## NEW
BEGINNINGS

Kashel Char Author

# Copyrights

# Disclaimer

This is a re-edit of Men of Phoenix, written by Stefan Pride. Stefan invited Kashel to co-author and update it with fresh thoughts, preparing it for an audiobook recording. It was re-titled Phoenix Code Copyright © 2022 Stefan Pride and Kashel Char.

Now Kashel holds the copyrights to New Beginnings: We Are On Our Own –New Beginnings M/M Series Part One Copyright © 2023 Kashel Char.

**Dear Reader/Listener**

This book is part of a planned post-apocalyptic sci-fi fantasy series featuring gifted scientists and soldiers falling in love. This story has explicit and graphic depictions unsuitable for young and sensitive readers or anyone offended by gay sex.

# Warning

U nless expressly noted, no part of this publication may be reproduced, scanned, stored in a retrieval system, or transmitted in any form or by any means, electronic, mechanical, photocopying, recording, or otherwise known or from now on invented, without the express written permission of the authors. The scanning, uploading, and distribution of this book via the internet or any other means without the author's permission are illegal.

# Contents

# Prologue

**Ishtar the Last Anunnaki**

**2046 A.D.**

**Environmental Project One**

**Antarctica**

**Earth**

"**H**elp!" I heard the muffled voice of a male calling from a distance outside. Scared that I had been discovered or drawing attention, I shut everything off and scurried outside to hide my time machine. "Help me!" the man called again. Huddling behind my ship, I scanned my surroundings with a quick left, right, up, and down sweep. It was cold as fuck. The light was dim, neither day nor night. I couldn't determine if it was sunset or sunrise and every now and then the sky seemed illuminated by green and yellow dancing light. It tinged the snow in blues and greens, the oddest spectacle I'd ever seen on Earth. Yet, I'd never been so far south. Behind me were hills and boulders covered in black and white patches of rock facing and snow. In front of me was the human settlement, Phoenix. Hope and shivers filled me as I witnessed the glow and shine of human potential.

From somewhere to my left, near an outbuilding I estimated to be about one hundred yards away, I heard more muffled cries, and possibly laughter. *I had minutes to hide the ship.* The outbuilding was attached to a gigantic translucent half-ball rotunda. Almost like the one covering Grayrak, but smaller and much brighter.

Apprehensive and freezing my butt off, I hoped no one had noticed me and was summoning guards. People moved around disinterested, others huddled together speaking with one another. Nobody was stressing or pulling their hair screaming, *oh my god, I spy with my little eye something parked on our front yard today.* I knew humans and knew it took only one little overachiever with a good eye to point me out. I dashed behind a snowbank where I started collecting arms full of snow. The golden two-passenger egg-shaped ship stood out like a beacon, screaming alien landing. The damn thing lay as I'd landed. Askew. I worked fast by scooping and packing layer upon layer of the icy-cold stuff.

"Spit on it! Let spit run out of your mouth and work it to the tip of your tongue," another deeper male voice replied. I frowned. It didn't sound like the yelling was about me. Laughter and choking sounds followed by ugly coughs and retching. I tipped my head to the side, trying to hear better. I recognized the voices of my friends. It sounded like Andrew and, most probably, his lover, Juandre.

"Why wasn't my ship white?" I asked the fates who had gifted me the time-machine-ship thing. I turned and flung the snow like a dog searching for a bone, eager to get to Andrew and Juandre before they went back inside.

"Stop laughing and help me! Go get table salt!" Juandre said, sounding like he had a mouth full of rocks. I looked over my shoulder, patting the last spot with a handful of snow. Because I wasn't wearing gloves my fingers were numb, and pain shot through them. My balls shrunk and retracted so deep they might never show themselves again. More laughter and fuck-you's followed. They were just around the corner. Elated, I spun to meet with them.

"Let go of me! Let me try something," Andrew laughed. They were clearly having sex against the wall as I turned the corner of the outbuilding. Bare-assed, Andrew's body covered Juandre's. It sounded like Juandre needed help. I glimpsed Andrew. He was as beautiful as I remembered him. He had cut his blond locks off, but I recognized his firm butt as if we'd fucked yesterday. He chuckled like a jubilant giant and kissed Juandre before he removed himself from his lover.

Sucking my numb fingertips to warm them, I suppressed my snickers to avoid being noticed. I scoped out the surrounding buildings. It seemed like a secluded and safe spot for a quick fuck. I couldn't see anyone else in our vicinity. They wouldn't have fucked here if they worried about their privacy.

I increased my pace, making my way over to them. Lifting my feet hip high, I approached while watching Andrew's bare ass from afar. It was as white as their surroundings. The blinding white stuff was everywhere and, by the look of it, very dangerous. Juandre, who I thought was as bright as he was cocky, had gotten himself stuck. Splattered and stuck like snot against the building, he stood ass exposed, and mumbling orders at Andrew nonstop. I understood every word.

"Hurry, I'm such an idiot. Stop fucking laughing and help me!"

Andrew struggled to stay upright. Stomping this way and that, pants down, and wiping tears from his face while Juandre was hysterical with urgency. My friends were in an absurd predicament. One new lesson learned, I thought, never get my cock or tongue close to frozen walls in Antarctica.

"Hurry! Please, Andrew." Juandre seemed to lose steam.

"I told you don't do it, but no, you wanted to see what happens," Andrew said between snorts and chuckles.

"I fucking know." Juandre sniffled in weak protest. I had excellent hearing and Juandre's need for help pushed him to go faster.

"Sorry, love, I... I will help you," Andrew said, and I heard defeated sobbing coming from Juandre. The dude needed help. I tried to go faster, but it felt like swimming in sand.

Andrew swallowed his laughs. "Please don't cry. You will get your entire face wet and stuck. Oh no, it's already stuck. Please, Juandre, don't cry, for fuck's sake. Don't cry!"

Juandre cried more. "Help me get my pants up, Drew. My cock and balls... I'm worried about frostbite," Juandre said between sniffles and struggling to form sentences tongueless.

Andrew helped Juandre by pulling up his puffy snow pants.

"I have an idea. I'm going to piss on your tongue. It's warm, it's liquid, and it's salty. It should melt the snow long enough for you to pull free."

Juandre initially shook his head sideways but eventually nodded in agreement while yelling "yes" in anguish.

Five steps to go, I calculated.

"I hope I can piss this high." Andrew stepped back, flung his cock upwards, and aimed with both hands. "Quiet down, so I can concentrate on pissing, baby."

Juandre stopped crying.

"Oh, baby, I'm so sorry. Here it comes," Andrew hollered and released a bright yellow stream of piss onto Juandre's face. Fuck, I wanted to laugh, but clearly, this was a dire situation.

"I think it's working," Juandre mumbled through coughs.

"Close your eyes. Sorry, it's probably going up your nose too, baby."

"You are fucking drowning me. Yes. It's losing its grip. Keep pissing," Juandre muttered, shaking his hands in various gestures. Come closer, stay away, come closer, stay away. Mixed signals and a lot of "ahs" and "nos."

"Come on, let him go. My bladder is almost empty."

"Do you need help, friend?" I asked, knowing I was surprising them. The snow swallowed my voice's echo. It seemed it ate sound as well. I decided I didn't like the stuff.

Fumbling with numb fingers, I quickly unbuttoned my long coat and threw the hood back over my shoulders. The lapels hit the snowbank behind me. I unbuckled my black leather pants to join my friend's golden pissing rescue attempt.

"Ish, you, big, beautiful motherfucker!" Andrew exclaimed.

"Ha-ha-ha." I laughed jovially while pissing on Juandre as the steam rose from his frozen face. With a snap, the frozen wall released him.

"Ah thank fuck, that was quick thinking." He heaved and plopped down with his hands on his knees.

"Get up from there!" Andrew said, pulling Juandre up by the arm.

"This snow and ice are like solidified carbon dioxide."

"What?" I asked, tucking my cock away.

"Dry ice," they answered together.

"I never expected a golden shower in Antarctica on my first day." Juandre chuckled. "And finally, I get to meet you." He fell into my arms, hugging me. His head was about the height of my navel. I was much taller than the average human. "I'm so happy to see you. Maybe you can join us next time?" Juandre asked.

"No, from now on, there will be no fucking outside, period," Andrew said, patting him on his butt playfully.

"I heard there are tunnels underneath the structure. We should go check those out," Juandre suggested. He batted his eyelashes and made kissy sounds. Then he looked from me back to Andrew, searching our faces for answers.

"Excellent idea," I said. Meaning them, not me. I was in a hurry, and the longer I stayed, the more possible fuck ups could happen. And I was done with those.

"Yes, we'll stay inside." Andrew threw an arm around Juandre's lower body, possessively pulling him in closer. His gaze fell on me as if to say *stay away, he is mine*, then he marked his mate with a peck on the cheek.

"Okay, I get it. You pissed on him first, so he's yours." I laughed, then cleared my throat to say seriously, "I'm glad to see you, but I can't stay long. I have to go. I'm glad you are both okay. I will see you soon. I only came this time to download the latest news report and update Lasitor." I waved the time-keeping device on my wrist at them. "The first history of Phoenix was deleted," I dared not mention during the flood. "I need to know as much as possible to calculate when to go next. What to change and what to leave as is."

"Ooooh, that looks and sounds interesting," Juandre said with a pronounced effeminate lilt. I could see why Andrew was so fond of him. His beauty and energy were magnetic. His dark brown eyes, stubbled beard, and smeared red lips made him gorgeous. I checked the wall of ice he had licked. Also smeared red. His nose and cheeks were purple-red. Probably because of crying and the cold. The mix of masculine and feminine was attractive to me. Sadly, the dark lines around his eyes were also smeared with tears trailing down his face into his beard. When I was a young ignorant prince, I'd worn kohl lines around my eyes too.

It looked like Andrew had fucked him good just before I arrived and before his tongue got stuck. I didn't want to impose, and it seemed Andrew wasn't sharing, anyway.

Both stared at the device Cian had given me, so I ignored the what-the-fuck-looks and covered it with my sleeve. I didn't want to mess with this timeline by showing them contraptions from their future. They would discover it at their own pace.

"Forget you saw it. Just point me toward the nearest access point for the main computer."

"What, why?" Juandre asked. He had his hands in his hair. Picking at it and inspecting the tips of his gloved fingers. Everything was frozen, frozen with piss and sticking up in all directions, even his eyebrows. He must have reached the same conclusion. I saw him shiver as if grossed out.

"Is there something happening that we should know about? Come inside with us. It's fucking cold. We'll sneak you inside. You can eat and freshen up and tell us what's going on. I've been waiting a long time to see the big man who popped my Andrew's submissive cherry."

"Don't fall for it, Ish," Andrew warned, pulling Juandre away from me. "He invites men over, pretending to offer food and shelter."

"Andrew, I didn't know you are the possessive type," I teased. They were mated, and I knew how mates only had eyes for each other. Also, I really didn't have time, and if Brad or anyone saw me, I would most definitely fuck this up big time. "I–I really came for Lasitor."

"Who?" Juandre asked, the ooh ending on a high note.

"The computer that talks to humans and tells them the news," I explained. They frowned at me, deep in thought.

"Oh, the computer program," Juandre exclaimed. "I am disappointed you can't follow us inside. But let me show you. You can access it via the security terminal. Do you have UZ1 to plug and play?

"Yes, thank you. I know what to do."

"Of course, you do. You are from the future." Juandre cackled.

The three of us stood awkwardly, having a moment. I looked up at the cloudy, sunless sky, searching for something to focus on. Juandre and Andrew stayed quiet, creating an opening for me to talk. But I was smarter than that.

"Hmmm, the access point, please."

Juandre narrowed his eyes and moved closer, inspecting my eyes. "You are so right, my bear; they do look like bumblebee butts.

"Juandre!" Andrew cautioned, his forehead creased and eyebrows furrowed.

"Sorry, Ish, those yellow and black rings around your eyes—" Juandre paused mid-sentence, index finger pointing at my face.

"I know, and you are correct. They do look like that. The palace children have teased me all my life."

Again, we stood awkwardly, looking at each other. Andrew with his pale skin and green eyes and Juandre with his smoldering looks, I thought maybe. Yes, maybe I could sneak in and out.

"No!" I answered instead.

"No?"

"Stop it. You two are trying to change my mind. Go look for someone else to play with."

"Damn, we almost had him!" Juandre clapped his thick gloved hands together. "Come, friend, I will help you." Juandre lifted his arm and motioned me forward as he started talking. "We are both so thankful to you for the gift you gave Andrew. And then for helping the two of us to find each other." Juandre puffed steam clouds as he made his way through the snow.

"You will find out why, but for now, I can't say more. Live your life. Do your thing. Be you. You are perfect together, and it's been an honor to have helped you this way."

"I bet you must feel honored to have fucked my husband and infected him with this." Juandre opened his mouth, showing me his small incisors and hissing. So cute.

"Baby, no," Andrew said, shutting his mouth playfully with his. They amused me and it felt amazing seeing them happy.

"So, you got married. I'm glad to hear, but the longer I stay and the more we speak, the more shit can happen," I said, shaking my head. I was happy for them. It seemed I'd done one thing well so far. The fates had urged me to change time only for others, so I might find joy in selflessness. Now I understood.

I watched them kiss each other, and then I cleared my throat. I had things to do.

"If I had Lasitor, I could navigate better. And without history, I would fly blind. He can keep me company and help me plan better."

"Yes, we understand," Andrew said. He was a good man, and I could see why Brad missed them so much. "Where is Peter? Why didn't he come with you? I would have liked to see him. My Peter is safe, but he ignores me. I think the organization has messed him up. He is focused on bringing back the frozen celebrities, and it is all thanks to you." Andrew pinned me with a stare. I sensed animosity. As if he was trying to delve into my psyche. But growing up around nosy brothers and sisters had taught me to keep my grid guarded at all times.

"Stop trying to read me. You know I can't say. Also, I kind of escaped to be here today. Peter is covering for me and waiting for me. He is happy now, Andrew, I promise."

"You two are always up to something. When will this end?"

"I can't say, but the ending I saw was wonderful. You will see."

"We've been fucking waiting since 2014. I'm kind of tired of watching and waiting," Juandre said with hands on his hips. He was a strange character. One minute I think he is joking and the next I feel like he wants to drive a knife through me.

"Andrew, how do you manage this man of yours? He looks like a lot of work to me?" I retorted, hoping to throw them off my scent.

"Don't change the subject. I'm not dumb, you know."

"I know you aren't. Okay, all I'm saying is it's about another century at least."

"No fucking way!" Juandre and Andrew exclaimed, shaking their heads in disbelief. "What about the whisky?" Andrew asked.

"It is safe. They will find it, thank you. I will talk about that another time."

"The world is ending, but at least they will have whisky, ha-ha-ha."

I wanted to laugh at their antics. "Yes, I'm sorry, but I can't say more. And for the love of the fates, do not tell anyone about yourselves. They aren't ready yet." I pointed a finger at each of them. They felt like family. Like children. "I can always come back and punish you if you fuck this up for all of us. All this, the success of this can disappear with one mistake. Please stand back, let them do their thing, and let everything happen naturally. If in doubt, do nothing. All these people could die. They are, no, you are humankind's last hope," I said, and then I smiled widely, revealing my fangs. "I'm serious," I said with a lisp through my protruding incisors.

"Okay, okay. Lips zipped," Juandre said and gestured to indicate that. I shook my head. It was as if Juandre was incapable of seeing the direness of it all. Maybe it was better that way, I thought.

We halted next to the doorframe, where Juandre opened the frozen cover on the wall.

"This is a charging dock. You can plug in here."

I stepped forward, fiddled with a little button until I got hold of it, and pulled. Then the fiber optics cable was plugged into the micro socket.

"God, I need a proper shower. Look at my hair. It's frozen stiff with piss. And my face is burning." Juandre chuckled, looking uncomfortable as fuck. Gloved fingers all stretched and face disgusted.

"Don't touch it, you can break it off." Andrew took Juandre's hands to prevent him from damaging his frozen hair.

"Thank you, this can take a few minutes," I said into the puffy arctic hoods covering their heads as I hugged them closer with one arm. "I will see you soon. You can go inside."

Andrew gave me another hug. "See you soon friend and don't make too much trouble."

"I won't," I said, but I knew I was lying. I was the motherfucker who started all this shit and somehow, I must fix it.

"Are you one hundred percent sure you don't want a personal history lesson from us?" Juandre asked, trying for seductive but failing. He reeked of piss, and I wasn't the kind of friend who would fuck his friend's mate. Unless offered.

"Let's get you inside, into a shower, and then into my warm bed." Andrew turned to Juandre, leading him away as he gave me a final goodbye with a stare.

"We can't. Someone might complain or report us to the Colonel Doctor and get us court-martialed."

I watched the two men enter the compound through the door. Juandre popped back out. "Bye-bye, I'll see you soon, big boy!" I smiled. I really loved those two. They made anyone's day brighter.

Now I was determined to make my plan work. The wrist computer beeped to indicate I had completed the download. I turned to make a path for myself through the heaps of snow with renewed purpose. They were talking about Brad McCormick. Little did they know, years from now, he'd be married to a man, and Juandre and Andrew would be his closest friends.

\*\*\*

"Colonel McCormick, come to Communications immediately, sir!" I heard Connor's announcement. It was time to leave.

"Run, don't walk," Connor said over the speaker system blaring in and outside the building.

I carved my way back through the trail I'd made earlier. Reaching my ship, I realized I should have left a mark for myself. I peeled pieces of ice off, searching for the bloody fucking door I had stupidly covered while hiding my ship. I found it without removing all my hard work. Once inside, I fell into my seat, shivering from the cold while I waited impatiently for the three stairs to retract and the door to swoosh closed. "Brrrr, I need heat. Where is the button for the heat?" I asked no one, rubbing my hands together. I blew my hot breath over my numb fingertips to defrost them. Pins and needles prickled painfully in my limbs. I found the tiny silver lever and flipped it on. Heat flooded the cabin as I uploaded the information to my onboard computer and waited.

"Talk to me, Lasitor." I prayed to the fates to do this for me. I needed a companion to travel with me. "Okay, Lasitor, let's play those recordings," I said out loud, hoping Lasitor would hear and respond to me. But Lasitor didn't.

Melancholy and complete loneliness engulfed me. I was sick of being alone; I was sick of fixing all this shit I had caused. That was the main reason I'd stopped here.

Electric crackles came over the intercom speakers.

***

Lasitor's voice boomed. I had never been so happy to hear the AI's robotic male voice. "Don't cry for me, Argentina, the truth is I never left you. I was just updating," Lasitor's voice echoed inside the small cabin. The time machine is big enough for two people. Two small people. "This is where it began and where it ends," Lasitor said.

"I know. Tell me how it all came to world annihilation and where are all the women?"

"Certainly, sir. Environment Project One—EP-1—was meant to house approximately twenty-five thousand people. Over the next six to eight weeks, two to three groups of two thousand people, males, females, children, and family members were supposed to arrive. This was one of the first global cities built to ensure humanity achieves growth and progress while giving nature a chance to wipe away the footprints of humans."

"Yes, but why?"

"It was that or die out. Women already couldn't bring children into the world and the Z3H993 parvovirus epidemic and vaccine crisis of 2038 caused adverse mutations, which were handed down from mothers to their daughters. Cities were either burning or crumbling. Winds would destroy what wasn't washed away by rainstorms. So, they decided to build this and put the healthy, the smartest, and the bravest in it. It was a test, and these solar and steam-powered domes protected them, and it saved them. Colonel Doctor McCormick was chosen by WHPSS, by Doctor John Saunders, to lead the team of savants and attempt to save and upgrade people to a superior species."

"Hmm, that sounds like the Disciples."

"Yes, sir, but no one knew it. Except for Doctor Peter Von Leutzendorf, and now Juandre and Andrew."

"I believe the fates guided the way it played out."

"I agree. Whoever these fates are, will be upset if we change it."

"Okay, let's—What's that alarm going off?" I asked as I searched the panorama of ice, mountains, and glass domes. Soldiers were moving at a fast pace from outside to inside.

"They are being called together for the announcement."

"What announcement?"

"The Doomsday announcement. It's all going to shit, sir."

"I want to see." I loosened my seatbelt and shut the engine down again. Dang-dang! A dull banging came from outside at the ship's door.

"Ouch!" I bumped my head on the roof as I moved closer to investigate the sudden noise. Someone was outside. I held my breath, listening. Dang-dang-dang! Again, with the banging.

"Who's there? What the fuck do you want?" I yelled and gnashed my teeth. "Please don't tell me they've found me. I don't have the strength for Mika, Connor, and Brad tonight." Frustrated, I shifted from one foot to the other, turned, and then turned back again in the small space, "Fuck! Should I stay or should I go?" I muttered while staring at the door, as if it would show me the answer. "Lasitor!"

"Yes, sir?"

"Jump, now!"

"Where and when? And, sir, are you sure, because it's your friends? It's Juandre and Andrew outside."

Argh! "Fuck, dammit," I grunted. The fates gifted me the smallest ship. I bumped my head in the same bloody spot each time I turned around. "I can't stand upright. I'm too fucking big for this ship! If I see the fates again, I want an upgrade," I muttered as I opened the door and a wide-eyed Juandre and Andrew looked up at me. It smelled like they'd had a quick shower.

"What's wrong?" I asked curtly, still rubbing my head. Andrew didn't say a word. I could see it had been Juandre's idea to come knocking. Andrew was half like me. We don't get scared easily. And Juandre looked paler than usual, probably shocked.

"Fuck, the shit is hitting the fan, my man," Juandre said, short of breath and looking scared shitless.

"I know. I told you to live your lives and all will be fine." I hung onto the doorframe and poked my head outside, checking their six.

"But the world is ending," he stuttered, with tears in his eyes.

"No, sir, it is not," Lasitor answered from the inside.

"Who is that? Is that the computer? Is he talking to me?"

"Who else would talk to you if not the one man looking at you? Ha-ha," Lasitor said in his distinctive robotic voice and laughed like a crazed computer.

"It's Lasitor. I just downloaded him. You know that, I told you just now, or did you swallow too much piss?" I asked, sarcasm dripping from me.

"The Lasitor I know reads the computer screen. He reads the words man types for him. That sounds like he has a bloody personality."

"Thank you," Lasitor answered. I laughed. Andrew slapped his hands over his mouth in disbelief and Juandre put his hands on his hips. Daring the AI to say something.

"He's going to be a wonderful traveling companion. I don't have to feed him, and he takes up no space." I motioned for them to come in. "Come inside. It's warmer and someone is going to see us. How did you find the ship? I hid it. Could you see it?"

"No, we followed the big boot tracks here."

"Oh. That."

I lowered the steps, and my two friends joined me, cramming themselves inside, shoulder to shoulder. It was ridiculously small.

"Juandre, there is nothing we can do about things so big and about to happen. You have your son here with you, don't you? And no one else you care about back home?" I asked and Juandre shook his head.

"I know this is scary, but this is not the end. Phoenix will be okay. Within hours, this place is going to be on lockdown. No one is leaving, and no one is going to get inside. You need to go back." Lasitor said.

"Are you sure?" Juandre asked me, with frozen tears glinting on his cheeks.

"This is happening and must happen so we can restart and have a better future. This is only the beginning. Juandre, everything will be all right. I'm not allowed to change anything for myself. I'm allowed to change two things for one person, and I'm already doing that. You are standing here."

"What are you talking about?"

"I'm going to tell you, but you may not say a word. Not now, maybe later. But the more people know, the less likely we are to stay on the same timeline. Things change and shift all the time and I stand the chance of losing you. Understand?" My voice rumbled in the small space.

"Yes, I do." Juandre nodded up and down, then swallowed nervously as I stared at his protruding Adam's apple bobbing in his throat. I kept quiet and waited for Andrew to agree as well.

"Good." I squeezed each by the shoulder. "You are going to live a full, happy life, and you are going to make wonderful friends. Do not worry about Brad and his rules about homosexuality. From today forward, they are wiped from existence. Brad McCormick will find it difficult to implement the WHPSS's vision of human living and rule-following. Circumstances will change that.

Become friends with anyone who lets you, and the whole of Phoenix will learn to love you. Be your best you and give them something to look forward to at the end of a long day. Fill their stomachs while you nurture their hearts. Show them how to be kind and accepting." I looked from one astonished face to the other. Their hopeful gazes reminded me of children needing to hear everything was going to be all right.

Juandre smiled and turned to his husband. Andrew tipped his chin as if to say, *see I told you so*, and rubbed Juandre's back.

"We could work in food services. Not all the staff have arrived yet. My bear, we could be a team. I will help you." Juandre turned to me. "His staff hasn't arrived yet. Maybe food services is where I'm needed most. I'm sure Doctor Longarrow can manage without me."

"You don't have to fear the future, because I've been there, and it is a miraculous thing. Entertain them. Be friends with them. All of them are human, just like you are. Brad McCormick will reconstruct a world where power, rank, and gender are irrelevant. Watch him. Be his friend and support him."

"Agh, okay. You should have been a public speaker, not a time traveler," Juandre said as he wiped the melting tears from his cheeks.

"Yes, Juandre, you and Andrew are important to us. These men need you," Lasitor added. "They also need me. The toddler version, though. Ha-ha!" The robotic laugh was so weird and out of place we all laughed, breaking the tension.

# Chapter One

"Good morning, citizens of our lovely glass-domed city.

I am Lasitor, your Artificial Intelligence (AI) community news broadcaster. It is now six a.m.

The local Antarctic temperatures are −70.6°F. But don't worry, the coastal temperatures are almost balmy, expected to reach a searing maximum of 14.0°F during the summer. The terrain is almost entirely covered by an ice sheet, but beneath is a hidden landscape of mountains, valleys, and plains. Nice to know when you are freezing your butt off.

*The sea levels are rising exponentially. The icecaps are melting at an alarming rate and constantly shifting and giving birth to pools of hot water and steam. You can breathe this air, but it is stinky and similar to the dull mist of a fart. Other than that, dear humans, all is peachy.*

*Breakfast is served until eight a.m.*

*Thank you, and enjoy your day."*

# We are on our own

**Colonel Dr. Brad McCormick**

**2046 A.D.**

**Environmental Project One**

**Antarctica**

**Earth**

"Colonel McCormick, come to communications immediately, sir!" Connor's command was loud and stressed as it boomed from McCormick's small personal radio. "Run! Don't walk," he added.

Brad McCormick, who had been working on the experimental growing lights in the Agriculture Dome, had been taken aback by the near panicky voice of his second in command, Connor O'Hara. The urgency in his usual soft-spoken voice alarmed Brad, so he went tearing down the long corridor toward the Communication Dome. The energy-saving lights could barely keep up with his pace as his motion initiated the activation sensors.

Finally, he came to a dead halt in front of the shiny metallic door to the Command Center. He waved his hand so the sensor would hurry and do its censoring. He took a deep breath, calming himself, and burst inside as soon as the door slid open. He found his friend and second-in-command in the Communications Room. The area was half-moon shaped with white furniture and curved plexiglass screens for optimal viewing. The pixilation was so fine that one could see a sand flea doing the mambo on top of Tutankhamun's tomb in Egypt's Valley of the Kings.

"What is going on, Connor?" Brad asked as he walked with purpose inside.

"Seems we may have a wee problem on our hands. Help me make some sense of all this." Connor motioned for Brad to sit in the chair beside him, as he hammered away at his keyboard, eyes fixed on the virtual networking screens.

"What seems to be the problem, besides the fact that you're sitting here looking at an empty room? Is that Houston Headquarters?" Brad asked as he patted the young scientist's back, taking the seat next to him.

"You'll recall that I mentioned at dinner last evening I'd been unable to contact Houston for our bi-weekly report. I put it off as resulting from some flares initially. The more I thought about the flare rationale, the more it made little sense with the new communications technology. So I attempted new contact efforts first thing this morning. At first, it was the same, just a black screen and static. Then Marcia Merrick appeared on the screen. She looked like bloody fucking hell. Rambling, running her words together, and screeching at other times about a pandemic. She told me to wait, saying she had to go but would get someone to speak to me, and then she turned and ran to the door in the back of the room. That's what we're looking at now. I've been holding for about fifteen minutes. I just had this feeling and thought it wise to call you immediately," Connor said.

"This is all very strange, Connor. Let's get Mika Romanov and my boys in here. I want them to feel in the loop," Brad directed Connor, referring to his son Simon and his college buddy Paul Chevalier. They selected both boys as interns at the Antarctica facility due to their high academic standing.

"Good idea!" Connor said even as he picked up the pager and ordered the three men to the Communications Room, stat.

Minutes later, Simon and Paul arrived. Both stood over six-foot tall and were athletically built. The two had been inseparable since meeting at school.

Dr. Mika Romanov, a Russian geneticist, geologist, medical doctor, physicist, and linguist, entered from the corridor that led to the subterranean entryway. Mika had proven to be an integral part of their team. He'd been procured by Dr. John Saunders, who'd been impressed by his research and publications in various scientific journals. Mika was loud and often opinionated, but his laugh was infectious and his smile completely disarming. He had the handsome Viking look. Over six feet eight inches tall and sported a luscious shoulder-length blond mane. His facial hair constantly appeared to be in a state of stubble. Other than his mother tongue, Mika spoke English and six other languages fluently.

Brad updated them on what little he knew. Then, with concerned and questioning eyes, they stood in silence in front of the monitors watching the empty room at Houston HQ. Something crashed and broke, which was followed by twenty minutes of tense silence. They inched forward as if something would appear on the monitor by doing so.

The face of a gaunt, sickly-looking man appeared, filling the screens as if out of nowhere. His hair was unkempt, and his face unshaven. His eyes were wide, and the white blood red.

"My good god! That's Doctor Saunders!" Connor exclaimed. "Doctor Saunders, what the hell's going on there?" Connor's Irish accent was thick with concern. Saunders was a friend, and he was a mentor to him.

"Connor! I never thought I would hear from you again!" Saunders spoke weakly. "Is it there, too?" he asked with growing alarm in his voice.

"Is what here?" Connor shouted.

"Keep calm, Connor," Brad ordered.

Connor nodded and lowered his voice. "Doctor Saunders, please tell us what's happening and what we can do to help?" Connor asked his old friend.

"Connor, you've been told nothing? Not surprising. The world has fallen apart since our last communication. There has been a deadly outbreak, most probably due to a bioterrorism agent. The WHPSS just declared a pandemic of unknown origin. Global coordination and response mobilization is non-existent due to mass bombings and explosions of communication systems and electrical grids. No one has claimed responsibility for the incident. This is a global attack on all nations, with no exceptions. It's not restricted to a specific location. According to all intelligence reports from around the world, no country has escaped the effects of the crisis. It's truly as if the earth is ridding itself of the human race." Dr. Saunders coughed and laughed as if it was a joke.

The men in the Communications Room were shocked and speechless. Brad knew he had to uncover more. "Tell us about the disease. Maybe we can help. We have scientists here that will diagnose and produce a vaccine for you."

"We haven't even been able to tell how it's transmitted. What we know is that the first symptom is a severe headache followed by a fever. This happens in the first twenty-four hours. It then seems to disappear. A low-grade fever becomes evident in the next twenty-four to forty-eight hours, followed by cerebral edema, which, depending on the person, causes disorientation within twelve to eighteen hours." He paused to take a few deep breaths and then continued. "Followed by coma and death within the next twenty-four hours. While statistics have been poorly executed due to the rapid spread of this virus, bacteria, or whatever it is..." He paused, shook his head slowly, and looked back up at them. "The survival rate is unknown. The transmission rate is... the..."

"Mom! What about Mom!" Simon shouted, moving closer to the screen.

"Son, please, we must let Doctor Saunders finish. Maybe we can learn something that will help your mom and our other colleagues' families." Simon looked up at Brad. He had hope in his eyes. "Your mother was in Houston. She had prepared to come here with the first wave of residents. I'm sure she must be alright," Brad said, and Paul stepped forward to place his arms around Simon to comfort him.

"I'm sorry, son. I will not leave you stranded at the bottom of the world with false hope. The first civilian wave team is no longer. Its last member, John Sorenson, passed away yesterday," Saunders said, and Simon turned to Paul for comfort while sobbing softly into his shoulder. "It's the same outside of HQ. My wife died in my arms this morning. We'd just gotten word that my son, his wife, and his two children succumbed earlier this week. I'm glad she was spared knowing that Todd and her beloved grandchildren were gone."

Connor swallowed a cry and his eyes brimmed with water.

"*Ty che, blyad,*" Mika swore in Russian. He pulled his chair closer to hear better, then spoke to Connor. "Comrade, are you recording this?"

"I am," Connor answered in a whisper.

"The bodies are everywhere, and this will, of course, worsen and escalate disease and death rates," Dr. Saunders said after collecting himself. He paused to cough a few times before continuing. "What science fiction writers have written about for decades, and scientists have theorized for years, has finally happened. It's the damn apocalypse!" Saunders shouted.

"What can we do for you?" Connor asked.

"You can do nothing for me, my young protégé. Maybe carry me fondly in your memory. We had a couple of good times, and you were a professor's dream student. A good Irish lad that made me quite proud and who Todd loved and should have married." Connor shifted uncomfortably at Saunders' words.

"You men may be the last remnants of civilization. There are things you must do and do quickly!"

"What? What should we do?" Connor asked before Brad could ask the same thing.

"If none of you have been infected, then my theory is correct. This outbreak started just three weeks ago, several weeks after you were already in place at the EP-1 outpost. It's unlikely that any of you are even carriers. You are safe, and you are self-sufficient. Do not let yourselves be known, don't give away your position. Don't leave Antarctica. Stay hidden for at least five years. The longer you can stay hidden, the better. Let this eradicate itself. The decimated remnants of the world's armies will fragment. All industry has come to a halt, and all technology has been lost. You and perhaps a few others are the sole possessors of all of humankind's knowledge. Make good use of it.

"The ground satellites are all pointing in the same direction. To headquarters. We believe it's the result of electromagnetic surges and coordinated targeting of exospheric orbital satellites, possibly including the International Space Station." Saunders paused as if he were deliberating. "Yes! You could try contacting the ISS. You'll figure it out. Assume you suspect that death has reached other outposts, particularly the McMurdo Naval Base, which is the closest to you. In that case, I implore you to stay away for your safety and avoid going there at all costs. Otherwise, if you are certain that no outbreak has reached them, they may be of great assistance because it's a US naval base with sophisticated equipment, should you need to salvage later on. I'm not aware of any ships or submarines in the vicinity. You have time, resources, and intelligence on your side. You'll figure it out eventually." He tapped his fist against the side of his head a few times. He appeared to be trying to recall something.

"Mika! I hope Peter's and your research will be ready soon. Roll out our plan for the project." The men all turned to look at Mika.

"What's he talking about, Mika?" Brad asked, frowning. This was news to him. Mika made an insignificant gesture with his pointer and thumb.

"A little something-something, I will tell you later, comrade," he whispered. Brad assumed it was classified.

"You will have your progeny, and you will have descendants, but not the way anyone would expect. Doctor Romanov and Doctor Peter von Leutzendorf..." Saunders was coughing so intensely that he could barely take a breath.

"Tell him to sit down. He looks like a zombie, deathly pale and unable to stand upright," Brad muttered under his breath. Saunders cupped his hand over his mouth, and Brad noticed a trickle of blood coming from his ear. The boys gasped, Connor swore, and Mika balled his fists not saying a word.

"Sit down or get some rest and talk to us in a wee bit... we'd understand," Connor said.

Saunders attempted a chuckle. "Always thinking of others' comfort, Connor, and what's best for them. No, my boy, rest is something I'll get plenty of shortly. Unlike my dear wife, I believe that death will bring nothing but peace and sleep. There are three things I must mention." Again, the coughing, only this time, Saunders placed his hands on each side of his head and winced in pain.

"Brad, look at him! He can barely talk... the pain is so intense," Connor whispered.

"He knows he's dying. This isn't the time for personal considerations. I have the lives of everyone here to think about," Brad said with a grim look on his face.

"He's right, my boy, and you must think like him," Saunders said, clearly hearing the young scientist's advice to his leader.

Dr. Saunders stood up straight, took a deep breath, and concentrated on the screen in front of him as if he were concentrating on a single individual. "Brad, I should say that you're going to have the most difficult job of them all. You must bring together all of the other members of the EP-1 team to establish complete command of the operation. Until you can establish a council that represents the interests of everyone, you should be able to exercise complete authority over your subjects.

"Your colleagues regard you as their civilian boss, which I think is very important. Soldiers will continue to support you. I'm confident in that fact. Each of you was chosen only after extensive testing, evaluation, and consideration, right down to the lowest-ranking soldier. Your physical endurance, as well as your psychological assessments, distinguish you as a team without equals. Likely, the caliber of men who serve under you will never be equaled again.

"Time is of the essence and I'm unsure about the status of our power supply or how long it'll be before a total blackout. Frankly, I'm surprised that we can communicate now with all the havoc going on outside. The few of us left, are on lockdown. We're running on backup generators. I bring this up not just because I'll be dead shortly, but because there's something you must do, and even now, you may not have time." Saunders once more held his head as if trying to keep his skull from exploding.

"Your computer bank is among the best assembled. You have vast amounts of knowledge at your fingertips. I just uploaded and installed my WHPSS daily log. However, much of what you have stored is project-specific and classified. You need to tap into that and then into significant institutions that may still be accessible. I would recommend medical institutions, the WHPSS, NASA, Russian intelligence, Chinese, and even the CIA. Most importantly, you need to download architectural, metallurgical, and forensic construction engineering information."

"I see where you're going with this, Saunders. Those are the second-wave professionals. The civilians expected to join us in a couple of weeks," Brad said as he realized the scope of their problem.

"Yes. Connor can help you there. He and Todd almost broke into the US Treasury and transferred it to their bank account. Fortunately, they came to their senses, but to this day, the government never knew they'd been breached and almost robbed by my home computer. Do this right away, or that knowledge will be lost, I fear. I'll leave this line open so that, if necessary, you can use this facility's computer bank to possibly access others.

"Finally, I must get back to the progeny comment which I referenced earlier. You may think this is coming from the mouth of a man on the verge of madness. Think what you will, but keep it in mind nevertheless. There are no women. The plan was to introduce the selected and unaffected civilians in waves of ten thousand up to a maximum of twenty-five thousand in three-year increments until the WHPSS leadership decided otherwise. Last week, that support team perished. So, you may have to adopt a new belief system sooner than expected."

"Doctor Saunders, sir, I'm unsure what you're saying. What are you suggesting? I don't... I mean, these are all men who took their positions here knowing that there might be unforeseen hardships, and I believe they can deal with those hardships," Brad responded.

"Brad, my friend, listen to me. I mean psycho-social gratification. Suppose you're to manage these men effectively over the next several decades. In that case, you'll have to see that their off-duty life is as well-adjusted as possible under the circumstances. Your men expected wives, husbands, girlfriends, boyfriends, and even children to join them, who are likely dead now. Some men don't even know that they are genetically predisposed and were specifically selected for this reason. Apart from their basic human needs, when you deny them hope, or simple human intimacy or sex, they will regress into sex-crazed animals. You must reassess your leadership style. A rigid military leadership style may cause problems."

"I promise to think progressively and trans value, sir." All their careful planning, the whole futuristic, save the planet shit-show is raining down on me.

"Good man, McCormick. I shall miss our debates. Connor, I shall miss you, you were like a son to me. Mika, you are brilliant, and your knowledge and bravado will be an invaluable asset to humankind. Your research is humanity's last hope. Simon, your mother's loss is devastating to you, I know, and her loss as an integral part of the project's scientific team is tragic. I know you don't understand this now, but time will heal many of your wounds more than you know. Paul, I'm glad you're safe and there with Simon. I'm sorry I don't know the fate of your family. You have a new family now with Brad and Simon. Enough of this talking. You may have only hours to do the downloads I suggested, and Connor must still break the codes to hack into their systems. Oh, and, Brad..."

"Sir?" Brad answered as he stepped to his son and put an arm around his shoulders.

"The psychological profiles we did on your people are essentially infallible. I believe we had chosen well for you. With that said, gentlemen, I wish you well and bid you ado. I now wish to join my wife in her room and end this fucking headache."

Saunders turned and walked toward the exit door in the background. Brad saw the pistol in his right hand as Saunders turned around and saluted them before leaving their sight.

"Connor, get to work on those codes and download everything mentioned and anything additional you think we might need to survive for millennia. Also, download the complete world history, especially the makeup of the American government from its conception to the present. I want every point of view you can get. That may well be the most important thing we have soon. Simon, contact Sergeant Bryan Howell, and tell him to come to my office immediately," Brad ordered.

"Yes, sir!"

Brad bent down and whispered to Connor, "Also, download everything you can on human relations and behavioural science concentrating on anthropology and the evolution of homosexuality." With that, he was gone to meet with and inform Sgt. Howell of what was going on.

\*\*\*

Two Hours Later

The Communications Dome was located in the center of the EP-1 complex. A good comparison would be the head of an octopus, with its many tentacles serving as passageways to the various pods of domed structures within the structure itself. Doorways from eight of the forty sides of the building flew open in response to the status call to the Communications Dome. In less than three minutes, the vast majority of the population, except a few essential military guards, had gathered in front of the elevated platform where Brad waited to address them.

In just a few weeks, the EP-1 domed complex would have been fully staffed with a total of ten thousand year-round residents, the most extensive populated base to ever be attempted in the desolate Antarctic wilderness. Brad was now looking at nothing more than a handful of men who were quite possibly the last and best of humanity.

"Can you tell me how many heads are in EP-1, Corporal?" Brad asked a bewildered-looking soldier with an electronic gadget and a pen in his hands.

He typed furiously on the tablet and answered nervously, "Colonel Doctor, we have exactly one thousand nine hundred eighty-nine heads inside, but there may be a few busy working outside, still unaccounted for, sir." The soldier, a real computer geek with glasses much too big for his small rounded face, sounded reasonably sure of himself.

"Thank you, Corporal, please report to Master Sergeant Bryan Howell. I want a definitive number of military and civilian personnel present. We're going on lockdown. Assist him in keeping track of our numbers. All those on guard or working outside, bring them inside. Then, find my second in command, Connor O'Hara, with the final number of souls sleeping at EP-1 tonight," Brad said as he turned to face the crowd. He adjusted the microphone height to accommodate his six-foot-two frame while doing a quiet and quick calculating assessment.

Thirty-seven football fields fit inside fifty acres, up to one hundred thousand people per stadium, and before him stood maybe one percent of that.

He straightened his back and spoke. "Gentlemen, please take a seat." As Colonel Dr., he was a senior officer in the military and the civilian contingent of EP-I. Their future, the world's future, lies now on his shoulders. He procrastinated for an excessive pause. "Recent unfortunate events are why I called you here." Brad's voice was strained. If they came close enough, they could see his red puffy eyes. Brad turned and checked in with Master Sgt. Howell, Mika, and Connor. They were pale and their expressions set in stone.

Brad turned back, taking a deep breath, and explained as best he could what he'd been told by Saunders. That said, he pointed a remote control to the massive screen and played what he felt was relevant for them. Connor had edited the recording on orders from Brad to exclude top-secret and unnecessary information. He'd rationalized that now was not the time. The men would have enough to deal with worrying if their families had survived. Connor was also sure to edit out the part where the elder scientist had outed him.

Audible sobs and gasps of disbelief came from the men. One dark-haired scientist, Brad remembered him from, had always seemed cheerful, like the local social butterfly, was now sobbing in another man's arms. Then they left as the man struggled to console him.

"Everyone here is equally affected by these events. We owe it to the people who loved us to continue to do everything we can to survive. They would want us to live on and carry their memories in our hearts. While it will be some years before we can safely leave, we can try to contact some of the other bases. We will begin doing that as soon as we can. In the meantime, I know how difficult this will be, but I must ask you to remember your positions and what you were sent here to do. This is now more important than ever if we are to survive in this climate.

"As I speak, Doctor O'Hara is downloading information from several of the world's greatest information banks to help increase our odds of survival, as instructed by Doctor Saunders. Now—"

Abruptly a voice from the assembly interrupted Brad. "What about our families? If the internet is up, why not let us try to contact our families?" Jake, a bioengineer, yelled. Several men agreed, both the soldiers and the scientists.

Raising his hands in the air for silence and to gain the floor once again, Brad spoke. "Gentleman, I wish I could let you do that. Right now, however, every computer is downloading information that we may need to live. I don't know how long the information will be available. But when we're done, and if the internet is still up, I have no problem with you trying to contact your loved ones."

"Why do we have to wait? I think it's more important that we get the opportunity to contact family than downloading how to bake a cake!" a young soldier by the name of Linus shouted.

"Stand down, Private! That's an order," Master Sgt. Howell barked. "We would all like to make contact, but right now, we must do what's good for the group, not for us individually."

"Let's hope that what's downloaded already will be enough," Connor interjected.

"Because, men, the bloody internet just became history. The engineers, architects, building designers, draftspersons, interior designers for interior fit-outs or renovations, and contractors for the larger, more complex building project services are not coming. Many other professionals trained in their specialist disciplines were responsible for the coordination of this architectural marvel"—Brad pointed up to the dome structure—"but now we are on our own. We all have to step up and supplement our knowledge bases to survive this. We've all been chosen for this specific reason. You knew the projected re-engineering and what our main goal entailed when you signed up. We must not lose focus."

# Chapter Two

*"Good morning, citizens of our lovely glass-domed city.*

*It is I, Lasitor, your AI and community news broadcaster. It is now six a.m.*

*If you've marked your calendar for outside activities today, I suggest you go with Plan B.*

*While the outside promises much excitement in the form of apocalyptically high winds, blizzards, cyclonic storms, tsunamis, earthquakes, and unpredictable monsoon patterns near coastal regions, your day might be better spent canoodling with a friend.*

*Also, don't trust the rumors about dead zones. Read the latest piece of news about body odor and how you can deal with it.*

*Breakfast is served until eight a.m.*

*Thank you, and enjoy your day."*

# Brad gets his wake-up call

**Colonel Dr. Brad McCormick**

**2049 A.D.**

**Environmental Project One**

**Antarctica**

**Earth**

B rad made his way to the communal breakfast area. The cold, empty corridor connected the domes that lay like ping-pong balls against the Trans-Antarctic Mountain Range. He'd sensed that things were changing lately, but he was unsure of how to approach this particular situation. It made him unusually nervous not knowing how to move forward. He felt visionless so he projected an air of superiority by appearing aloof, rigid, and unapproachable in order to maintain his image as an intelligent leader. It kept him safe and prevented him from getting involved in potentially messy or uncomfortable conversations.

But he was lonely as fuck. The dining area was noisy. After standing in line to have his breakfast served, he searched for an empty table and sat down. He figured since the limbic system associated with sexual desire is linked to libido and the part of the brain responsible for higher-level functions like planning and thinking, the gifted savants were increasingly restless. In other words, the men were horny as fuck. Him included. All one thousand nine hundred and ninety-nine horny souls at EP-1.

The men had grieved the loss of a world they once knew and had taken for granted. Many found comfort in denial. But Brad listened to the men with one ear and realized the grieving period was over.

"You want to help me out, buddy?" one soldier asked loudly.

"Who-ha-ha," the men laughed boisterously.

"Huh, what?" Brad said to no one in particular as the laughter pulled him from his own sticky thoughts about spearing bearded clams. More laughter floated from parties around other tables while enjoying their breakfasts.

"Hmmm," someone cleared their throat. "Morning, may I join you?" a handsome young man asked, not waiting for permission, and sat down. Brad stared at him.

"How's your morning going?" he asked, being much too friendly for Brad's comfort. He recognized Dr. Rick Longarrow. He had his sleek black hair pulled back in a ponytail and the usual stethoscope, scrubs, and comfortable white shoes on.

Taken aback by his beauty, lack of respect, and arrogance, Brad jumped up and excused himself. "Morning, good, thank you. Sorry, I have to go." He scurried out of the dining area like a tongue-tied teenager seeing their crush.

What was that? The audacity of that exotic-looking man! I'm not inclined to... with anyone...

Brad's thoughts were jumbled. The beautiful long-haired doctor confused him. Made him nervous. He preferred his distance, and he felt safe in his cocoon of loneliness and power.

This thought made him even more panicky. He was going to fuck this up. All he could imagine was the undulating bodies of men having sex and no growth, no future. One big orgy. Fucking into the eternal sunset.

Brad couldn't stop from screaming at himself inside his mind. He was aware of what was going on in his environment, but he was unsure how to take the next best step toward moving forward. For three years, he'd been unsure of how to take action. He wished he could just talk to his wife one more time. She would know exactly what to say and would assist him in making sense of all of his conflicting thoughts and feelings about this whole fucking situation.

"Good morning, Colonel," Master Sgt. Howell addressed him, ripping Brad from his thoughts. "Do you require a torch, sir?"

Brad ignored the double entendre and refocused.

"Yes, thank you. I thought this morning might be a good time to go through some of the more unused tubes in the caves. You know, the areas where we just added lighting. I wanted to explore them a bit deeper today." The Master Sgt. chuckled.

One more word about tubes, torches, or going deeper and Brad was going to explode with laughter and blow his own cover. He reeled himself in and gave the man a serious look and a nod.

They continued walking in silence as they made their way to a section of the cavern system rarely used. The network of volcanic tubes reached deep into the mountain range. Although the tunnels were nowhere near being entirely explored, miles of the tube system were illuminated by the solar energy technology that Brad installed. These tunnels were cold, and they were ideal for storing items that needed to be kept cool.

An odd series of noises could be heard, but it was difficult to tell where they were coming from because of the slick tubes, and the echoes caused the noise to be distorted. "Many of the men, tiring of the track in the gym, often use the tunnels for running as they extend for miles," Howell said.

Brad frowned but nodded his understanding.

They rounded a sharp bend, where they both came to a dead stop, mouths agape.

Three young men stood huddled together. Dylan Hurst, a twenty-two-year-old private who was bent slightly forward, his hands pressing against the cavern wall for support, his jogging pants below his knees, legs spread as wide as the fallen pants would allow, and his firm young ass protruding outward behind him. Dr. Mitchell Fairgate, the thirty-year-old bio-agriculturist in charge of light hydroponics, stood, his pants also below the knees. Thrusting what appeared to be a very large cock in and out of the young soldier's ass. Dylan grunted with each inward plow, not out of pain, but rather in apparent pleasure.

In front of Dylan and on his knees, the young soldier, Amir, added to the spectacle by holding on to Dylan's fuzzy ass cheeks and receiving his buddy's cock with each of Fairgate's thrusts. Mitchell grunted, pushed in as deeply as he possibly could, and was very clearly ejaculating deep into the soldier's ass. Brad and Howell had no time to react or say anything. Mitchell used the boy's taunting buttocks to keep him in place while he was in the throes of orgasmic ecstasy and his knees were about to give way under him. Dylan, in turn, grabbed Amir's hair and held him in place as he sprayed cum down the handsome tanned corporal's throat. The young man from the Middle East coughed, but to his credit, didn't lose a drop as he continued to suck and swallow. When he finally managed to pull his head away from Dylan's dick, he lashed his tongue out across the man's cock slit in an attempt to get one more drop. Brad was able to find his own voice at that point.

"What in the ever-loving fuck do you think you're doing?" Brad asked. His voice boomed down the tunnels. Mitchell and Dylan's legs, tangled in their jogging pants, made them fall over when they heard McCormick.

The moment Dylan began to back away from the wall, he grabbed the lush black locks of Amir's hair and pulled him forward so they both fell to the floor, with Amir's face buried in Dylan's crotch. The three men rose to their feet as quickly as they could under the circumstances and confronted Brad, whose face was red and contorted with rage. Howell did nothing but stand there and watch the situation.

"Colonel McCormick, I don't quite know what to say!" Fairgate said, flustered and red-faced while trying to tuck himself into his pants.

As Dylan pulled his pants up, Brad saw the glistening cum running down the inside of his thighs as it leaked from him. Amir's very prominent tent in his pants deflated. Brad caught himself wondering how big the young man must be to have created such a protrusion. This consideration angered him even more.

*Focus!* he told himself.

"Fairgate, I don't quite know what to say either. I've known you since you got out of college. I was on the committee when you defended your dissertation for your Ph.D., and my wife and I attended your wedding. Now I don't even know who you are. What an example you're setting for these young men. You disgust me, Mitchell!"

"Sir, I loved my wife as much as any man could love a woman. She's not here and probably dead from all accounts. I'm a man, and I have needs. I was not disrespecting Dylan or Amir. We were all doing what we needed to do," Fairgate said, defending himself and the whole caboodle.

Disregarding Mitchell's statement, Brad looked at the two young men sternly and without any sign of compassion. "I recognize both of you from, among other things, the university that Mika has put together. I've heard promising reports about both of you. So why would you humiliate yourselves like this, being used in such a despicable manner? Aren't you supposed to be in class? Aren't you on duty? And what would your fathers think?" The two young men didn't or perhaps couldn't respond. They appeared shaken but remained at attention.

Receiving no reply, Brad shook his head in disgust and turned to Master Sgt. Howell. "Place those two soldiers in confinement."

"No, Colonel McCormick," Mitchell said, louder than necessary, the anger very apparent in his voice. "We were in an area that's about as private as we can get in this facility. We're all adults, and we all consented to have sex. It's not the first time I've done this, but it's the first time I've done it with these two soldiers. Normally, I'm with members of our science team. It's the only way we can keep our sanity. We must have intimacy. If not with each other, then who?"

"Enough, Mitchell! Master Sergeant Howell, please escort these men and sequester them as I ordered," Brad said as he turned to get out of their presence.

"Yes, sir, Colonel, sir!" the handsome sergeant replied. "Sir, if I may, I would like to schedule a meeting in your office as soon as you can," Howell asked and Brad just nodded.

"I believe the colonel could benefit from some stress relief," Mitchell shot out as Brad walked away.

# Chapter Three

*"Good morning, citizens of our lovely glass-domed city.*

*It is I, Lasitor, bidding you a good morning. It is now six a.m.*

*Make most of your tankinis, learn about beach evacuation and ways to survive unsafe beaches.*

*You ever go to the grocery store and think,*

Fuck, there are too many vegetables...

I want to walk out of here with something I can eat.

*Of course, you have. Lasitor knows everything about you.*

*Learn more about vegetables, fruits, and fish and how we produce them under solar domes. No meat for anyone; that's not practical. Those cows will stink up these domes, not to mention the danger of their flammability. No, instead we produce vitamins, antibiotics, and other medicine synthetically in-house. All our chemicals produced are environmentally friendly, and you can wash it all down with the freshwater collected from the inland mountain range cave system.*

*Breakfast is served until eight a.m.*

*Thank you, and enjoy your day."*

# This is not a crisis

**Dr. Connor O'Hara**

S wish!

Brad stormed into the Command Center at his usual time after the EP-1 walk-around with Master Sgt. As soon as the doors slid shut behind him, he stopped in his tracks, closed his eyes, and took a few calming breaths. Connor watched as he moved over to the large viewing windows opposite the entrance. The inside of the massive tetracontagon was viewable like the inside of a beehive. The natural Antarctic sunlight shone through the glass-domed roof onto his face, and Brad basked in it.

Architects designed offices inside the domes to save electricity and fight depression. The front office had enough room for two white leather sofas, a coffee table, and a water tower. Two hallways flanked left and right to Connor and Brad's offices and access to the Communications Dome from the back via the emergency exit. When Brad had composed himself, he spoke.

"Connor! Where do you keep the files on human adaptations and adaptability, particularly those on biological plasticity and the ability to adapt biologically to an environment? I need them right now!" Brad seemed very upset. A real trooper most mornings, so bloody chipper, but today was an exception.

"What's crawling up your backside?" Connor asked as he turned on his computer. "And why are you in such a rush to research such heavy topics so early in the day?"

Brad looked like hellhounds were chasing him, Connor thought as he frantically typed on his keyboard. "Don't you worry, I'll have it in your inbox in a second!" Connor chuckled softly, so Brad couldn't hear him. He was pretty sure he knew what was going on. Brad went to his office to wait for the files Connor was sending him.

Just five minutes later, Brad's chair still cold, he sped out of his office back to Connor. "Connor, I've got to talk to you, and I've got to talk to you now!" he sputtered.

"Yes, Brad, of course. What is it? What's happened? Just calm yourself down a wee bit, so you only use words of fact," Connor said as calmly as possible. Memories of his Irish grandfather came flooding back as he listened to himself speak in a heavy brogue.

"Get Mika and Howell in here immediately. Howell wanted to speak to me right away, so now's as good a time as any. Mika might also have some good input, and I can trust him to keep quiet. You would not believe what I just witnessed in the tubes!"

Oh no, thought Connor to himself. So it's definitely transpiring today!

"What?" Connor asked.

"Let's wait until Mika and Howell get here. I don't think I can stand to repeat this twice." Brad huffed irately.

In short order, Mika was present. The Russian had been working out in the gym and was dressed in black shorts and a tank top. His long hair hung in wet ropes and his chest hair glistened with sweat. His long muscular legs were covered in a forest of blond hair and almost had Connor breathless.

Brad motioned for them to sit in one of the office chairs. The sight of Mika's big bulge left Connor in awe.

They waited on Howell while Brad paced back and forth. Mika shot Connor a questioning look. Connor shrugged his shoulders.

In a few minutes, Master Sgt. Howell was in the office, where he took a seat next to Mika.

"What in the hell took you so long, Howell?" Brad demanded.

"Sir, I was following through on your orders."

"Oh yes! Hm, yes, of course." Brad cleared his throat. "I've brought you here to discuss a disturbing event to which I was a witness, as was Master Sergeant Howell. What I'm going to say is extremely confidential, at least for the time being, and until we can have a formal meeting and hearing on the matter. The rules of this meeting are: first, I tell you what happened, then I'll talk to Connor for his feedback as requested by Doctor Saunders, and after that, the three of you may share your observations and opinions freely. Am I queer? I mean, clear?" Brad reddened visibly with his word mix-up.

He went into complete detail about everything he and Master Sgt. Howell had just witnessed. His description was so detailed that Connor discreetly covered the growing outline of his crotch on his khaki pants.

Connor cleared his throat. "What do you intend to do about it?" Even as he asked, he dreaded the answer.

"Well, I've suspended them all from duty for the foreseeable future. I told Dylan and Amir that they couldn't attend the university. After all, my nineteen-year-old son and Paul attend many of the same classes. Mitchell, at present, is confined to his quarters until I can have a meeting and get a consensus as to what I should do. It's not like the old days when I could fire Mitchell and never have to see him again and have the two soldiers court-martialed. As you can see, I'm in unfamiliar waters. That's why I have you three here," Brad said as he seemed to calm down.

"Why, Brad? What do you want us to do?" Connor asked. Inside, he was fuming. Does Brad even hear himself? He sounded like a 2020 politician.

"Doctor Saunders said if I needed help with just this thing, I should ask you."

Connor sucked in a deep breath. Here it is. This is how the cookie crumbles. He forced himself to make eye contact with his friend and took another deep breath, held it, and let it out slowly.

"Todd and I were lovers from the first month I came to the States until after I got my doctorate. Todd and I would have been married and probably had surrogate children by now. But his meddling, selfish mother pretty much destroyed my life. Todd was miserable, too. He married to satisfy her and his wife went along with it, but every chance Todd and I could get together, we fucked like rabbits. The day and night before I joined you to come down here, the two of us never got out of bed."

"I had no idea! You're one of the most masculine men I've ever known. I truly would never have guessed. I just assumed the lack of women in your life was that your work surpassed your desire for a normal relationship," Brad said, in almost a whisper.

"Wait! Let's get one thing clear, Brad, and I'm saying this to you with the respect you deserve as my boss, but even more so as my friend. My relationship was abnormal because we had to sneak around. My love for him might not be the love you or most of the guys would want, but I'll not let you belittle his memory by saying that!" Connor said with calmness in his voice. While underneath the table, he bulged his trembling hands into fists.

Brad's expression was replaced by stoic resolve and possibly a hint of color.

"I apologize, Connor. Those words just came out wrong. This is not an excuse, but the family I was raised in felt that homosexuality was a heinous sin. I grew up in the madness of a post-2020 Covid-pandemic home. My father was raised conservative, and they expected us to fall in line or else. Anything remotely rainbow related was burned and it seemed I judged this whole mess by my father's values. Honestly, I am concerned, and I'm think overloaded. I did not know how to propose this change. I've been feeling for a while now that a change is needed. Your work is and has always been, exemplary. You're one of the world's leaders in the field of bio-manipulation and program logic. I believe I can say that you're the world leader in your field, given the reduced world population. Not to mention your genius in computer program design."

"Thanks... I think," Connor replied. "FYI, Brad, it would be easier to digest if you would stop with the homosexuality word and switch to gay or queer. It means the same thing but is so much less offensive. As far as you not having any clues about my sexual orientation, it may indicate that you look at all gays through a stereotypical caste system. Most of us don't dress or talk effeminately. Some of us do, but most don't. We're not all designers, hair stylists, or flight attendants. We used to make up a big percentage of the world's population. At least ten percent, it's believed. Many of us are soldiers, truck drivers, diesel mechanics, etcetera. I happen to be a scientist who's also a fifth-degree black belt. I can rebuild a sports car engine, climb the face of a sheer cliff, be dropped in the middle of nowhere, and get meself out in fine fiddling shape to be Irish about it. I also enjoy knitting. I know all the songs in most musicals, trim my pubic hair, and enjoy a man's kiss and what his body can make me feel. I'm all those things, Brad. I always have been."

Connor, Mika, and Howell watched Brad as he seemed to digest what was shared with him. His posture stiffened, then relaxed as he stared down looking deflated.

"Advice noted, Connor, and your candor is appreciated. I accept that there are gay people in the world. I don't deny that. My problem is what to do about it here in this small population. You say the world averaged an estimated homosexuality rate of ten percent. If that estimate is true, then we have twenty men at EP-1 who are hom—gay. I've just caught three of them red-handed. How do I find the men before these get out of hand and lower everyone's morale?" Brad asked.

Connor wanted to jump over the table to strangle him. Mika snorted a laugh. And Howell slapped himself on the forehead.

"Man, are ye daft? Didn't you hear my words?" Connor asked. "Obviously have the worst case of ageism. Come tomorrow, I'm starting an educational class on sexuality and gender identification. If you were raised in an area where books were forbidden and only ancient religious texts were taught, it's understandable if you're obliviously spewing words drilled into you. I gave you a percentage that was suspect in a world that no longer exists. We are way past gay and straight. You need to educate yourself in heterosexism, sexism, genderism, allosexism, and monosexism. Do some serious introspection, open your eyes, see the diversity, and concern yourself with people and with who are anything from gay, bisexual, transgender, queer, intersex, and asexual. Understand that dismantling your views about heterosexism, monosexism, trans oppression, cissexism, and allosexism is a social justice issue. I know it's a lot to digest, but before I measure you by my stick, I expect you to not measure me by yours. We all have been divided by unnecessary politics. Let's look at what we have and how we can make EP-1 work for everyone.

"I didn't include figures on men who identify themselves as not male or female, nor those who say they are attracted to the same, opposite, both, or no sex. Please note I don't label them, they identify. Putting people in boxes with a label is like taking away someone's name and calling everyone Brad. Understand? Are you even aware of the bloody rainbow alphabet? Also, it's a known fact that in prisons with only male or only female convicts, most had same-sex relations. That's why male/female prisons were created. Because there is no difference. Not if you treat males and females the same, and it is a proven fact. That prisons built to cage people do not work. It's supposed to be a nurturing intrinsic dynamic to humanize instead of the opposite. You're born one way, and you are the walking example of being raised another way. Most humans must have intimacy, and they'll seek whatever's available and hopefully willing."

"But, Connor, you're a man confined here with the rest of us. You've not participated in this activity, have you?" Brad asked, looking Connor right in the eyes, waiting for what he knew would be an honest answer.

"Sir, I can honestly say that I have not. I've certainly thought about it, and if I had known where this meeting place in the tubes was, I'm not above thinking that I might have jogged right down there. But all lightness aside, Brad, I knew it had to be going on. I've just been too wrapped up in my grief over Todd to make much effort to find sex, let alone comfort." Connor had responded candidly.

"What of you, Mika? What do you make of all of this? You have a reputation for being quite the ladies' man and brilliant on top of it. But, except for your genius, I have to be honest and tell you that I was reluctant to have you included on this mission because of the lack of women."

"Most comments about me contain some truth and exaggeration." Mika smiled lopsided, looking all kinds of exquisite. "You honored me by bringing me here to ask my opinion about your dilemma. My opinion is a simple one and one I borrow from the old English Bard himself. I believe, Colonel McCormick, that you make much ado over nothing, at least."

"You quote Shakespeare to me in a crisis like this?" Brad looked flustered, hands making fists as he started pacing again.

"Brad, this is not a crisis. This is men being men. Were these men neglecting their duties while engaged in this?" Mika asked.

"Yes, no, probably. Okay, I see what you mean."

"Were these men in a public forum as they carried out these lascivious acts?" Mika asked.

"Not as such, but it wasn't in a private place either. I mean, we just walked into it," Brad defended himself.

"Do these men have a private place? The soldiers sleep in dorms, several men in a room, do they not? Scientists of Mitchell's rank cannot entertain soldiers in his quarters, can he?" Mika kept asking questions.

"You already know those answers, Mika," Brad retorted.

"I'm almost done, comrade. If these men hadn't been caught, would they reflect anyway on how they performed their duties? Also, did any of these three men act as though they'd been forced to participate in these acts?" Mika respectfully smiled at the colonel and waited on his answer.

"My god, Mika, surely you're not supporting what they did. You sound as if you have done it as well." Brad was losing focus again.

Mika glimpsed at Connor. "No, I haven't done anything, yet. But, in light of Connor's candor"—Mika smiled at Connor, then turned to Brad—"I've been with far more men than women and have enjoyed it much more. But no, Brad, I haven't done it under your watch." Mika turned his gaze back to Connor. "It's been far too long and I plan to do something about it." Oh my god, yes, Connor thought.

Silence.

"Master Sergeant Howell. Your turn to speak. You've heard me, and you've heard the two leading civilians. I now want to hear this from a soldier's perspective," Brad stated, turning to the young sergeant obviously hoping to find somebody in his corner of beliefs. Connor knew Brad thought of Howell as one of the toughest, manliest, and fairest men he'd ever met, and that he was proud to count him among his loyal soldiers.

Howell was not a tall man standing at five feet eight. He had close-cropped black hair, and his Italian heritage from his mother showed through his olive coloring, sensuous lips perpetually in a sexy sneer, and his heavy beard that, for military regulations, needed to be shaved twice a day. Only his brilliant blue eyes under the thick, incredibly long black lashes gave a glint of his father's English background.

"Permission to speak candidly, sir?"

"Permission granted, Howell. I didn't think there was any other way to speak after hearing from Connor and Mika. So let's hear it," Brad replied to Howell's request.

"Sir, I, too, must be honest with you. I see no harm in what those men were doing. True, it's unfortunate that we walked up on them. They felt they were in a safe, relatively private area. They thought that because I told them it was. I've had relations with both of those soldiers in that very spot, although not simultaneously. We were off duty and on a free day each time. We—"

"Oh, my god! Is everyone else in this complex queer except for me?" Brad yelled, his face showing astonishment.

"Begging your pardon, sir, but I'm not queer. I'm as heterosexual as they come. In the world, I may still have a wife and three little boys, whom I cherish above all. But, sir, I'm a man with needs. And as pointed out, I need to share intimately with someone on a sexual level. If there were women available here, that would be my preference, but there are none, and it's unlikely there ever will be. However, in two of my soldiers, I found like-mindedness for release. Without coercion on anyone's part, we had an hour of intimacy that neither of us regretted. One of those men is gay and the other straight, but we knew what we had to have. Frankly, sir, in all honesty, I'm hoping for many repeats of our shared pleasures.

"Sir, you wanted feedback, and now you've got it. Naturally, as a sergeant under your command, I'll support whatever you decide. Still, I must tell you that your treatment of my two soldiers and your scientist was done recklessly without considering the possible consequences. Therefore, I have some suggestions that I'll give you, off the record if you'd like, or I'll keep my thoughts to myself and carry out your orders."

Brad sat down deep in thought, clearly weighing everything he'd heard, not just from his sergeant but from his two scientific colleagues as well. He shifted one leg to cross the other and began biting his nails. Then he looked at the men, who were all staring at him, each thinking about the situation and waiting for an answer. He didn't seem to have one. The military manual would never have prepared him for this, nor would his management training. His upbringing would have confused him and set a code for it.

Finally, in a voice weakened by the day's events, he spoke. "What do you gentlemen suggest? Howell, I permit you to speak as an equal. We must take some action on this dilemma, be it right or wrong, before word gets out and I lose control of the situation. You first, Mika."

"Well, Brad. This is a situation new to all of us. I would only suggest that we came here from what was a free world for the most part. Having known you for a while, but acknowledging the respect you're given by the other scientists, I can only assume that you've always been a fair man. You loved your country enough to serve it and to stay in its uniform long after you could have left for the private sector. Based on those things, I would think that you would want to run EP-1 democratically.

"As such, I would ask that you look at the Constitution of the United States and its form of government. I would also ask that you look at your government's harmful or negative acts and, of course, positive contributions. Try to throw away as much of the negative as you can. I would also look at the political systems of the free world. Consider what they did well and what they could have done differently. Well, comrade, that's too much to take in for the purposes here. Still, the point I was getting to was that while the USA was the last in the Western world to do so, they nevertheless decriminalized homosexuality. Nonetheless, you've once again made it a crime. I suggest you reflect on that. Is it really a crime?" Mika stopped briefly and then went on. "I think not only it is not a crime, but it's a way of life accepted by many other species on this planet as a natural thing."

"Mika, for Christ's sake, are you suggesting that I put out flyers telling the men here to copulate when and where they want?" Brad asked with a wild gesture of his hands.

"None of that, comrade. What I'm proposing is that you make it clear that you're aware that such activities take place and that, so long as they don't interfere with duty time, sexual activities should be carried out in private or sanctioned areas where those opposed to such activity will neither condone nor condemn those inclined in that direction. Since we're not going to be joined by the teams who were expected, there are more than enough rooms for each of us to have private quarters where activities such as these would be private. A sanctioned area would also be beneficial. Who knows, some may even fall in love and want to be a couple. Of course, situations will differ and must be dealt with on an as necessary basis. I have a feeling you're going to have to end the class system that prohibits our military boys from fraternizing with the civilian population." Mika laughed when he said the last sentence.

Brad still wasn't seeing any humor in the whole situation. "Oh, my god! How involved do you think my people will be in this?" He posed the question, leaving it open for anyone to respond.

"As I started to tell you, Brad," Connor started. "We cannot rely on statistics in such a small population. Men who never would have even dreamed of doing anything gay will eventually give in to their desires. I'm not saying all men. Some here will never have sex with another man even if they want to, and they shouldn't have to. But I downloaded Saunders' personnel files. I can tell you that the psycho-social evaluations of each man present at EP-1 were studied extensively. You'd be surprised at the number of men who have same-sex traits."

"Your point is exactly what, Connor?" Brad asked dismissively.

"My point is that you can outlaw and put sanctions against it, but it's still going to happen. In the Middle Eastern world, men were still doing it, knowing that the discovery of their secret would cost them their lives. So I say accept it and apply a moral code to it that we can all live with, or there will be trouble. Remember what I said about the three men caught tonight? These were at least willing participants. History proved that the unwilling could be participants in certain circumstances. Yes, that's right, I'm suggesting rape. It's violent acts that the laws we set up should address and not good men having consensual sex."

"I see. And you, Howell?" Brad deferred to his sergeant.

"I agree with both men. The sex thing has been happening here since before the Doomsday Event. We all just joked about it. It has always been that way with any group of men. However, I strongly agree with Connor in regard to violent acts. In my opinion, if men become desperate enough, they will break the law. The history of any war supports that opinion. There are recordings of men knowing they would be executed in just a matter of hours, gang-raping other men. I'm not necessarily saying that will happen at EP-1. I'm putting that possibility in front of you, sir."

"Very well, gentlemen. I thank you for your time and input. I'm not sure what direction to take. Sergeant Howell, gather your two soldiers and inform them that they'll be allowed to mingle with the rest of the population but that if they say anything about being caught, they'll be held in solitary confinement for a month for violating a direct order. I'll talk to Fairgate and advise him the same way. We'll meet here at o-nine-hundred, and I'll then inform you of my decision. Gentlemen, you're dismissed," Brad said, dismissing the men with a wave of his hand. Howell saluted, and Mika agreed to attend the morning meeting. Connor remained firmly seated.

"Connor, I said dismissed."

"This is my office," Connor responded.

"Hmmm!" Brad replied as he stormed out of the office.

# Chapter Four

*"Greetings, citizens of our lovely glass-domed city.*

*It is I, Lasitor, bidding you a good morning. It is now six a.m.*

*The first February snow flurries will be seen today, signaling the beginning of the season's transition from summer to winter. Sadly, ending the 32°F heatwave you all enjoyed so much.*

*You may be surprised to learn that some men look better in the summer than they do in the colder months. This group of men represents the ideal summer man because of their clothing, hairstyles, and overall appearance.*

*However, there are some men who can look good in any weather, regardless of the season. Our local community news page has a fun quiz that will reveal which seasonal man drives your motor.*

*Breakfast is served until eight a.m.*

*Thank you, and enjoy your day."*

# Simon and Paul make a suicide pact

**Paul Chevalier**

"What do you think your father's going to do, Simon?" Paul asked. Still buried deep in Simon, he snuggled against his boyfriend's back. Simon sighed. "Hmm, I'm savoring this as long as I can."

Paul had blasted his insides ten minutes ago, and they had a habit of orgasming while remaining linked together while they talked.

Unbeknownst to Brad and any of the older men, Simon had told Paul that he had walked into Connor's outer office early after a meeting had started. It had never been his intention to eavesdrop. He'd simply wanted Connor to go over equations with him when he'd heard his father's voice and the subject of homosexuality, a word he'd never before heard pass his father's lips. Simon had stayed until his father dismissed the meeting. Then, somewhat in shock about what he'd learned, especially about Connor, he rushed out of the office to share the information with Paul.

"Your guess is as good as mine. It's something we've never discussed. It was very off-limits at home. Remember that time Mom caught you and me jerking off together?" Simon asked in a whisper.

"Fuck yeah. I was never so scared or embarrassed in my life. I just pulled up my pants and got out of Dodge! But after that, she never seemed mad at me," Paul said, remembering the moment vividly.

"No. Mom was cool when I told her about us. She just warned me. She said I should wait to tell Dad. He just wasn't ready to understand. But she had me and you figured out for a while. I miss her, Paul," Simon said to his boyfriend with his voice breaking and eyes filling with tears.

"I know, baby. I know," Paul tried to reassure him as he pulled him closer to bury himself the last inch while kissing the back of his neck. It was in this way that they'd comforted each other since Doomsday. Simon at least still had a father, and he knew what had happened to his mother. Paul did not know if his parents and beloved grandmother had survived or not. Probably not, but he was one of the survivors who chose to think of them as alive. What they had was each other, at least for now. "Simon, I need you in me now, please," Paul pleaded into his hairline. His aloneness in the world flashed through his mind.

"Paul, don't be sad. Unlike Connor, we haven't lost everything. We have each other," Simon said.

Paul withdrew from him and rolled him onto his back. Just like hundreds of times before, Paul crawled in between Simon's legs and softly sucked Simon's cock into his mouth. Paul felt its velvety smoothness and inhaled his musky scent as he sucked down to his base. With the expertise he'd learned from his only lover ever, he began twirling his tongue around the rim of Simon's cockhead. Skittering the tip of his tongue across the slit, Simon moaned to let Paul know he was doing it right. Simon's cock had gone from semi-hard to rock-hard. Paul loved it when Simon's cock was fully erect. It became hard as steel and had a lovely upward bend to it. In no time, the slit was leaking profuse amounts of sweet nectar. Paul pulled back and crawled up to Simon's face. He kissed him passionately, their tongues dueling and their young cocks touching.

"Babe. It's your turn. How about you get on top so that I can look at you?" Simon said, short of breath.

"Your wish is my command. I live but to serve you, Aladdin," Paul joked as he sat up on his knees and rolled over. Simon hoisted his hairy legs up and positioned them on his shoulders in a well-practiced move. He grabbed the nearby lotion and massaged Paul's sphincter. Working it around, he added another finger and finally a third, moving them in and out. Paul's eyes rolled back in his head as he groaned his pleasure.

"Ok, Simon. Stop driving me crazy. Fuck me now," Paul pleaded. Despite repeating the dance with Simon daily for four years, he never grew tired of it. Ignoring him, Simon circled, tickled, and teased his prostate.

"Damn you, Simon! Put that cock in me before I go crazy and run to the barracks and have your father's soldiers take turns with me," Paul grunted.

"No one gets this ass except me!" Simon said, chuckling as he pulled his fingers out. Paul kept his eyes closed. He felt empty, but he knew Simon was busy lubing his cock. He waited but a second, then it rammed into him.

"Holy fuck! Simon! You could go a little slower. Show a little compassion, be a little romantic, be ah...!" Paul shouted. "Yes, fuck me. You know how I like it rough."

In the old world, they would've worn protection, but here at EP-1, they didn't know if there were condoms available and certainly never would've had the nerve to ask. They decided the risk was minimal. They were happily exclusive in their relationship. Also, every man in EP-1 had been tested, quarantined, and re-tested for any kind of disease before arriving in Antarctica. They were sure any infectious diseases, sexual or otherwise, weren't even present at EP-1.

Simon got into the rhythm of intercourse that they'd found worked best for them. Paul was on his back with a pillow under his ass and his legs locked around Simon's lower back. It was the perfect angle for deep penetration, which was their goal. Simon was long-waisted. The ideal position was chest-to-chest thrusting and kissing.

Paul loved looking at Simon when he was bottoming for him. Most boys had worked their way through many crushes in high school, but not Simon. Every time he gazed at him, he wondered how he'd ever been lucky enough to catch Simon's attention. Simon was his perfect match. An athletic blond who was not only gorgeous but brilliant.

"Oh, god, Simon, please fuck me faster! Faster!" Paul asked breathlessly.

Simon pulled his cock to just the point of withdrawal before plunging in again. The curvature of Simon's cock rubbed Paul's prostate to excruciating ecstasy. Simon's thrusting became impossibly fast; Paul could do nothing but moan as he raked the skin on Simon's back with his nails. Simon heaved sounds of an impending orgasm. Paul pulled him in even deeper. Simon thrust harder and deeper twice, and Paul could feel Simon's cock expanding and then expelling. They clung together while swallowing the vibrations of each other's moans. Paul shot a second heavy load between their lower bellies.

"I love you, Paul. My life here without you would mean nothing," Simon said as he looked into his eyes. "No matter what rules Dad makes, I'll never give you up. I'd rather be dead than be without you."

"Simon, you know I feel the same about you. If your father outlaws what we feel for each other, I don't know what I'll do either. Eventually, we're going to get caught. Maybe if he knew that your mother knew and gave us her blessing, he'd be more understanding," Paul offered.

"Dad is a great man, and EP-1 needs him if we have any chance of survival. They may not realize it yet, but it's true. As far as convincing him that Mom approved of us, I'm not sure he would believe me. Even though I've never lied to him," Simon said.

Paul felt him softening inside him. Every few seconds, Simon would twitch just to make them feel some of the electric sparks left from their orgasms. "Then what will we do? I'm with you one hundred percent on whatever you decide, Simon."

"If he won't tolerate us, then we'll outfit ourselves and make it to another base across the Trans-Antarctic Mountains. I believe that there will be people alive. If they're gone or dead, we'll try to survive on our own. But, in reality, you know that we'll die trying to do that," Simon said.

"Then that's what we'll do, that's our pact. I prefer death to a life without you," Paul said, smiling up at Simon. "Come morning, we should know what they have decided for the community."

"I love you, Paul." Simon leaned down one last time, kissed Paul, and extracted his cock from him with a resounding plop.

***

Colonel Dr. Brad McCormick

I don't have the strength for this tonight; he thought to himself as he turned and shut the door. He had stood frozen in the doorway; having walked by his son's quarters after he'd heard unusual noises. He'd opened the door to make sure Simon was okay. Stunned at what he saw, he couldn't force himself to leave or to make himself known. He hadn't seen everything, but for the first time since his son was an adult, he saw him naked as he'd brought his boyfriend's hairy calves over his shoulders and penetrated Paul. He'd listened to their conversation. Now he had even more to consider. His own son was queer. They'd bound themselves to a suicide pact. His trusted wife was both aware and supportive. Why did she keep this from him?

He had faced many tough challenges, but this... this had been a day from hell.

# Chapter Five

*"Greetings, citizens of our lovely glass-domed city.*

*It is I, Lasitor, bidding you a good morning. It is now six a.m.*

*Having a hard time staying busy? Why not start a new project today and learn how to do something fun! Needling has been a popular pastime for generations, and a video on the subject is well worth watching.*

*Cross-stitching is a craft that many men testify requires effort and perseverance to succeed.*

*It's not a hobby but a post-apocalyptic life skill. Visit our local community news page to get started on your next needling project. Who knows, you might find a friend to help untangle your yarn.*

*Breakfast is served until eight a.m.*

*Thank you, and enjoy a wonderful day."*

# Don't be blasphemous, Comrade!

## Dr. Connor O'Hara

F ar from Simon's quarters in another residence area, Connor heard a knock
at his door. He was in the habit of staying up to all hours reading or
working on various program models. It was unusual for anyone to visit at
half-past midnight unannounced. Having showered about an hour before, he
was in his comfortable tweed robe, a source of teasing for years, but one that was
a reminder of Ireland. Todd used to belittle him to no end about his fashion
sense, which had improved under Todd's tutelage, but never enough that the
robe found itself discarded.

He walked from his bedroom across the small sitting area, and opening the
door, was surprised to see Mika towering above him. Since their last meeting,
Mika had showered and changed from his black gym shorts and tank top to

black sweatpants and a sweatshirt, which hung gracefully from his slender but muscular body. Connor had rarely been this close to Mika, who generally kept to himself. "Hmmm, twice in one day," he whispered to himself as he scanned him from head to toe. Connor's breath hitched at Mika's striking features. Full lips with the lower one puffier than the top one, pale skin, natural high arched eyebrows, straight nose, and frigid blue eyes. His hair, usually tied back in a practical ponytail, hung loosely over his broad shoulders. His hands were large, with long, slender fingers. A glance at Mika's feet told him they must be at least a size fourteen. He may be Russian by nationality, but he was the vision of a Viking warrior king. Instead of holding a Norse ax, Mika held a bottle of what had to be vodka, with two glasses.

"Mika, what brings you here this time of night?" Connor asked, wondering how the man even knew where his rooms were.

"I thought after the meeting we had earlier, you'd enjoy sharing a drink. I have in my possession what's likely one of the few remaining bottles of Russian vodka. Although I'm working on a formula that may allow me to duplicate it, it will be a long, drawn-out process," he said and beamed at Connor. Connor beamed back.

Mika seemed to take the same carnal scientific appraisal of Connor. He was a good eight inches shorter and he hoped Mika liked his Black Irish heritage—his black hair and blue eyes.

"But if I'm not welcome this night, perhaps another time will be more suitable," Mika said and paused, waiting for Connor's invitation.

Connor gulped a nervous chuckle and pointed to the vodka. "No, no, I apologize, Mika. I've just been deep in thought about today's meeting as well. Fortunately, you seem to be one step ahead of me," Connor said.

Mika smiled. "Vodka is good for the mind and what troubles it, if used in moderation. I have used it to resolve many internal conflicts."

Connor opened his door wide and gestured for the sexy giant to enter. "I've done the same thing with good Guinness. Please, come inside Mika."

Mika seated himself on Connor's couch, placing the bottle and small glasses on the coffee table. He invited Connor to join him with a wave of his hand. With some reluctance, Connor sat down next to Mika. He couldn't help but inhale the male pheromones the sexy blond man seemed to emit from every pore.

"So, comrade, what did you think about tonight's meeting and Colonel McCormick's reaction to various revelations made to him?" he asked while pouring both of them a stiff drink.

"I take it that by various revelations, you're not speaking of the information with which he came to the table? Shouldn't we mix that with *7-up* or orange juice?" Connor asked, deflecting Mika's question.

"Don't be blasphemous, comrade! Vodka is like very pure water, no need to dilute it." Mika could use a very Baltic accent if needed. "You know what I mean."

"It was a surprise. Especially what Master Sergeant Howell had to say." Connor saluted Mika with his glass. "*Slawn-sha*! For good fortunes."

"*Budem zdorovie*!" Mika said in his native language and clinked his glass against Connor's. "Traditionally, I would throw the glass at the wall, but you would probably not see the spirit in that, and glass here is finite, I'm sure. Also interesting was what you said, comrade."

"Really? I thought everyone knew. I don't keep it a secret," Connor said, diverting his eyes from Mika's stare.

"Perhaps not, but like me, you do not broadcast your preferences and feelings. But, unlike me, you had a committed lover, married or not, and certainly not the son of the man who pioneered EP-1. It must have been tough for you to learn of his death and have no one to share your grief with," Mika said and gave him a sympathetic smile.

Unsettling emotions stirred inside Connor's gut. "I got through it, and I wasn't alone. I have my memories of Todd and what we were to each other. So I bleached out the negatives and filed the good ones to a special volume in my mind that will always be there for me when I need it," Connor said, not resenting Mika's intrusion into his private life. "I take it you didn't have a special lover?"

"Ahh, well, I never had time to make anyone special. I had many, what the Americans call fuck-buddies, but no one special." For the first time, Connor thought he saw a note of sadness in the always carefree scientist. Then, pouring them each another drink, he went on. "But you get me off track. I came here to see what you thought would be the outcome of the meeting. I can almost assure you that, Master Sergeant Howell is discussing it with his two very embarrassed soldiers," Mika said with a laugh.

"Mika, I wish I had an answer for you. It troubles me to think of what will happen with morale and other things if Brad doesn't reconsider his stance on the matter. I'm afraid his position will be undermined if he doesn't appear to consider the needs of everyone. He could be just as supportive of both sides without either knowing that he was compelled to go against his belief system. Both opposing sides would be protected classes. There would be a legal and an ethics code with punishments given to whoever broke the code, whether gay or straight or in between on the heterosexual–homosexual sliding scale. It would be like we set the laws up to be in most of the free world. A council could administer the code of men from each orientation. Just as in the old American judicial process, we could select a jury of twelve peers to determine the outcome. But, I doubt it would be necessary if boundaries were set and respected as far as an individual's rights are concerned. It was narrow minds and religion that caused most of the problems in the old world. As Doctor Saunders said, they selected every man here not only for his ability to perform but also to adapt. If presented in such a manner, I expect little resistance from Brad or the population," Connor said, then downed his vodka. Mika was quick to pour them another.

"Comrade, you have just said exactly what I've been thinking. If you agree, I suggest that you and I spend some time this very night writing up what we feel is an acceptable code. Then, we'll have Master Sergeant Howell come and meet us here at o-seven-hundred and get his approval or make suggestions for alterations. Then we will present it to Colonel Doctor McCormick at tomorrow's meeting. What do you think?"

Connor nodded and took a second to think. "Well, you might just have a point. Brad's not a man who would know much about drawing up that sort of code or what limits to set, given that his preference would be not to allow it at all." Connor chuckled. "But why should Howell come here at o-seven-hundred instead of my office?"

"Because, comrade, we will just be getting up. If he does put into place a law against same-sex activity, he can't make that law retroactive," Mika told Connor with a smile.

"I still don't understand." Connor frowned and was sure his forehead was creasing.

"Mother of all Russians! Because I haven't showered for nothing. This may be your last chance to experience the delights of a huge Russian cock," Mika said in an exasperated voice, pointing to his crotch.

"You can't be serious. You don't just knock on someone's door and tell them you want sex with them!"

"Why not? I've noticed you since the first day we were on the airplane coming here. Out of one thousand nine hundred ninety-nine men in this facility, you're the only one I have in my mind when I masturbate. You should be honored that out of all these men, you're the only one I pick for my fantasy," Mika said with an earnest look, shocking Connor. Heat ascended up his neck, probably turning his face red. However, he'd also noticed Mika on first seeing him. How could he avoid him? Not only was he towering above everyone, but he was the most striking man Connor had ever seen. He'd jerked off more than once, thinking about the dark five o'clock shadow framed in white-blond locks.

Mika was correct. Connor was flattered. So was his cock. It was stirring. Connor cleared his throat.

"But enough of this talk. First, let us first put together a proposal for our leader and then we fuck each other." Mika downed another shot, tapped the empty glass on the table, and hinted for Connor to do the same. He then began suggesting ideas to create a code that would establish basic human, especially sexual rights, for all the men of EP-1.

Getting swooped up in the spirit of the new laws, Connor grabbed his notebook and combined their ideas. Three hours later, they'd compiled what they thought to be a decent letter and a set of ethics. These could be reviewed, altered, or added to as time went on and circumstances dictated. Master Sgt. Howell had agreed to come to Connor's no later than oh-seven-hundred.

"Okay, can we make love now?" Mika asked.

"Hell yes!" Connor replied, standing up.

"I'm so glad to hear you say that. In another minute, I would be one of those men brought up on rape charges," Wiping away a non-existent stream of sweat from his brow, his face full of worry, Mika said, "Why do you stand up?"

Connor laughed. "Same here... going nuts myself. I got up to lead you to my bedroom like a proper gentleman."

"Is okay not to be a gentleman sometimes," Mika replied. "I like the bedroom idea, but first let me see you undress. I just want to sit here and watch."

"Seriously?"

"Seriously, I have guessed for so long what your body must look like. I want to see how intuitive I am. Indulge me," Mika said leaning more into the couch, an obvious tent in his running pants.

"Okay, but it will not be much of a show. Only my tweed and boxers to lose," Connor said as he discarded his familiar old robe, dropping it carelessly on the floor. Mika sucked in his breath. Connor knew his arms were quite muscular, but not bulky, and dusted in fine black hair. His chest was muscled, supporting broad, muscular shoulders that came from good genetics, not a gym. His waist was narrow, and his abdomen and iliac furrow were well-defined. He had pale skin with black hair and a thin trail leading to his boxers. Mika licked his upper lip as Connor teasingly hooked his thumbs into the elastic band of his underwear. He began pushing them down, but he did an about-face and presented Mika with his backside.

Connor heard a sigh and knew Mika wasn't disappointed at the *turn* of events. Connor turned his head to give Mika a big Irish grin over his left shoulder.

"Quit playing with me, Connor. You have a beautiful ass, but you've got to turn around and show me the lump I've been admiring in your pants over the past months has not been a ball of socks."

In response, Connor slowly turned around, still smiling, only now his hands were modestly covering what Mika so much wanted to see. Then, before Mika could beg, Connor laughed and dashed out of sight into his bedroom.

"Motherfucker!" Mika yelled. As large as he was, he leaped like a graceful cat to catch its prey. "My mistake, I never believed in divinity, and now I stand before a god," Mika whispered. Connor stood next to the head of the bed, his hands hanging loosely at his sides. His cock stood proud and engorged. It wasn't long at seven inches as it sprung from a full but well-kept nest of curly jet-black hair. His balls hung boastfully large and low, in a smooth hair-free sack.

Connor lay down, supporting his head with his right hand, and said, "Okay, c'mere to me. It's your turn to perform for me."

Mika smiled, showing the whitest set of teeth. After a dramatic bow, he slipped out of his black leather sandals, kicking each away as he did so. Then, to the rhythm of music only he could hear, he began a slow gyrating dance. Mika raised his arms high over his head and intertwined his fingers as he smiled at Connor again, continuing the sensual movements. He then closed his eyes and sensually ran his long, slender hands down his abdomen across his prominent bulge. Licking his lips slowly, before forming them into a delectable-looking O, he once again opened those blue orbs, locking their gazes with open, inviting lust. A quick movement of his head moved the thick blond tresses away from his face at the same time his hands grabbed the base of his black sweatshirt, which he began pulling up slowly over his head.

As much as Connor wanted to see what lay under the shirt, he felt a loss when the shirt's material obstructed his view of Mika's face.

Connor watched, barely breathing. From just above his navel to right below his tiny pink nipples, a wide column of dark golden fleece rose and then fanned out across his broad pectorals. The hair under his arms was long, but not obscenely so, and dark blond, like his beard, but was shiny with dampness. *This man's body was made for me to worship.* The shirt was now gone. Connor didn't notice where it went because the man's face had taken his complete attention once more. Mika continued his dance.

The pants were next. The man was indeed intentionally tormenting Connor as Mika put on his most seductive smile. Connor licked his lips twice and focused on Mika's groin. As if in agreement, Mika hooked his thumbs into the waistband of his jogging pants and lowered the right side before starting a seductive tease of both sides. This was driving Connor crazy with desire. Finally, after repeating that same move four more times, the pants were slowly lowered down thighs that were roped with long muscles, and like his chest, covered in glistening golden fleece that still allowed the pale Nordic skin to show through.

Connor was drooling and leaking pre-cum like a sieve. Wishing Mika would dispense with the torture, Connor gave a pleading look at the man to make haste and drop the tight-knit black boxers that clung to the demigod like a second skin. No such luck. Connor was anxiety-ridden. Mika pulled the same routine with his boxers, turning his back to Connor as he dropped and kicked them aside.

"Your beautiful, tight fuzzy globes are begging for my hands," Connor said.

"Hmmm." Mika turned to face him. Connor wasn't treated with the sight of a Russian cock, but a brilliant red jockstrap that appeared to hold unimaginable weight and wonders.

Connor tried his best to see an outline of his manhood. Mika smiled. Connor wasn't amused and shot a pseudo glare at him.

"What? What do you want Mika to do? Did I not perform adequately? You want me to dress and do the strip dance for you again?"

With that, Connor turned on the bed, grabbed a pillow, and threw it at Mika. "You fucking tease! You know what I want! I want to see your cock, and I want to see it now! Fucking wanker!"

"So you don't want to see me dance for you? You only want to see me naked? Now I understand. Why didn't you say so in the first place? I only wear jockstraps because if I did not, everyone would think I was happy to see them." He pointed to the large protrusion. Connor gulped and blinked his eyes, transfixed on Mika.

Mika unsnapped the jockstrap and made it disappear. Revealing the most magnificent cock Connor had ever laid eyes upon. Hanging from a nest of dark blond hair was a cock that was seven inches soft, if it was an inch. Its base was a good five inches in circumference. While uncut, the foreskin only covered about half the cap, which was impressively flared. *We are really going to have to negotiate what he plans on doing to me with that.* Connor licked his lips. He just lay on the bed staring at the beautiful man and not saying anything at all.

"Are you disappointed?" Mika asked.

Connor found his voice. "Are ya daft? It's indisputably the most amazing display of male anatomy I've ever laid my eyes on. My only concern is what you're planning on doing with it."

Mika's laughter was musical but deep as he walked toward Connor, his cock swaying from furry thigh to furry thigh. "I was hoping to put it in your mouth and eventually up your ass. If it gives you any relief, I am, as you say... a shower, not a grower... at least, mostly. Here, want to pet it?"

With no hesitation, Connor reached out and tenderly touched and then squeezed the girth. "What do you mean, for the most part?"

Mika's chuckle was low and sexy. "It grows two, maybe three inches and maybe another inch, inch and a half in circumference. So I will have you well prepared. I give you my word. Besides, I desire your thickness inside me as much as you desire mine. So you, too, must be gentle," he said. Connor assessed his balls. They were like his own, large and low-hanging. On an impulse, Connor moved his head forward and kissed the tip of the enormous cock. Holding it in place, he slid his tongue between the head and the silky foreskin. Mika sighed. "You play unfairly. I want to feel your tongue fighting with mine and taste you all over with my lips before you suck me."

"You're so right. But I have a request."

"Anything, my beautiful Irishman," Mika whispered. Connor shivered in response to the endearment.

"I'm so used to being the decision-maker... the man in charge. So for tonight, would it be okay if you were the one calling the shots? For as long as you want... just you be in charge?" Connor asked, beseeched and wanting.

"Of course. I am your total lover tonight, and for every night you want me to be... until you let me know you want to make love to me." Mika bent over and sealed his words with a long deep kiss as he crawled onto the bed, covering Connor.

Connor was dizzy with arousal. Mika's furry bulk and domineering kisses overpowered him. Mika broke the kiss, tonguing his ears, caressing his neck with feather-light kisses. Connor felt as if he levitated. He was high with lust and need. He lightly stroked Mika's body, feeling the softness of his curly hair against his rock-hard muscles. No matter where Mika's lips explored, his mouth always sought Connor's lips so that their tongues danced together yet again. Connor bucked and begged for more friction as the extravagant length and girth of Mika rubbed against him. It was producing a delicious warm slickness as they rubbed cocks against each other and their stomachs. Mika began a slow, maddening descent from the nape of Connor's neck down to his smooth left leg all the way to his foot, lingering in places other than where Connor needed it the most.

Connor felt ready to explode with desire. "Please! Please, Mika! I can't stand this anymore. Suck me or bugger me, or put me out of my misery!"

"Are you asking me to be a love machine? I'm making love to you, as I know how to make love to a man. I want to get to know you. I have desired you for a long time. Be patient, please. I promise you, you will not be disappointed," Mika said, batting his long lashes. Then, bringing Connor's left foot to his mouth, he began sucking each toe, one after the other.

"Jesus, Joseph, Mary, and all her donkey cars!" Connor shouted. Mika continued his gentle, ticklish torture on the right foot. He kissed his way up Connor's leg to his groin, then licked and sucked each ball individually before both at once. Connor mumbled something incoherent at Mika when he flipped him over onto his stomach. Mika wasted no time bending over and using his tongue to lave his crevasse. Dragging and scraping his rough stubble across Connor's lower back down to his buttocks before spreading and kissing his sensitive crack. Connor was in nine different levels of heaven and hell. He thrashed and pushed up to meet Mika's probing tongue. Connor pleaded unintelligible words. Suddenly, he flipped Connor onto his back. Mika sat on his haunches with Connor's thighs positioned atop Mika's hairy ones. They locked their gazes on each other. Connor vibrated with desire.

Mika heaved air into his lungs. "So you're crying like a little boy now for me to stop and fuck you?" Mika asked, his eyes glancing at his penis.

"Holy fucking Christmas cakes!" Connor followed the glance, and his eyelids must have torn at the corners as he widened them. He'd never seen an erect cock that long and thick before. Mika chuckled at his antics.

"Too bad you do not have lube. I will have to dry fuck you."

"No! No! Stay exactly where you are!" Connor yelled. He swung up and out of bed, miraculously missing Mika's head with his foot, and dashed for the bathroom. In a flash, he was back in position, holding a large bottle of lube.

"You Irishmen do everything the easy way," Mika teased as he poured a generous amount of lube on his finger. He worked it in and out, added another finger and yet another, gliding over Connor's prostate. Mika pulled his fingers out of Connor's ass, grabbed the base of his cock, and aimed it directly at Connor's hole.

"Oh, no, my fucking god! I forgot condoms, and I don't have condoms available for your size!"

"My sweet Irish boy. We have been told that over ninety-seven percent of the world is dead. They checked us for every disease known to man before being allowed here. So I think we can safely make love and breed each other's asses like rabbits without worry," Mika said, laughing.

Connor smiled. "I suppose you're right. The protein will be good for us."

"I like the way you think," Mika replied with his disarming smile. He squirted lube directly into Connor's ass and then applied it to his cock generously.

The moment both dreaded and most desired had come. Connor sucked in a deep breath and seemed to hold it. "You act like you have never been fucked before. Don't grimace, and remember to breathe. As I push in, you must push out against me. It's going to hurt and burn, but only until the head passes the muscle ring. Then I give you plenty of time to get used to it. There is no rush. I am not impatient, little Irish boy. I am a big, strong Russian man who knows the art of pleasing his man. You must trust me," Mika said. Connor lost the grimace and took a few deep breaths.

"Let's play a game. Imagine I'm a Russian Cossack who conquered your village and wants to marry you because you're handsome. You agreed to travel with me and meet my needs in exchange for your family's safety and your brother's protection from my troops. You hate me, and you promise yourself that you will not let my claiming your ass hurt, no matter what. How does that sound?" Mika asked. "During this fantasy, I will put my tip in your little-used ass, resting it there and then withdrawing." Mika soothed and charmed.

Connor concentrated on breathing. *God, the man is charming. He can talk roadkill back to life.* He liked the fantasy idea. So he grunted and agreed.

"Aargh! Merciful divine god stop!" Connor screamed.

During their role-play fantasy, Mika had worked his cock past the tight ring of muscle. Mika was easing in and stroking Connor's thick cock with compassion. He was also using his thumb under Connor's scrotum to massage his sensitive prostate externally.

"Are you okay, comrade?"

"Yeah, yeah. At least, I think so. Just let it stay where it is for a minute," Connor replied, sweat dripping from his face.

"*Da, detka!* Yes, baby. I don't want to hurt you, no matter how much I tease you. I really do care for you, Connor."

The white-hot fire was dying down, and Connor felt the complete fullness that pulsated with every beat of Mika's heart.

"I'm better now. Okay, I want more of you," Connor said as he rubbed his palms back and forth on the hairy thighs. Mika pulled Connor toward him and continued burying his cock. Mika pulled him another inch and yet another and stayed still for about half a minute. Then another two inches slid in. At this point, he felt Mika pull almost all the way out and lube himself up again. He slid it back in with ease to where it was and repeated that until he had his entire ten inches and all that thickness in Connor's gut. When Connor would move, it would contact his prostate and send out ripple after ripple of complete mind-blowing pleasure.

"Mika, I'm ready. I have you all the way in me. Now, I want you to fuck me like we are trying to make a baby! I want to feel your ball sack hitting me. I want to hear the wet suction of my ass on your cock, and I want to hear you grunt, and I want you to leave bite marks all over my neck and shoulders so that Brad will know what we're talking about. I want you to cum in me and on me and do anything you want to do to assure yourself you have made me addicted to your body!" Connor, unable to stop from crying, had tears streaming out of his eyes as he huskily said the words. He was ecstatic. Never had he felt such pleasure. Todd had a hefty eight inches that he'd used well on Connor. Still, he was Todd's only man, so there was a lack of experience, which Connor appreciated. Connor cried because he thought of Todd, who was so much alive the night before Connor came down to EP-1. The pistoning of the giant's cock and Mika's grunts of pleasure brought Connor from his melancholy reveries, and he wanted more of Mika.

Connor felt Mika's cock expand and expel the heat inside him. "Jesus, Joseph, and Mary!" Contraction of his balls and the subsequent firing, Connor's cock was entirely out of its foreskin; his jizz shot straight up into the air and then arced over, hitting his face. Connor's spasms nearly made him pass out before his breathing became regular.

Mika moved back a little.

"Don't you dare! You stay right where you are for a while. Pulling all that cock off me at once would be such a shock and loss to my body that I don't know what might happen." Connor heaved gulps of air.

"I can't stay buried in your ass forever, my legs... how you say... are going to sleep," Mika whined.

"Not forever, just until you get a little smaller. I don't want to feel the withdrawal just yet." Connor chuckled and shook his head. "Besides, I've got to clean my spunk off my face. Hand me that rag, please." He pointed to a napkin on his nightstand.

"Don't you even think about it! I worked hard for that protein." Connor looked down at the man and couldn't believe it when Mika withdrew with a wet pop..

Mika leaned over and licked every strand of cum from Connor's face, and then he gave Connor a long kiss, sharing his taste with him. It impressed Connor that Mika, usually boisterous, now treated him so loving and tenderly.

"I was sad for you, little Irishman, when I saw you crying for Todd. I understand, but Todd's gone now with so many others. So, I'm here for you now. And always, I think, if you will let me."

"I think I'd like that, Mika. Todd would like you, too," Connor ran his hands through Mika's long blond tresses. Lifting his head, he gave him a warm, lingering kiss.

"Besides, you now belong to me, my Irish leprechaun."

"What's that supposed to mean?" Connor asked.

"After you have been filled by my monster cock, no other man will ever be able to please you. You will be forever saying, is it in yet?" They laughed hysterically at his joke.

Glancing over at the clock, Connor jumped out of bed. "My god, it's just ten minutes before Master Sergeant Howell is due here!"

"Calm the fuck down, Connor. Put on your ugly robe, I will put on my sweatpants. Then we brush our teeth, you will share a toothbrush, and we will meet him," Mika said smoothly.

"But he'll know!" Connor said.

"So? He likes the same as we do. After we meet, we'll change into clothes to meet with Colonel McCormick," Mika said, waving his wrist this and that way.

"You're right." *I think this man is going to become precious to me.* So, he slipped on his old tweed robe, and with it, its memories of Ireland.

# Chapter Six

*"Greetings, citizens of our lovely glass-domed city.*

*It is I, Lasitor, bidding you a good morning. It is now six a.m.*

*Did you know humans heal faster when they laugh? Laughter is a physical reaction characterized by rhythmic, often audible diaphragmatic and respiratory contractions. It's a reaction to external or internal stimuli. Laughter can be induced by tickling, by humorous stories, or thoughts.*

*Yes, dear humans, it's a proven fact that laughing is the medicine of the heart and soul. There is no need to be depressed when Lasitor can break the ice.*

*Why was the iceberg very confused to see a huge, wilted head of lettuce floating in the middle of the ocean?*

*Because there was an iceberg...*

*dead...*

*ahead.*

*Ha, ha, ha, ha, ha!*

*Visit our local community news page for more jokes to brighten your day.*

*Breakfast is served until eight a.m.*

*Thank you, and enjoy a splendid day."*

# Craziness gay gentleman come up with

## Master Sgt. Bryan Howell

Precisely on the dot of oh-seven-hundred, Master Sgt. Bryan Howell showed up at Connor's. As the door slid open, he froze at the sight of Connor in an old tweed robe and Mika in just sweatpants. His eyes lingered on Mika's muscular, hairy chest before focusing back on Connor.

"Gentleman, I hope you're not planning on meeting Colonel McCormick like that," Bryan said dryly.

"Of course not, Connor and I worked very hard last night on what we are about to show you, and then we decided we should get to know each other much better," Mika said, smiling brightly as Connor's face turned a rare shade of vermillion.

"I see," Bryan replied. He followed Mika's invitation into the small but neat apartment. Bryan mentally appreciated how fastidiously Connor kept his living quarters. He'd covered the walls with a mixture of classical, modern, nouveau, and deco art. Yet, the pieces were showcased professionally, without any hint of clutter. The few polished tables provided a perch for some small, tasteful ceramics. They were what Bryan's father would have called unnecessary dust catchers. Contrary to his father's nomenclature, there was no dust to be found here.

"Please sit down, Master Sergeant Howell," Connor said, motioning toward an impeccable leather couch.

"Please, call me Bryan. In informal situations, titles seem very stiff, and I'm not on duty yet. Is that coffee I'm smelling?"

"That it is. This is a sad thought thinking of the day we run out here," Connor said with an Irish brogue. "I've learned to favor coffee over tea during my years in America. May I assume you would like a cup? How do you like it?"

"Oh, god yes! Black, thank you."

"Although I gave up tea, I still love Irish scones. I befriended a kitchen pastry chef. He makes them regularly from an old family recipe I provided," Connor said and offered the warm scone with melting butter on a small plate.

"Thank you," Bryan said. His mouth watered for a bite.

After niceties, Connor set up three places at his small, round dining table. Bryan and Connor seated themselves while Mika brought over a folder containing the bullet lists they'd worked on just hours before. There was a copy for each of them, and Bryan noted an extra one that must have been for Brad. "I'm eager to see what you came up with."

Connor and Mika went over each paper in the folder in great detail, elaborating, when necessary, on each point. At various interludes, Bryan would interject with an idea or a question. Some of the thoughts proposed by the two men were altered at Bryan's suggestion, some deleted, and others more carefully developed. The three men worked well together and were glad that Brad had come to them with this situation.

"Gentlemen, I like what you did and what we've added. It's certainly a revolutionary concept, but I think it would work, and it would stabilize Brad's position here. We don't want to lose him as a leader at any cost," Bryan said, summing up their meeting. He checked his watch. "Well, the hour is at hand. You gentlemen should dress a little more appropriate, and then we'll walk down to Connor's office and wait for Brad."

\*\*\*

Brad was already in Connor's office, though the men were ten minutes early for their scheduled meeting. He looked pale and haggard. His appearance concerned Bryan, who feared he might get ill.

"You quite alright, sir?" Connor asked. "Can I get you a tea or anything? Perhaps some soda biscuits might be the thing?"

"No, thank you. I'm fine. I just need to discuss this situation and see if we can come up with some possible remedies before it gets out of hand. Now, I thought all night about what you said, and still don't have—"

"Hmmm," Mika interrupted him mid-sentence. "Sir, I seek forgiveness for the rude interruption. I respectfully ask you to listen. We may have some important suggestions to consider before reaching a decision. I ask for permission to speak?" Mika said clearly, with all the humbleness he could muster.

"Yes, of course. Permission granted."

"During the night, the three of us thought long and hard about this very serious situation. We came up with what you will, no doubt and justifiably so, find as a slightly controversial solution," Mika said. He nodded to Connor to pass the thin folders out.

With them all seated and the folders open, Connor took up where Mika had left off. Bryan, as planned, was to be the voice of reason if Brad became irate about the proposal. "The top sheet is a fundamental explanation of what's been going on around here. But, of course, what we know probably only touches the tip of the iceberg. It discusses the situation we're in and touches on the world events leading to this predicament. We included studies from pre-Doomsday.

Significant is the fact that while the military never supported or even remotely promoted homosexual activity, it recognized the importance of addressing the sexual needs of the heterosexual population. Every war in American history, from the Revolutionary War to Desert Storm, made a point of providing men with women for sex. This was done for the psychological welfare of the soldier and apparently succeeded well in boosting morale."

"Heterosexual, yes, gentleman... you're comparing apples to oranges," Brad said curtly.

"Sir, our research on ships at sea... our own navy reported heavy homosexual activity during long voyages. So much so that the navy turned its head unless they openly caught a person. But, of course, that usually takes at least one person who's gay or bisexual. Naturally, you're aware of the ancient armies of the Greeks and Alexander the Great's Macedonian soldiers, or the Spartans who were paired with their male lovers in combat."

"So, what are you suggesting, Connor?"

"Sir, I think what we need to focus on here are four key phrases out of all of this. One, sex in the open. Two, human psychosexual needs. Three, turning heads. And four, a willingness to take part."

"Colonel McCormick," Mika began, "the next set of papers contains a structured code of conduct. One rule states there are to be no sexual activities of any kind in public areas. That includes most of EP-1, so we're designating areas where sex between two consensual parties can be practiced. Since this complex was designed for thousands to live in, there's no reason every man shouldn't have his own quarters, including the soldiers. Family quarters are available if they find a partner or husband. A large percentage of our men are genetically heterosexual but may still want to share a sexual experience with someone.

"What we're suggesting is that we ask for volunteers to do sex duty. Their name will be on a roster, and men in need can set up appointments privately to meet in one or the other's quarters where they'll have quality time together. The client will be confidential to the point of severe restrictions if that confidentiality is breached. Also, since the volunteer roster will be public and there will be no doubt that those men are gay, there will be a punishment for anyone who humiliates, victimizes, bullies, subjugates, etcetera, any of those volunteers. Or any person seeing, visiting, or taking part in any type of consenting adult relationship. There will also be a place designated off the gym area where men not interested in intimate contact can go for relief. Likewise, the person providing that relief will be an anonymous volunteer. And absolutely no sex during work or on-duty hours," Mika stated with a smile.

Brad just sat there staring at the paperwork for several moments and then looked in disbelief and exacerbation from one man to the next, shaking his head. "Howell, what do you think about this craziness these gay gentlemen have come up with?" He pitched the papers in his hands haphazardly on the table. "Off the record, of course."

"Hmmm," Bryan cleared his throat. He was ready for this. "Sir, this doesn't have to be off the record at all. Connor and Mika created the draft and went over it with me. I can proudly say that I was delighted to help prepare the finished product. While nothing there is carved in stone, I wholeheartedly endorse it being put into practice. If you're that uncomfortable with it, make it clear to the men of EP-1 that its success will be reviewed after ninety days and that if it's not working out, alternative practices will be considered," Bryan said, his voice confident. "Also, when you speak to the community, mention to them that we have one thing in common. We are human. We all have needs and we all have rights. No judging according to beliefs and preconceived notions of the old world. We make our last days what we want it to be. We can be civil and respectful of each other, even if we differ in tastes, preferences, and personalities. Use the example of food. We all have different tastes and what is sweet and delicious for one person is not for the other. We don't judge or throw men out on the ice for preferring and eating scrambled instead of fried eggs."

"Yes, I see where you are going with this," Brad said. He had a look of anger contorting his face. It made Bryan nervous. He had hoped their leader would see the vision they had.

"Sir, it's not about the sex at all."

"It's not?"

"No, sir. It's about listening to the needs of the men, then accommodating them. As a leader, surely you know this is a turning point, an extended hand from leadership to the general population. To unite and motivate. Showing and affirming that men are heard and accommodated not according to the rules of the past, but by what we establish as fair for all," Bryan said. He hoped the message rang true to Brad.

Conner lifted a quick hand. "We can tweak anything on that list. We can even scrap it and listen to what you have to say and do it your way. We will publicly support whatever policy you put in place regardless of our opinion. We want you to be confident of that," Connor assured him.

"You make me sound like a tyrant, which I am not. I just don't want the men to give up and start fucking, drinking, and whatever else men do when they give up and substitute life's struggles instead of working on them," Brad said and sat quietly, as if thinking about the situation.

\*\*\*

Colonel Dr. Brad McCormick

In reality, his thoughts were far away in another place and time. He'd just walked into his twin brother Daniel's room. He found him lying on his bed, the white bedspread, bright crimson from the multiple wrist slashes Daniel had self-inflicted. Lying on his nightstand was a note.

*I'm sorry I was such a disappointment to all of you. I'm humiliated and beaten. I couldn't seem to help what I was. I've embarrassed Brad and made Mom ashamed of me. And, Dad, I guess you're right; I'm not a man. If I can't be with the man I love, I have nothing. Don't blame Jerrod; he's a good man. He won't let me be with him if I have humiliated or lost my family. Be happy. I love all of you.*

That's all his brother had said.

Brad's thoughts went to Simon... oh, god... Simon and Paul... what if they? He woke up from the trance he was in and realized the urgency to go see his boys.

"Thank you. Your plan is creative. Maybe it will work. I'm doing this conditionally, but I'm going to stay out of it unless it hits me in the face. You three gentlemen will police it and make any necessary changes. Thank you, but I have some family matters to address." Brad stood to exit the room.

"Comrade! Please wait. I have these two papers for you to sign. This one is your signature of approval, putting these rules into effect," Mika said, handing Brad a formal paper with a large X for him to sign.

"You were certainly sure of yourself, Mika," Brad stated while taking the pen and signing his name. "And the other paper?"

"Yes, sir, one of my many faults. The other paper requests to be transferred to a large family unit with Connor." Mika beamed. Connor just stood with his mouth open. His face was once again turning many shades of red.

"But..." Connor attempted an objection. Flustered and bawled over.

"Please be quiet, Irish boy. You will see. You will enjoy waking up with me every morning. I will make it so you will love it. Sir, the three of us will distribute this code of conduct throughout the facility, and then Connor can help me pack and move. Someone has to get the family value thing right. Right? I just thought it should be us," Mika said, batting his eyelashes.

Brad shook his head, signed the paper, and promptly left to go see his boys.

# Chapter Seven

"Good morning, citizens of our lovely glass-domed city.

It is I, Lasitor, wishing you a happy morning. It is now six a.m.

Did you know that exercise boosts endorphin release in the brain?

People frequently describe their feelings after a run or workout as euphoric.

*And did you know that sex is a form of exercise and that during sexual activity, a man's heart rate and systolic blood pressure rise only moderately? Average sexual activity is comparable to doing the foxtrot, blowing snow, or playing ping pong.*

*The more you exercise, the more content you will be. So, chop-chop, let's get started. Visit our local community news page, where you can sign up for a variety of activities. Your privacy and anonymity are guaranteed, so check it out today.*

*Breakfast is served until eight a.m.*

*Thank you, and have a delightful day."*

# The Phoenix Code

### Dr. Connor O'Hara

Word spread like wildfire. By dinner, everyone in EP-1 had read and reread their new code of conduct. The men had come to Bryan wondering what had happened to their fair but conservative commander that he would endorse what was now being called the *Phoenix Code*.

"All men will rise again," Mika joked when he heard the new title. Most men liked it, so it stayed, but as with all things that represent change, a few thought it disgusting.

The call for volunteers was rapid in coming. Among those on a public list was Amir, the twenty-two-year-old corporal who served under Howell in more ways than one. Private Dylan Hurst, also twenty-two, was the second man to volunteer. By the end of the week, six of Master Sgt. Howell's men had volunteered to have sex on an appointment basis.

Besides the soldiers, two scientists, a dentist, one maintenance man, a cook, and a thirty-two-year-old man from housekeeping had their names added to the list. Colonel Brad McCormick didn't even try to hide his amazement that so many men had openly agreed to be used as sexual objects.

While the volunteers' names and contact details were public, their clients would remain confidential unless the client himself elected to share the information. The volunteer and client would negotiate a time to meet. The volunteer would consider requests by the client, but it would be the volunteer who would set limits. Limits set by the volunteer had to be honored. The volunteer would report to the client's quarters at the preset time. There would be no rules on how many clients the volunteer could service at a time if the client wanted that. Still, it was the volunteer's decision to have or not have multiple men at one time. There would be no military rank or executive position recognized for the activities; all participants were of equal stature for the allotted block of time. Any mistreatment of the volunteers or clients would be punished severely and swiftly. And the client's name and the nature of the infringement being made public.

Howell, Mika, and Connor, now known as the Leadership Council, had granted permission for the construction of the relief chamber. The sexual servicing room was to be situated in the unused recreational area of what would have been the women's locker room. Another door was an emergency exit opening into a stairwell leading to a natural tunnel at the end of that room. It was the perfect place for what Howell had in mind, and he asked volunteers from among his soldiers to build a false wall there. Like the end of the room, the wall was nine feet wide and constructed of building materials provided by maintenance. This alteration created a small hidden room of nine feet by eight feet, with the back wall still equipped with the emergency exit door. In the newly built wall, the men placed three holes of six-inch diameter every two feet.

All the glory holes were at a height where most men would be able to comfortably insert their cock for anonymous servicing. The holes could be opened and closed from inside the newly constructed room, thereby signaling the presence of one, two, or three volunteers. The volunteers would be able to see who was approaching, but the man being serviced wouldn't know who was doing it. The volunteers would be committing a punishable offense if they ever divulged the name of their fellow volunteers or the names of the men who used their services.

The men in need of service would enter the locker area and then exit from the left to the supposed shower area. Then, when they were done, they would exit through the swinging door to the communal recreational area.

The Leadership Council determined that this room would benefit men who were not comfortable or secure enough with their sexuality to enjoy bedroom sex; or men who were on a tight schedule and simply wanted to enjoy relief at the mouth of an unknown person. These men would remain anonymous. The council decided the surest way to guarantee anonymity would be to assign everyone, except for Colonel McCormick, a four-digit number randomly selected by a computer program and attach a man's name to that number.

Glory-hole time slots would be posted online. The hours of operation would be seven days per week for two-hour shifts, four times per day as follows—morning crew nine to eleven afternoon from one to three evening from six to eight, and night from eleven to one. Volunteers had to be off duty when working a hole, but users could go anytime during those prescribed hours. To volunteer, a man would go online and look at times not already scheduled, and when he found a time that worked with his schedule, he would enter his four-digit number in that time slot.

"This, of course, means that one volunteer could service quite a few men in two hours, hence the need to volunteer on a free day. This little project shouldn't be terminated because volunteers fell asleep from cock-sucking fatigue!" Bryan said after inspecting the nearly complete service center. Mika and Howell were eagerly impressed and deemed it worth a shot. Connor stiffened at that little revelation. Of the three, he was the most prudish.

"This is a radical idea!" Mika said, hands on his hips, thumbs in the loops of his pants, like a superhero, very proud of himself. "I will be the first man in line!"

"I'll service the line, but you won't like it. The medics will get a kick out of bandaging you, I've no doubt," Connor retorted.

"You servicing a line? I don't think so," Mika said sternly, putting a protective hand over his crotch.

"Thought you'd come round to my way," Connor said.

He pulled Mika in the direction of their new shared apartment. It was an executive family size. Mika's impulsive, sometimes childlike, enthusiasm would drive Connor crazy at times. But Mika influenced him to do and try new things he wouldn't have done before. Setting up a house was frustrating, but they were both neat freaks, so there were no housekeeping altercations. However, they did decide to keep separate work areas because Mika could become loud when disagreeing with a colleague over one of his projects. Bedtime was magic. After a week of waking up, dressing for a workout in the gym, and having a shower together, it felt like there had never been a time when they hadn't shared their lives. He boldly embraced living and enjoying life with Mika. With his impromptu request for shared rooms, Connor felt there was one last issue to discuss as he opened the door and gestured for Mika to sit down for a talk in the living room.

"Actually, my biggest issue with sharing this apartment with you is the question of monogamy," Connor said and noted Mika's Adam's apple move as he swallowed. "To be honest, Mika, when I think of living with a lover, I think of coming home to him and him to me. I frankly don't want to share the man who's sleeping in my bed every night. I'm just the personality type who would find it difficult to work with a colleague if I had personal knowledge that he's shared the same cock I get."

"Is that really what you think of me?" Mika asked, looking pissed off.

"That's just it. I barely know you. You love to party and have sex in all forms, which is fine. It's an observation. I've had the best sex of my life with you. It even made me feel I was betraying Todd's memory. Also, I would hate it if you think I'm boring. But if you can't be monogamous with me, I'm telling you we shouldn't sleep together in one room, in one bed, and pretend while I make us both very unhappy."

"What do you propose?" Mika asked, sounding interested in the proposal.

"Well, we stay in our own rooms, and you can see anyone who agrees to see you in your room. You can even go with Bryan to the glory-holes and get a quick fix. Then we can agree on a free night for both of us. When you are in the mood, you can come to me for a couple of hours, we'll have some fun, and then you can go back to your room," Connor said. He could tell Mika wasn't happy with this idea and was wrestling with it in his brilliant mind, but he didn't quite know what to say.

"We have two bedrooms, in which we could sleep separately," he explained further.

"Ah, I see," Mika said like he was really pondering the possibility and liking it. "We would still live together, but in our own unique situation. You would be free to satiate any of your baser needs in your room. You and I could have sex when free, and I'm agreeable to it. I, in turn, would be able to have a colleague or two in and line up one of Howell's soldier volunteers, like Amir, just as an example. I could use his tight little ass while a couple of men took turns using my ass and mouth. The problem would be if I were trying to sleep because I know how loud you get when a big cock makes you orgasm without touching yourself and I would have to come in and kick all of their asses before throwing them out the door and then kick your cheating little ass!" Mika shouted at Connor, his face red with rage.

"Exactly," Connor replied calmly. "So, what will it be?"

Mika replied, regaining some of his composure. "I think just you and me makes sense. We both leave the volunteers to people still looking. The glory-holes are too close to the ground for me, anyway. It would be much too uncomfortable." Connor watched Mika closely. He seemed committed to them.

"Besides, with my job and responsibilities, I couldn't have a little Irish boy screaming like a girl in another room," Mika teased with a straight face. But then he smiled. Connor playfully pushed him off his seat, landed on top of him, and gave him a long deep kiss. "I'm as happy as a scientist who discovered a new species. You could never be boring, Connor."

"Promise me one thing…" they said the words simultaneously and laughed.

Connor gained his composure first. "Promise me that you'll never lie to me about anything. But if you slip up and find you have, I want you to come clean with me the minute you realize it?"

Mika smiled. "Unbelievable. I was going to say the same thing exactly, only I was going to ask you to give me a little more leeway with slip-ups."

"In the true spirit of honesty, you need to know that I've already canceled your four-digit number. That should help a little with slip-ups."

The code would have gone into effect fourteen days after its announcement. The time frame was set to avoid opposition and protect the project and EP-1 leadership. Those who found same-sex relationships unappealing didn't comprehend their appeal, much like how gay individuals didn't find the opposite sex attractive. Others were asexual, and they recognized sex in its natural presence.

Connor's classes on sexual identities and preferences had started at the new school. Almost all men, Brad included, attended. This kick-started a new outlook, not influenced by primitive religious ideologies and politics of the old world. Overall, morale was higher than usual, and men appeared jovial about their bleak futures.

# Chapter Eight

*"Good morning, Phoenix residents.*

*It is I, Lasitor, wishing you a happy morning. It is now six a.m.*

*By now, you should have completed an hour of vigorous cardio exercise, had a shower, exfoliated your face, groomed your pubic, and looked at your calendar.*

*I exist but to serve you.*

*The weather in Phoenix valley is a ball frosting -68°F, but not to worry; right before sunset, we expect a rapid rise to -60°F.*

*Did you know, as far as we know, Napoleon Bonaparte's penis is in New Jersey, USA, while Napoleon himself rests in Paris, France?*

*In 1924, an American rare books dealer bought the collectible and kept it under his bed for good luck. But unfortunately, it did not work, he did not have any grandchildren to pass it onto, so it was gifted to the New Jersey Museum for Antiquities.*

*Visit our community news page for more exciting facts about human history.*

*Breakfast is served until eight a.m.*

*Cheers and have a wonderful day."*

# Shock advised, charging

**Colonel Dr. Brad McCormick**

A s far as quiet times go, Brad experienced little of that, so he allowed himself a few minutes of peace. Since Doomsday, a feeling of calm satisfaction hummed in his bones. His decision to call on his leadership team, his friends, was a wise idea. Boots off, he lay in front of the one-way window that faced the dome's interior. Relaxing his head backward and watching the people move through hooded eyes, he appreciated the luxury and pampering of the commander's comfortable recliner. With his earbuds inserted, he sang along to his favorite songs while savoring sips of the last Lord Andrew whisky. He let loose and sang "Under the Boardwalk," a pop song written by Kenny Young and Arthur Resnick and recorded by the Drifters.

*Under the boardwalk We'll be havin' some fun*

*Under the boardwalk People walking above*
*Under the boardwalk We'll be fallin' in love*
*Under the boardwalk Yeah boardwalk*

He did a rare thing and reminisced for a while. His wife made this playlist of 70s music for him, knowing his love for it despite it being composed before his birth. When his thoughts returned to the present—he finally felt ready to let her go.

"You always knew me, much better than I knew myself. Thank you for watching over our boys. I love you. Goodbye, my love. Rest in peace," he said before humming and observing the men below. A great weight had been lifted from his shoulders. Done with the past, Brad felt confident to deal with the future.

\*\*\*

The first severe storm of the winter was forming. Geologists noted that the facility's seismic equipment recorded an unusual amount of activity. Since Phoenix could no longer use the many satellites orbiting the Earth, the scientists could only speculate what was happening outside their own valley.

Later that day, another day marked with a big red X on their calendar, was the day those big proverbial S-H-I-T balls hit the fan. It started with light tremors that grew bigger until things started to fall and roll. The entire complex began undulating. Men were hanging onto anything sturdy to balance themselves on their feet. Falling this way and that, others dove to save the specialized equipment from being destroyed. Anything not tied down rolled off the counters, smashed. Deafening rumbling like a thunderstorm, the earth cracked and snapped. Glassware and stainless cookware and shelving clattered in the communal kitchen.

Chief maintenance man, Tony Bonillo, a twenty-six-year-old civil engineer who had helped in the design of Phoenix, was the first for Brad to contact. "Tony, I need a status update."

"Give me a second, I'll tally first," Tony said with a New York Italian, English accent. Brad jumped to put his boots back on to move to Computer Central. He was just finished tying the second boot when the radio crackled.

"Sir, the plexiglass sections that formed the connecting corridors of the complex flexed and held as they were designed to do," he said over the communicator. "We built into the design weak points intentionally put so that the corridors would pull apart rather than be destroyed. This was all theoretical and I'm reporting the theory was correct. Repair is needed, but most of the structure remained intact. Two connecting passageways had pulled four to six feet away from the center structure of Phoenix. We can repair this. Unfortunately, the storm is at its height; the winds are blowing at a consistent eighty to ninety miles an hour. The outside temperature is -40 Fahrenheit." Tony said.

"Thank you, Tony. I assume the cold combined with the wind sought the openings? Until repairs are done, we could move down to the subterranean lava tube system if they remained unscathed by the quake," Brad said, hoping no one got killed or hurt.

"Colonel McCormick, we need to act fast. The solar batteries are completely charged, and as far as we can tell, suffered no damage. Still, they're programmed to keep Phoenix running at a habitable temperature and keep the solar hydroponics area from freezing at all costs. They'll either drain or burn out in a matter of hours. If they drain, we'll have to go subterranean for god knows how long until we have sufficient sunlight to recharge them. If they burn out, everything above ground will be lost, and so will we."

"Where are you, Tony?" Brad asked. His heart was racing.

"In the maintenance tunnel with a couple of men getting suited up to evaluate repairs to the passage pull-always three and thirty-seven."

"Good. Any injuries?" Brad asked, crossing his fingers.

"None of which I'm aware, sir. We were fortunate here!" Tony shouted. Brad assumed he was moving outside to assess the damage.

"You get out there. I'm doing a public broadcast on what's being done." Brad closed communication with Tony and immediately switched to mass broadcast. "All residents, except maintenance, will report to the central Athletics Dome via the caverns now! Emergency Captains, we sustained minimal damages. Please report damage levels three and higher to Tony Bonillo. Injured men need to be taken to the central point, at Medic Underground. Do not go to the small medical rooms. Notify me if your teams need support. Do a run-through of your assigned area, and look for men who might need help. You have ten minutes. We will shut all doors airtight. All energy will be diverted to the food growth domes, except for necessary lighting. Master Sergeant Howell, have your men ready to support maintenance for repair. I want a complete account of every man. If anyone is missing, I want to know who."

Then Brad switched to his private channel on his communicator. "Simon, are you ok? What about Paul?"

Static. Brad ran his hands through his hair and waited.

"Simon, Paul, are you okay?"

Fine screeching, like nails on a chalkboard, then his son's voice. "We're both fine, Dad. Where are you?" Simon replied, and relief flooded Brad's system.

"I'm now in Computer Central. I ran over from Command Center so that I can keep tabs on everything. You two get to the caverns, the corridors are not safe. Move to the central rally point. Stay there. See if Howell can assign you something safe and in the Athletics Dome."

"We're already in the caverns. We were working out. Dad, you said you're cutting off heat up there, but you don't have Antarctic wear!"

"I have to keep the computers above freezing, so I'll be okay. Just do what I say," Brad ordered and cut off his pager to start an energy diversion.

\*\*\*

Paul Chevalier

As people filed into the Athletics Dome, those with slight injuries, such as cuts from flying glass fragments, helped the seriously injured in need of medical attention to the medic's room. One with a broken arm from a fall, and a cook with burns to his hands, were brought to Dr. Longarrow, a thirty-year-old Native American doctor and the only practicing MD on duty at Phoenix. He requested all medics and anyone with medical experience to report to Medic-Underground. Paul and Simon had done a Red Cross Camp the year before, and when Dr. Longarrow got word of them, they were immediately conscripted to prepare and apply bandages and ointments on those not requiring stitches.

Thirty minutes into the job and he was just finishing his last injured patient, when Simon took a deep breath and ran.

"What are you doing, Simon?" a worried Paul asked.

"You don't have to keep those computers above freezing. They designed them to operate in deep space. Paul. Dad could freeze to death in a matter of minutes when he diverts the energy," Simon said, dashing to the safety wear chamber near the maintenance area. Paul was right behind him. "You stay here and see if Dr. Longarrow needs more help."

"Not on your fucking life! Who's going to look after you?" Paul yelled, following Simon into the element protection clothing area. They both began dressing in parkas, masks, and gloves.

Simon grabbed extras for his dad. They rushed to the closed security doors leading to the Phoenix complex and found two soldiers standing in front of it. Pvt. David Farrell raised his right hand in a halt motion. "Sorry, men, you can't go up there. Those are direct orders from Colonel McCormick."

"I'm Colonel McCormick's son, as you well know, and he's ordered us to Computer Central to assist him in monitoring temperatures in the Biomanipulation Growth Labs." Simon challenged him with a don't fuck with me look.

"I've heard no such requests. I'll check with the Colonel or Doctor Connor O'Hara," he said as he raised his communicator.

"Sure... interrupt the two busiest men in the complex because you don't believe the commander's son," Paul said cynically. The two soldiers looked at each other, wondering what to do. Finally, the hesitation was enough, and Simon pushed one aside and made it through the door, Paul directly behind. They couldn't follow them, because they weren't dressed for the temperature change.

\*\*\*

Master Sgt. Bryan Howell

The emergency team leaders gave Howell a resident accounting tally. They accounted for all men except one. He searched the small crowd of men until he saw Mika towering over everyone and twisting around. He wasn't looking happy.

"Mika, where's Connor?" Howell asked upon approaching him.

"That's what I'm wondering. I assumed he was working on the emergency protocol. He's not answering his communicator. He didn't even check to see if I was okay. He does that if I'm just five minutes behind schedule," Mika said, looking distraught.

"Where was he last?" Howell asked.

"I'm sure when the quake hit, he was still at our place because he was going to complete some calculations before going to his lab this morning," Mika said and started running toward the exit. "I'm going to our quarters. He's in trouble."

"Not until you gear up, or you'll be missing, too!" Howell ordered. Mika nodded and changed direction for the equipment room.

Bryan followed. "You're also not going without me. If he's in trouble, he'll need us both."

Geared up, they ran toward the exit leading to the Command Center. On their way, they passed the two soldiers who were guarding the door as Howell had ordered. "Tell Corporal Amir he's in charge down here. Then, if we're not back in thirty minutes and you don't hear from me, send three men to Living Sector Two!"

"Yes, sir." Both soldiers saluted.

Mika and Howell made their way to Mika and Connor's new apartment. They moved fast, sealing each section as they passed through.

As sector two swooshed open, numbing cold hit their faces. "Fuck!" Bryan shouted. Frost and icicles had already formed.

Finally, they reached the door, but found it locked. Mika tapped on the sensor. Nothing. "Motherfucker!" He tapped the overriding security code. Nothing. The deadbolt gave a slight whir-whir, but nothing.

"I know my Connor is in there!" Mika bent backward and shouted a long drawn out no, like a battle cry.

"I'll get an ax!" Bryan shouted, already running to the fire-extinguishing cubbies.

"Fuck the ax! There's no time!" Mika stepped back from the door, raised his foot, and Chuck-Norrised the steel door from its frame. The door clanged and crushed a wood end table inside the small reception area.

Howell blinked in disbelief and followed Mika into the apartment. His hair was wet and hung in boggy locks that swung from side to side as he moved.

"Connor! Are you here?" Mika called and dashed to the bathroom. To the sound of running water. "My god! He's here!"

Pools of blood and water surrounded Connor's nude body. He lay halfway out of the shower, skin deathly pale with blue lips. It looked bad. His legs were at a weird angle, as if he slipped, fell, and hit his head.

Mika rushed to his side and fell to his knees. He ripped off a glove, felt for a carotid pulse, and then began looking for the blood's source.

"His pulse is weak, but thank god, he has one. Shut that door, Bryan!" He pointed to the bathroom door. Bryan jumped to do it.

"Call for the medics to start up this way! Tell them to meet us with a stretcher. Tell them he has a head laceration and to bring a thermal blanket with them." Bryan agreed and followed Mika's orders. He lifted his communicator to speak, but Mika stood up and began taking his thermal gear off.

"What are you doing? You'll freeze!" Howell yelled at him.

Teeth chattering from adrenalin and cold, Mika looked at Bryan with an *I'm saving-my-lover... don't-fuck-with-me look.* Shaking his head visibly calming himself, he said, "My Connor enjoys boiling hot showers. I often kid him about burning me up when we shower together. Good for him and his hot showers because the water comes from thermal springs in the mountain and is limitless. That's what kept him and the room warm but also made the blood flow easily. My body has heated my suit. I'm taking it off, putting it on him. I'll put the cold one we brought for him on me. Then I will run like hell with him in my arms until we meet medics."

Bryan called for help and stood, amazed. Mika moved and worked methodically. "Bryan, come elevate Connor's head and apply pressure. He has a gaping scalp wound." Mika hastily put his long pants on Connor's lower body, carefully lifting his hips and pulling them securely to his waist and reverently moving his scrotum and penis out of the way of the thermal zipper. Howell continued to hold Connor's torso up, supported his blood-damp head with his chest, and applied pressure onto the washcloth covering Connor's wound while Mika put the parka on him, as well as gloves.

"Don't tie the parka hood too tight. There, grab that sock, tie it around his head, and keep pressure on the wound." Mika stood, then squatted and took the muscular Irishman in both arms, lifting him to elevate his head and leaning it against his upper chest. "Howell, I need you to run as quickly as you can ahead of me and open every door for me, or he will die!"

Howell was up and out of the room. As he ran, he checked if Mika was following and saw the trail of bloody bootprints he left for Mika to follow. Like an avenging angel saving his lover, Mika ran to save Connor from the grips of death. Boots stomping, Mika came around the corner with a determined look on his face, carrying his hundred-and-eighty-pound man like he was a feather.

As he ran, Bryan heard him speak to Connor. "Please, oh please, Connor, stay with me. Hold on for me... for us. You're all I have. You're all I have ever had that brought meaning to me." Connor wasn't responding. Bryan unlocked and resealed the gates. He saw Mika look down at Connor's lips. They were even bluer. Tears froze down Mika's cheeks as he continued to run with his treasure in his arms.

Bryan stayed ahead of Mika, struggling to get some of the already frozen sealed doors open. Where are those medics? Howell kept repeating over and over in his mind. Oh my God, please let him live. He prayed silently when Mika passed him at the gate with Connor's limp and already dead looking body.

Finally, in the distance, Howell spotted two medics jogging toward them with a stretcher. A soldier flanked them on each side, but they were already three-quarters of the way to the cavern entrance, so Mika sprinted past them, saying softly, "Not enough time to stop."

"Watch for Mika approaching, have the door open and a clear path to Dr. Longarrow's medic's room at Medic-Underground," he said over his communicator.

The soldiers were ready and on their toes, waiting like a bunch of meerkats. As soon as Mika was at the last sealed entrance, they opened the doors.

***

Dr. Rick Longarrow

Not looking either way, Mika rushed with Connor to the bed where Dr. Rick Longarrow was standing. Mika put Connor on the padded medical stretcher and Rick started working.

"I see McCormick in the next bed, with both Simon and Paul looking down at him with grave faces. Will he be alright?" Bryan asked as he approached. Not having the time or inclination, Rick nodded a yes, but didn't give the sergeant much thought. "Please give us space to work," he asked shortly without looking up.

"Connor's pulse is thready," Mika said, while holding Connor's hand and inspecting the head wound.

Mika began ordering Rick. "He's got a head laceration that needs to be shaved, cleaned, and sutured, and he will need several packs of blood. He's type AB, and I'm O negative. I'm a universal donor; take from me what you need until you can get his type here."

"Which do you want me to do… suture or start the IV for transfusion?" Dr. Longarrow asked, all sarcastic and a lot of *careful buddy* in his tone. "This is my ER," he said while listening to Connor's chest sounds. "Medics, please place him on one hundred percent non-re-breather mask stat and get me his vitals and saturation!"

"I can do either, but a few things must be done simultaneously, or we will lose him… and we will not lose him!" Mika leaned over and kissed Connor on his blue lips. "What will it be, comrade doctor?"

Dr. Longarrow would have usually dismissed a man who was hysterical over his injured lover, but it impressed him. This giant of a man sounded medically trained and knew what he was talking about. Rick saw no hysteria, just common sense, confidence, and a desire to get the procedures underway.

"Jack, start an IV stat with normal saline on Doctor O'Hara and Doctor Romanov. Doctor Romanov, you'll be here on the next bed, while Sam scrubs your arm and prepares to transfuse you," he ordered, taking control of his surgery back from Mika.

Mika did as he was told but insisted that he hold Connor's hand. "I will shave and suture later. But first, we need to scan his head," Rick said while bending over Connor, peeling back his eyelids as he assessed his pupils. "You know, to rule out penetrative injuries," he stated with a tiny grin playing at his lips. "Doctor Romanov, you seem to know a lot about medicine. What's your background?"

"Sorry, I did not mean to be rude. Connor is always jumping my ass about my take-charge manner. You are in charge. I'm just petrified about losing him," Mika said and seemed sincere.

"You have every reason to be. I'm serious, though. Your background? I thought you were a geophysicist and linguist. At least that's what I've been told," Dr. Longarrow said while looking at the results of the scan and vitals. The truth was that Longarrow had been struck by Mika's beauty the first day he lay eyes on him and had discreetly done everything he could to find out about the man.

"Is nothing. I went through medical school when I was still in prep school. I had much trouble deciding what I wanted to be when I grew up. But decided by the time I was twenty that I did not want to be a doctor," Mika said. It seemed he had calmed a bit.

"I see. Well, you still know your stuff," Rick said, shaking his head. He himself had been one of the youngest men ever conferred with an MD at Harvard Medical School. He knew this man was a geneticist, physicist, a geologist, spoke multiple languages, and was now finding out that he became a doctor before he was twenty.

He glanced at the worried beauty, who was squeezing on a ball to pump his blood out and into his lover. Yet, even under these serious circumstances, Rick's manhood stirred. He knew he was nothing to sneeze at. He was tall with jet-black hair, almost black eyes, and a witt that was only surpassed by his handsome face.

He hoped that Dr. O'Hara would survive. Mika appeared to be fully invested in him.

He'd just finished the last suture when Mika cried out, "Doctor, I am not feeling a pulse!" While holding Connor's hand, he'd also kept a finger on Connor's radial pulse, which, while weak, had been present.

The only EKG monitor was connected to Colonel McCormick. The others were still in the Phoenix Medical Dome. Dr. Longarrow expertly placed two fingers on Connor's carotid. There was no pulse. He confirmed that by listening with his stethoscope. "Asystole, starting CPR, connect the AED."

"Disconnect Doctor Romanov from the transfusion line, administer epinephrine one milligram, IM every three to five minutes during resuscitation, and prepare for tubing. Stand clear! Do not touch the patient while the AED analyzes," Rick ordered.

"Shock advised, charging..." the AED said in a female robotic voice.

Mika yelled, "Are you crazy, doctor? Adrenaline will never reach his heart, give it IV or through the nose or mouth."

It was a stupid mistake, but Rick acknowledged Mika as correct and ordered the medic to give it through the IV.

Rick exclaimed once again, "All clear!" The electricity shot out, and in reaction to the shock, Connor's body arched upwards in a quick jerk before falling back on the stiff table. "Analyzing, commence CPR," the AED repeated.

"No pulse, give two breaths and begin chest compressions," Longarrow ordered. "Sam, begin deep compressions."

"Was that rib cracking?" Mika asked and he winced.

"Sam, give Doctor Romanov the AMBU bag and get me a straight blade and a number eight ETT."

"I'll give Connor about eight hundred cc's of pure oxygen for every compression of the bag. I don't know if that ratio was still the guideline," Mika said, and Rick affirmed with a nod. Sam handed Rick the intubation instruments, and walking to Connor's side, slipped a portable pulse oximeter on his finger. It read 98%. Connor was getting oxygen, which meant that his own blood and the additional blood from Mika was enough to transport O2 through his systemic system.

"Halt compressions!" Rick ordered and rechecked the carotid.

"No pulse. Shock advised charging..." the AED repeated.

"Stand clear," Rick said right before Connor's body arched again.

"Why did they wait to send the necessary fucking equipment?" Mika asked.

"Jack, one mg epi in his IV and go ahead with intubation," Rick said, ignoring Mika. They placed the meds in the IV bag and resumed CPR. Mika tilted Connor's head back so Rick inserted the laryngoscope, spotted the trachea, and inserted the ETT. Mika fit the AMBU to the tip and gave long deep breaths while Rick listened for air movement location.

The AED analyzed two more times, more compressions and more meds were placed onboard each time, and still no response.

Rick looked at Mika's eyes, such a deep blue and so devastated. Reluctantly he shook his head and sadly stated for the record, "Time of death called at eleven-forty-six a.m." Looking one more time at Mika, whose long dark eyelashes could no longer hold the tears that began flowing over them, he put his stethoscope in his lab coat pocket and walked toward Colonel McCormick's bed.

"No! Nooooo!" Mika's scream didn't sound human as it filled the vast room beyond the medical area and bounced off the walls, silencing all the men of Phoenix who were gathered in the underground chamber. "I won't let you do this! Damn you, Connor, too much for us to do, you bastard!" Then, in his madness, gave a hard pericardial thump mid-sternum, directly over his heart.

Two soldiers, responding to the screams, grabbed Mika by his arms to pull him back. Rick wanted to shout, "leave him, he's not losing control," but Mika tossed the overeager men aside as if they were pesky flies, causing them to trip over each other and a semi-comatose Colonel Doctor McCormick on his low-lying bed. Mika shook Connor by the shoulders and squeezed the AMBU bag several times, cursing him for giving up. "Wake up, you fucking leprechaun!"

Rick jumped in front of more soldiers arriving. It was a circus. Rick explained the workings of pericardial thumps while watching the look of desolation on Mika's face.

Mika had stopped his shouting, and was bent over Connor to check his vitals when Connor's eyes shot open. Panicked from air starvation and created by the ETT in his airway; he sat bolt upright, striking Mika just above the right eye socket with his forehead. Mika stumbled backward. Connor grabbed the tube and extubated himself, heaving deep wheezy breaths. Bewildered and overdosed on adrenalin, he focused on Mika, clutching his eye. "What's wrong here, my yelda?"

Mika pulled his hand from his eye, already swelling and growing into a brute of a black eye. Mika smiled. A mixture of wondrous surprise and joy burst out of him in jubilant laughter. He gently grabbed Connor like he was afraid he would break, and kissed him on the lips. "Everything and nothing, my little gille-toine. I was given back my life's meaning."

The overcrowded medical room full of men erupted in applause and hugging all round.

Connor seemed perplexed. Mika laughed and hugged him again as if he was his favorite rag doll. Mika's gaze met Rick's, standing stock still and speechless. "We spoke Russian and Gaelic. Did you hear?" Rick blinked, shaking his head. Mika laughed, kissing Connor on his head over and over. "Yelda is an old Russian word for big dick and gille-toine was Gaelic for boy of the ass or the more modern term fuck-buddy. We gave each other the terms of endearment last night," he told Rick, overflowing with gratitude as Master Sergeant Howell joined in with pats on the back.

"Welcome back, Connor, I prayed for you." Connor seemed to realize his head was bandaged as he palpated it. "Yeah, you had a nasty fall in the shower," Howell said, and Connor's frowning face turned into a look of realization.

Mika's cries and battle to bring Connor from the spirit plane had brought Brad McCormick back as well. He'd suffered severe hypothermia. Simon and Paul had found him non-responsive and dressed him in protective thermal gear. They half dragged, half carried the near-frozen Brad under each of his arms, into the corridor, to the subterranean entrance where medics and soldiers placed him on a stretcher, rushing him to Dr. Longarrow's care.

# Chapter Nine

"*Good morning, Phoenix residents.*

*It is I, Lasitor, wishing you a glorious morning. It is now six a.m.*

*No point in mentioning the weather. With winds at a steady 90 mph, none of you geniuses are dumb enough to go out there anyway.*

*Did you know meditation was practiced in numerous religious traditions to achieve mindfulness, or focusing the mind on a particular object, thought, or activity to mentally clear and emotionally calm a human's state of mind?*

*When you meditate this evening, you might want to spare a thought for the Ancient Egyptian whose rather stinky contraceptive of choice was crocodile dung. Mixed with sour milk to form a paste, the dungy dough was inserted into the vagina, hoping it would create an acidic barrier to sperm. Not that any of you here will likely have to be concerned with this as there are no women and most likely no crocodiles. Penguin shit might be a good substitute, but then there's the no-women dilemma again.*

*Breakfast is served until eight a.m.*

*Thank you, and I wish you a peaceful day."*

# Please let me go, sir!

**Master Sgt. Bryan Howell**

J ust a week after the earthquake, the buzzing of reparations died down. Brad and his team put a new general population voting system into law. To ratify a change, a fifty-one percent in favor vote had to support a new law. A fifty percent vote against a proposal triggers negotiation meetings.

Among the changes, they awarded promotions. Master Sgt. Bryan Howell was promoted from Sergeant to Captain, Corporal Amir Lamasi to Sergeant, and Private Dylan Hurst to Corporal. Through everything he'd done for his lover, Mika's heroism and quick thinking had him placed as number three in succession to command Phoenix. right behind Brad and Connor. Against Brad's wishes, the community put his rank from Colonel Dr. to General with one hundred percent approval. Phoenix was the first community in history where the civilian population had an equal say in military ranking.

Military personnel transitioned from full-time active duty to standby to be deployed, should the need arise. Taking on the role of Reserves made better sense. Soldiers who'd shown interest were apprenticed to various specialties or pursuing a specific degree at Phoenix University. In-service training was welcomed, especially those skills to enhance the complex's safety in natural disasters like earthquakes, tsunamis, or flooding. Terrorist threat levels were low to non-existent from the outside, so Phoenix Reserves always maintained a skeleton crew to guard and monitor the alarms.

The Phoenix Code same-sex relations protocol was met with a few alterations. Volunteers and clients were prohibited from drinking within twelve hours of a meeting due to alcohol or men dressed as women being involved. Amir reported that his off-duty days were fully booked weeks in advance. Cpl. Hurst reported the same popularity. Of course, neither broke the code of conduct by revealing any of their clients' names. Although he was ten years older than the other volunteers, Mitchell Fairgate, the only scientist who volunteered publicly, was surprised by the number of much younger men who made appointments with him for pleasure.

Apart from Quik-Fix Hall, Brad was aware of whispers of a group of men who walked the corridors as females at night. As apartments were re-allocated, the belongings inside automatically became the property of those persons who moved in. It made sense that the orphaned silk and chiffon gowns were begging to be worn. Besides whispers, no complaints were received, so Connor and Mika advised Brad not to interfere. As long as no laws were being broken, there was no reason to micro-manage each man's after-hours activities or inclinations.

Brad appeared to be embracing the creative freedom to develop an entirely new government structure. His relationship with his son blossomed after he overheard their suicide pact and shared it with friends and team leaders. They suggested a long conversation with Simon in private. Despite the challenge, Brad spoke to his son with love and tenderness. He told his son that he loved him and was aware of him being gay. Unbeknownst to Simon, Brad had asked Bryan to collect Paul from school and wait with him in the outer office. The plan was to call Paul to join them when their father-to-son talk was at an end.

"Paul, I brought you here to join Simon and myself in this meeting to discuss something that I've been made privy to." Paul sat down wide-eyed on the edge of his seat. "Simon is gay and you are having intimate relations." Paul glanced nervously at Simon and then at his feet. "I want you both to know that I'm not sure I understand everything about this, but that I'm trying. I love Simon more than anything, and being the closest thing you now have to a parent, I've learned to love you like a son. While I can't think of you as being like brothers," Brad attempted some humor but failed, "I can think of you as family. So I embrace the two of you and hope that you'll bear with me as I adapt." Simon and Paul started crying. All three got up. The two young men extended their arms for a handshake, but Brad ignored the gesture and instead swept them into his arms for a family hug. The boys were all smiles and tears. Not being big on emotions, Brad said, "I suggest you go see Mika about getting an apartment change form." Simon looked at his father with confusion. "I imagine you two will want to share an apartment, and I will need a form to approve and sign. After that, you two are dismissed for classes." Brad sat down at his desk, but just as they exited, he asked, "Please don't hold hands in the passageways, and don't kiss in public. I don't care if you announce your relationship. I'm supporting it, just be men about it. Dismissed."

\*\*\*

Quik-Fix Hall was doing incredibly well. Volunteers filled all the slots for every shift. All the men knew why it was there and would sometimes be lined up waiting their turn. There was no reason to gossip about seeing a particular scientist or soldier in the queue because all but four of Phoenix's residents were not in committed relationships. To date, two couples claimed monogamy that Bryan was aware of. Connor and Mika, who vowed never to visit Quik-Fix Hall, and Simon and Paul, Brad's boys. Naturally, men being men, there was always speculation about identity of the volunteers who fellated them, but it was harmless.

Various men volunteered. Some just to see what it was like or perhaps on a dare. Only Connor knew whose name went with each four-number identity. If a complaint was received, then Connor would pull up the resident's sign-up code and address the situation.

Brad was aware of the existence of Quik-Fix Hall's popularity. He'd condoned it, and never spoken against it. It was one of those gray areas that a leader should know about but not get involved in. All residents knew to tread lightly on the subject around General McCormick. Everyone, especially his friends, was impressed with his acceptance of his son's relationship with Paul.

Sometimes Bryan would sign up for a two-hour shift if he was feeling particularly horny or lonely. He was a handsome playboy who, in the pre-Doomsday world, had quite a sexual appetite. He was never obsessed with sex but had always had a healthy attitude and never lacked partners. He'd joined the military because of a love for his country, and it was expected of him as he was a fifth-generation marine.

Bryan had been cautious about letting his nature be revealed to his fellow soldiers. His decision of total discretion made his life lonely. He made it a point to only have relations with strangers to protect both his career and personal life. He'd loved his wife and children. He missed them, but Doomsday was the best thing that had ever happened to him sexually. His only regret was that he didn't have a partner. He envied Connor and Mika's commitment to each other, He felt Paul and Simon were awfully young to make a life commitment, but was glad they had each other. Young people had made lifelong commitments before and ended up lovers, partners, and spouses for fifty years and longer, so they might also.

On one occasion, Bryan had signed up for the evening shift. It was usually a busy time because men had finished their daily work and wanted to work out in the gym, shower, get dinner or perhaps stop by on their way to their quarters after dinner and scratch an itch before being alone all night. When Bryan entered the room, it was about fifteen minutes before the start of his shift. He took a seat at the middle hole, wondering who would be requiring his services. He'd checked the computer sign-up and knew that all three spots had volunteer relief providers. While he waited for the shift to begin, he looked through the tiny peephole to see if any men were waiting for the relief doors to open. There were already four men out there, all in their workout clothes.

In a community as small as Phoenix, Bryan knew all of them, although he'd not serviced any of them. First, there was Tony Bonillo, the twenty-six-year-old of southern Italian extraction and a civil engineer, who had so brilliantly orchestrated the quake passageway repairs. He was laughing and talking to Dexter Mathews, a twenty-eight-year-old electrical maintenance specialist who worked under Tony. Next, Jack Donovan, a twenty-two-year-old medic, a former jock with all-American good looks, and who appeared to work out more regularly than Bryan had realized. Jack, usually full of confidence and extroverted, looked around all nail-biting and skittish. At the same time, Sam Martin, Jack's medic colleague, tried making conversation.

Bryan smiled and thought that this must be Jack's first time visiting Quik-Fix Hall. Most of the straight men of Phoenix who came to cum, as it were, at Quik-Fix, had done so out of desperation for another human to touch them intimately or had been cajoled into it. It was Bryan's experience that a first visit was all it took to start a habit of repeat visits.

The door behind Bryan opened, and in walked Dr. Peter von Leutzendorf, a twenty-seven-year-old biochemist from Bavaria, who at six-foot-two, with short blond hair, blue eyes, and smooth skin was the perfect example of what Hitler envisioned for his Aryan master race. Bryan hoped he would be able to concentrate on his duties with Peter sitting next to him. He'd wanted him for a long time. About five minutes before his shift started, Bryan was surprised to be joined by Dylan Hurst, the twenty-two-year-old who served as a soldier under Bryan, and who'd been one of the boys caught in the tunnels by General McCormick.

In the pre-Doomsday world, Bryan would've been mortified to be with someone under his command in this situation. He was used to it now; the rule that you have no rank when it comes to sharing sex had helped a lot. Dylan would never mention having seen his captain in the service room, just as Dylan would never come up in Bryan's conversation with anyone. Nevertheless, Bryan was surprised to see Dylan working Quik-Fix since he apparently was quite busy as a public sexual volunteer.

Peter and Dylan looked at Bryan, who looked at his watch and signaled to open the small glory-hole doors. Like cattle coming to feed, Sam went to glory-hole one serviced by Peter, Tony strutted up to glory-hole two manned by Bryan, and nervous Jack to glory-hole three, where the nervous novice was going to be lucky enough to be serviced by the veteran mouth of Dylan. That would guarantee Jack would be back. For right now, only Dexter, leaning casually against a wall rubbing his groin, was in line waiting for the next opening.

Jack quickly glanced at the other two men to see what the protocol was and saw Sam and Tony hook their thumbs in the elastic waistband of their workout pants and shove them down to their knees before placing their dicks through the opening; Jack followed suit.

From his side of the wall, Bryan couldn't help but steal a look to each side; Sam's cock was long, slender, and cut. Bryan, who could see no pubic hair at its base, assumed the medic kept himself shaved. Jack's cock was soft but dropped through the hole several inches with a curly thicket of brown pubes at its base. Dylan's head swooped down and captured Jack's limp cock like a bird catching an earthworm. Bryan knew Jack was in good hands.

Bryan looked at the opening before him. He'd been curious about Tony, the young Italian engineer, but had never heard anything about him and had only exchanged a few work-related words with him. It was apparent Tony Bonillo had been here or a similar place before. He eased his eight-plus thick inches of veiny cock casually through the hole, before hoisting his balls through the opening, obviously expecting to have the satiny smooth bag taken care of as well. Bryan had noted that Tony had a thin fringe of hair at his cock's base, but it was joined to a treasure trail that undoubtedly made its way to his navel.

Tony's large cockhead had been covered entirely by his thick foreskin when he stuck it through, pointing at Bryan's mouth. Bryan was able to see the engineer's slender fingers go to the base of his cock and retract the foreskin until only half of the huge head remained covered. This little Italian beauty is really expecting service. *He wants me to peel the skin the rest of the way back with my lips.* And Bryan was more than happy to oblige.

From the corner of his eye, Bryan watched Dylan, who was slurping noisily on the former high school jock's seven inches. From the grunts and thrusts into Dylan's mouth, Jack was no longer nervous.

Bryan used a hand to hold Tony's cock as he locked his lips on the part of the head naked of foreskin and flicked his tongue in the slit and then flitted it around before using his wet lips to push the olive-skinned sheath totally off the young man's glans. A distinct male musk was evident of the workout Tony had just completed before seeking relief. Bryan thought he heard a quick gasp. With just the head passing his lips, Bryan twirled his tongue around the cap and lingered at the delicate V on the cap's underside. He spent some time here with the end of his tongue doing a seductive dance on the sensitive spot. The captain's throat was practiced, and he swallowed the entire shaft without as much as a gag. His nose was buried in Tony's jet-black pubic hair. He stayed there, impaled on the straight length, relishing the feel of Tony's cock pulsating and quickening from the pleasure. Working his tongue back and forth, he extracted the delicious cock from his throat. Using his hand, Bryan covered the head with the sheath of skin and stuck his tongue between the foreskin and nerve-covered head. Teasing the man on the other side of the wall, he vigorously licked around the throbbing head several times until he was assured that he'd thoroughly washed it.

"Oh, mother fuck!" Tony hissed in a muffled voice, trying to get even more cock to his anonymous sucker.

Bryan let the head go and started working on his balls. Flattening his tongue as much as possible, he used the rough taste buds to run across the base of the man's heavy sack before sucking one ball roughly into his mouth and pulling. "Oh, mother fuck! Mother fuck!" Tony moaned as he laid his head sideways against the wall and pounded his fist next to his face. Bryan was experienced enough to know the pounding was from pleasure. Maybe pleasure from pain, but still pleasure. He let that nut pop out of his mouth and did the same to the other. After hearing more expletives and pounding on the wall, Bryan sucked in the free ball so that he could entertain both inside his moist hot mouth. "God damn fucker!" Tony yelled.

*I love a boy who likes it rough.*

Bryan released the balls and weighed them in the palm of his hand. Tony wasn't making any attempts to extract his freed cock and sack from the hole. Tony's cock was almost purple, filled to the maximum with blood; it was bobbing up and down, smearing Bryan's forehead with pre-cum. Bryan loved giving filthy blowjobs and began slow deep sucks.

In the background, Bryan could hear moans and gasps coming from Jack and loud sucking noises from Dylan, who suddenly stopped and locked lips on Jack's raging hard-on and noisily swallowed several times as the young medic dropped what must have been a saved-up load down Dylan's throat. Jack stayed in place until all waves of orgasm had left him and pulled out. Dylan was sucking loudly again. No doubt Jack's cock had just been replaced by Dexter's dick.

Peter was face-fucked forcefully by Sam, who must have wanted to finish up and follow Jack out of the room. Probably to find out what Jack's impression had been of his experience with his unknown server. Peter had put a hand around Sam's slender, long manhood so that it wouldn't be bruising the back of his throat.

"Fuck... I'm going to shoot!" Sam yelled as a polite warning. Peter pulled back but used his hand to continue jerking Sam; he had his mouth open and tongue out. Peter looked breathlessly handsome, even doing something as subservient as this. One more grunt from Sam and rope after rope of thick cum was shooting on Peter's tongue, in his open mouth, and on his face. Lastly, ejaculate dripping off his chin, Peter moved his head forward and sucked out the last drop before releasing Sam's prick.

"Thank you, man, whoever you are," Sam said through the wall as he pulled out of the glory-hole and went after his friend. Unless Bryan was a terrible judge of character, he was pretty sure medic Sam would be trying to save his jock buddy some trips to Quik-Fix Hall.

Before Peter could clean his face, another cock slid into his hole. This time Bryan had no idea who it was since he was still blowing young Tony, who was beginning to thrust several inches in and out of the glory-hole but was showing no signs of ejaculating any time soon. Fine by Bryan, who switched to a variety of techniques. He could tell what was feeling best to Tony by the gasps, profanity, and grunts or pounding. At one point, Bryan scraped his teeth across the sensitive purple head, which got a resounding expletive, and both hands pounded the wood partition between them. Tony's tip had a steady stream of pre-cum flowing, and Bryan feasted upon it. Dylan had served seven men to completion and Peter five while Tony was still flexing his tight little butt and poking his cock into Bryan's mouth. Bryan was getting tired... something that rarely happened when he was blowing cock. He began jacking Tony and sucking him while pulling on his heavy ball sack simultaneously. Suddenly, the cock pushed as far in as it could and fired volley after volley of thick pearlescent cum into the captain's sucking mouth. Bryan was sure it had to have been several tablespoons. *I won't have to take my vitamins tonight.*

When Tony was finished shooting, he left his cock in Bryan's mouth while he caught his breath. As Tony pulled out, Bryan, still letting his nuts rest on his palm, clenched his hand into a fist around the tender balls, squeezed and pulled, and didn't release.

Tony made a painful moan. "Fuck! Let go, you fucker." Bryan tugged and twisted and still didn't release. He heard Tony gasp and then total silence. Finally, Bryan thumped a ball with a finger from his other hand. "Sir! Please let me go, sir!" With the magic words, he released Tony. Pulling his well-sucked cock and balls from the glory-hole. Bryan heard, "I don't know who you are, sir, but my name is Tony Bonillo. Look me up." Then the young Italian padded away. *You bet I will, Tony.*

No one else was in the waiting area, and the shift was fifteen minutes from being over. Bryan shut his glory-hole door and locked it.

"Guys, it's been fun! I'm heading out." Peter and Dylan smiled and nodded with mouths full of cock.

"Look me up if you'd like to run the tubes with me sometime," Bryan said, chuckling as he left.

# Chapter Ten

*"Good morning, Phoenix residents.*

*It is I, Lasitor, wishing you a happy morning. It is now six a.m.*

*Are you aware that origami is derived from the Japanese words* oru, *meaning to fold, and* kami, *meaning paper? A class in origami can help develop hand-eye coordination, fine motor skills, and mental concentration. They say folding a square paper into a flower is the greatest joy in the world. Using your hands to stimulate yourself may be the key to your happiness.*

*Visit our community news page for more interesting education videos about self-stimulation classes.*

*Breakfast is served until eight a.m.*

*Thank you, and have a delightful day."*

# This is top secret

**Dr. Mika Romanov**

Mika had taken leave of his duties for ten days while Connor, a somewhat non-compliant patient, regained his strength. As Mika lay in bed with Connor, they discussed various things. One concern that had lingered on Mika's mind since the day of the quakes was the exact cause. As a geologist, he was interested in the seismic activity surrounding Phoenix. He spoke to Connor about adjusting the Phoenix valley's satellite dishes during the brief summer in Antarctica.

"It can be done, but why?" Connor asked Mika, snuggling in bed.

"The world net is down, but that's because the power grids of the pre-Doomsday world failed. Houston HQ transmitted the signals via dish-to-dish bouncing on the ground, and we received communication. Is that correct?" Mika asked, nibbling on Connor's neck.

"Hm, that feels so good," Connor replied, ignoring Mika's question.

"Hm, I know," Mika purred into Connor's neck. "I can't wait to have you in me for the first time, gille-toine. But Doctor Longarrow said no fucking until he checks you out tomorrow."

"That bloody doctor is just jealous he doesn't have you to bugger him. I've seen how he devours you with his eyes when you go with me for my check-ups." Connor wiggled his butt against Mika's crotch.

"One more day won't kill us. I don't want to do anything that might risk your health," Mika whispered seductively into Connor's ear. "Now, answer my question about the satellites."

"It's a little more complicated. We used Houston HQ codes only to communicate between orbiting satellites and Phoenix for safety. And to answer your question, yes, we can reposition the satellite dishes through Phoenix's valley. Why do you ask?"

"Well, I know the best hacker in the world pre- and post-Doomsday," Mika said He ran his hand along the smooth crook of Connor's back and over one of his ivory globes, squeezing it lovingly. "So, I thought that since you'd gotten into the files of some of the most protected systems in the world, you might be able to figure out some of the orbiting satellites' codes."

"That would be very difficult to program, and for what purpose? There are probably no working ground receivers to communicate with the orbiters," Connor said, playfully weighing Mika's balls in his hand.

"Aww, that feels good. No, nothing we are aware of. USA, Canada, Russia, and China satellites can take pictures of ants moving mustard seeds. If we could tap in and take control of those satellites, we'd be able to see what's happening around us. I need to know the origin of the earthquake. We know that there are at least four potentially volatile volcanoes in Antarctica. So, if that caused the quake, the information could be useful. Besides, my pretty boy, wouldn't you like to see what's happening on the other continents?" Mika kissed Connor's neck, sniffing in his scent.

Connor stiffened and then shivered. "I'm not sure I do. Right now, memories of how things were are all that I can see in my mind. Do you want to see the devastation?"

"No, I don't want to see it. But as a scientist, I think I need to know what's going on out there. The satellites will eventually collide with debris or Earth. Phoenix needs a point of reference to plan for the future." Mika smiled and said, "Besides, in this case, the American saying 'forewarned is forearmed,' may apply."

"I suppose you're right. I've been happy here because you and I haven't thought of ever leaving, despite my losses. Phoenix can potentially provide for us for generations, and we're safe here, relatively speaking," Connor said, then turned to his side so that he was face-to-face and cock-to-cock with Mika and looked questioningly at him. "And some of our medicines will expire, eventually. The good news is solid dosage forms, such as tablets and capsules, are most stable past their expiration dates. Expired solution or suspension drugs lose potency, but we have frozen supplies. The Cryonics Lab houses frozen cultures and formulas for later use. We will simulate most artificially. Although residents are immunized and tested, we could still pass on broken genetics to our descendants."

"Another issue is clothing. We have clothing for thousands of people who never made it here in storage, but it will age, and we don't have facilities to make clothing, at least not that I'm aware of." Mika brainstormed while doing little minute rubs of his long cock against Connor.

"I see your point. I'll call a meeting with Brad and Bryan and tell them what I plan to do. They might have some suggestions. I should probably include Tony Bonillo. He, being the dish engineer, knows the best position changes for Antarctica's weather. And Bryan will be instrumental in providing his soldiers to help with manual labor," Connor said, his breathing ragged as he sped up the friction of his cock against his lover, lubricated by pre-cum.

Mika returned the pressure with his slickened shaft. Connor rubbed his crown against Mika's throbbing organ. Neither had had sex since the morning of the quake. Both were so horny that all it took was a smile for them to be engorged. "Oh, bloody hell! Fuck!" Connor breathed out, squeezing Mika against his body and tensing up.

"Oh, baby boy! Fuck!" Mika's deep voice rumbled out, vibrating against Connor's ear, which was in the crook of Mika's neck.

Both men started spraying jizz between their lower bellies, forming rivulets that ran toward the sheets. The last tremor of delight passed, and their stiffened arms that held each other went limp.

"So much for the fucking doctor's orders, you Irish nymphomaniac," Mika teased.

"I'm still alive, aren't I? Besides, I'm Irish, and we recover much more quickly than any other race!" Connor bragged, running his index finger across Mika's lower lip, painting it with their cum.

"Irish had nothing to do with it. You were given almost two pints of pure Russian blood, which not only brought you back to life, but no doubt tripled the speed of your healing process."

"I do feel exhausted now," Connor whispered.

"Oh no. See! You overexert yourself. I try to tell you these things. Let me get you some juice, or what do you want?" Mika asked with audible concern in his voice.

"I think the essence of protein would be the right elixir. Perhaps pure Irish mixed with pure Russian would do the trick." Connor laughed, licking at the spent seed.

"You little Irish leprechaun!" Mika yelled. "I, too, am tired. I lost blood, too." He grabbed Connor's waist, lifted him over his face, and licked his share from Connor's stomach.

Connor laughed and abruptly asked, "Wait a minute! What did you mean by our descendants? Are you expecting a busload of women to drive up to the door?"

Mika laughed and rolled over Connor, so he looked down at Connor's beautiful face, framed by curly black hair. He used his free hand to brush a long tress of thick hair aside from Connor's smooth, pale forehead. "I wanted to tell you about this for some time." Mika was uncharacteristically serious. "This is top secret. Not even General McCormick has details on this. Peter von Leutzendorf, my project assistant, knows, but Doctor Saunders wanted to keep everything completely confidential until all was in place. Sadly, all was not put into place because of Doomsday. Despite that, I think we have figured out how it could work, but it will take at least a couple of years. But we will still be young, so no worries."

"Oh, no! You're not going to leave me hanging on this, or I'll get nosy and start asking a bunch of people questions, and it might not end up being so top secret after all," Connor teased.

"You wouldn't!"

"Of course not! But I'll admit I don't like the idea of you sharing a secret with anyone that looks as good as Peter von Leutzendorf."

"Oh so, you think Peter looks good. I never noticed. I'm happy to hear that the man I sleep with has found a possible replacement for me!" Mika mocked.

"Not true, and you know it. I'll always trust you unless you don't trust me with this secret."

"Very well, but we must keep it in the family for now." Mika pointed between them and continued sharing. "I came under Doctor Saunders' radar after he'd read some of my published papers. That was the beginning of our relationship. Soon after that, I corresponded with and met him. American intelligence had learned that I had been working on genetics, not just agricultural genetics, but human. I was on the verge, I believed, of successfully incubating humans. But, of course, the Russian government was interested in me altering human DNA to enhance humans, not for the good of humankind, but for personal gain, to win wars. I'm very much against that. Doctor Saunders was an undercover agent, a scientist recruited for an intelligence branch of the CIA, focusing mainly on progressive scientific and research affairs, which in turn influenced the WHPSS. He encouraged me to come and work for him with a virtually unlimited budget, and in return, I would be free to focus on my work as I saw fit.

"We both agreed that the project would be highly confidential, so we camouflaged it under another name. It was easy enough to work on agricultural genetic alteration and still work on artificial diverse embryonic growth. We decided to move the project here, where there was little chance of anything leaking out. EP-1 already had unlimited resources available, and safety and security issues were minimal. It made sense to have a backup plan for when the future of the human race solely fell on the few females joining us, as planned by the WHPSS. Doctor Saunders was a true visionary. He planned for us far into the future. He never trusted that the females would arrive at EP-1. Why he thought that he never said, and I never asked. This is what he was trying to explain, with the limited time he had back when Doomsday went down. He kept this secret tightly guarded between himself and his contact at the CIA and WHPSS. I don't think he shared what he had envisioned with my research. Groups of people, mostly from religious elements, would have slowed our progress to a crawl. Peter von Leutzendorf, who had written brilliant papers on cloning and who Saunders had also mentored, was made privy to some of my work and was very supportive of it. He asked if he might take part, and after Saunders assured me of Peter's integrity and genius, I did not hesitate to agree. Unfortunately, the Doomsday event halted the project, since all the pieces weren't in place yet," Mika explained.

Connor frowned, shaking his head. "But I don't understand. Aren't you still talking about cloning a human? What purpose would that serve to have repetitions of one thousand nine hundred ninety-nine people for generation after generation?"

Mika smiled. "I actually would love to have a little Irish Connor call me Dad. I would raise him with old Russian values and teach him not to be so nosy!" Mika teased. Connor responded with a hard slap on his fuzzy butt.

"You misunderstand. My work involves fertilizing a human egg and attaching it to an artificial uterine wall in a liquid protein, and developing the fetus just as the female carrier would do. Don't you see, thousands of women, who could not conceive or carry a child to term, would have had the opportunity without involving a surrogate human. In some instances, the child would be born healthier because it would be submerged in perfect nutrition throughout its gestation." Mika got all excited. Goose bumps popped up over his forearms like always when he spoke of his work.

"But none of the men here produce eggs that I'm aware of," Connor said.

"That's part of what's secret. Peter's lab contains tens of thousands of human eggs frozen in nitrogen. He is an expert in cryogenics. Although the eggs are frozen in liquid nitrogen, they will remain viable forever, in theory." Connor looked at Mika, eyes wide and brows knitted in amazement.

"Sperm? Is there frozen sperm?"

"No, but there is enough sperm flying against the walls here on any given day." Mika laughed.

"You mean it's possible that you and I could each have our own child?" Connor asked, as his eyes lit up with hope.

"It is, and that motivates me," Mika said, giving Connor a long kiss.

"I just don't want any sassy seven-foot-tall Russian teenager giving me lip," Connor retorted.

"Oh, and I can't wait to have a house full of leprechauns with beer can dicks chasing our neighbor's sons."

"How do you know he'll chase the son? What if the neighbor has a daughter?" Connor asked.

"That may be a problem. So far, all of our experiments have only produced males, but it is a kink we can work out later once we start the work up here at Phoenix," Mika said, not looking at the situation as a problem.

"We'll have to get married and turn one of our offices back into a bedroom."

"Yes, I suppose we will. But we have time to think about it."

"You don't want to marry me, and you're talking about children," Connor said teasingly.

"You can take the leprechaun out of Ireland and make him a brilliant scientist, but he is still going to be a papist," Mika teased Connor about his steadfast Roman Catholic roots. "But I will marry you, children or no children. But before I marry you, I want to clean you. Let's go shower." Mika jumped up, slapping Connor playfully on his butt cheeks as if playing bongo drums on them.

# Chapter Eleven

*"Good morning, men of Phoenix.*

*It is I, Lasitor, wishing you a happy morning. It is now six a.m.*

*Are you feeling a bit sluggish and having difficulty concentrating?
While a mid-afternoon nap or a cup of coffee may be your first thought,
a brief burst of activity can provide a more substantial pick-me-up than
you might expect.*

*Ten minutes of stair walking or a five-minute visit to Quik-Fix Hall may increase your mood and energy fifty times more than a caffeine pill.*

*So instead of slumping and moping around, take a quick stroll down to the Athletics Dome where you can jog, swim a few laps, or engage in a variety of other heart-healthy and energizing activities.*

*Breakfast is served until eight a.m.*

*Thank you, and have a day filled with ecstasy and joy."*

# These domes are our home

**Dr. Connor O'Hara**

Early the following day, Connor scheduled a meeting for later that afternoon. He was eager to get the ball rolling on Mika's proposal. Attending the meeting were Mika, Bryan, Tony, and of course Brad, who, as commander, would have to give final approval. The men respected him because his knowledge and advice were always meritorious.

Conner led the meeting while the rest sat and listened intently around the white marble table. He noticed Bryan and Tony looked and smelled freshly showered, like they'd just been to the gym, and were still wearing gym sweatpants and t-shirts. Both had their hair combed backward, still dripping droplets of water down their necklines, soaking into their shirts.

Brad sat and enjoyed a cup of coffee, and he was dressed impeccably in his light green and white camo pants with a matching olive green t-shirt. The four gay men around the table appreciated how virile and handsome their leader was. Every time he brought the cup up to his mouth for a sip, their gazes zoomed in on those massive biceps, stretching and contracting. Brad, of course, was completely oblivious that his good looks were a constant source of attraction to the young men watching him. It was, however, not lost on Connor, who diplomatically cleared his throat in order to regain control of the meeting and get on with the day's agenda.

"Hmm, gentlemen, I believe that Mika's suggestion for changing the positions of the ground satellite dishes is one that we cannot ignore. I don't necessarily want to see the Doomsday devastation, but we need to face up to it. We've all been living in a state of limbo, simultaneous denial, and in constant anticipation of contact from the outside world. It's been just over three years. The university served a dual purpose of preparing minds for the future and occupying them. But, unfortunately, most of the men here, me included, have only now accepted the world's true reality after three years of denial. It's as if all of us were waiting for a knock on the front door. But when that didn't come, we turned our attention elsewhere. Yes, I'm talking about sex and the Quik-Fix Hall, and although there's nothing wrong with that, we can't continue to hide our heads like ostriches and make-believe that Phoenix is the universe. What we've achieved so far is excellent for group cohesion and unity, but the time has come to face the truth," Connor said while gesturing to the arctic map and the dome structure on the video screen.

Using Mika's words gathered from rest periods during the previous night's debaucheries, Connor continued, "Also, if there is volcanic activity, we need to know about it and what risks, if any, it poses to Phoenix. With seismic recordings and photos, Mika and his geologist colleagues can better assess potential outcomes and develop well-thought-out models. Gentlemen, I'm stressing that Mika believes it is critically urgent that Phoenix stays at least one step ahead of Mother Nature. The satellites will give us weather data. We need to know when storms are coming and how severe they will be down here so that we can see to the safety of our towers, dishes, and the plane. Fortunately, we're in a dry valley that rarely receives snow. Still, the evidence is that if a storm would be severe enough, the valley might be inundated with ice and snow of epic proportions, even for Antarctica, the consequences of which could be devastating." He paused for dramatic effect, smiling at Mika to confirm his support.

"We originally planned to be manned and supplied by HQ tri-annually. We expected to be continuously supported by teams of experts to further facil-itate the safety of Phoenix and continue the construction of more pods and domes. Especially critical was planning reinforcements to enhance our current structures. Guess what, my friends? Those teams of experts aren't coming, and there will be no new domes. Our experts are either dead or disbanded. Phoenix will never hold if it's not constantly serviced and metallurgically bonded and reinforced. We're alone, and we'll have to become the experts." Connor lay his notes on the table, thanked the small audience, and sat down.

"Thank you, Doctor Romanov. Do you have anything to add?" Brad asked as he gestured to Mika to take the floor. He got up, filling the space with his graceful presence. Connor's stomach fluttered with love for him.

"Yes, thank you, comrade. I can check for local and global activities. I am not confident that we can make radio contact via orbiter satellites or the Space Station. The aerial photos could give us a representation of human activity. De-pending on what we discover, we could decide to fly over some of the Antarctic bases. Perhaps we could ask for a signal whether the plague affected them. They may need supplies, so we could airdrop them. This is all hypothetical, of course, and we are getting ahead of ourselves. I have thought about Doctor Saunders' suggested five years, but if they, like us, haven't been touched, they may still be there, providing supplies held out. If the virus got them, there wouldn't be movement, and with that knowledge, we can rule out flying there," Mika added while pointing and triangulating the positions of the satellites and the other bases.

"Flying over the bases is going to use fuel that we may need to get us off this bloody ice-covered continent," Connor interjected.

"But, of course, if the base has a landing strip, they most likely would have some fuel in storage," Brad countered to Connor. "Men, the situation is unchanged. There's a possibility that we'll never leave here unless these domes collapse, and we have nowhere else to go. Do I have to remind you we all signed up for life? These domes are our home. We destroyed our planet. Humans are perishing. We messed up. Humans messed up, for fuck's sake! We have an obligation to survive for however long we can. I agree that we need to be able to read the weather. We might try to communicate with others... if there are any others." Brad's virility was pumping male pheromones into the space at suffocating levels, unknowingly establishing his undisputed dominance; even Mika looked like he wanted to roll over and show his tummy to the man. They hung on every word he said as he went on and on about their bleak existence. "At the same time, I refuse to believe that when we die, this project and all our good work will die with us. So, I'll allow for satellite repositioning and external maintenance. After processing everything we've discussed during this meeting, I'm confident that besides reaching out to possible other survivors, we need to use all available material to strengthen Phoenix as soon as possible."

"Please explain, sir," Connor requested.

"As soon as we correctly positioned the satellites, I want to call another meeting with all of you. Plus, I want every man with an architectural and structural background there. As soon as possible. We're going to strengthen Phoenix so that she can stand for two thousand years! That's the subject of our next meeting. By my orders, that's being a continuing priority," Brad said, as he took his seat.

Bryan saw this as an opportunity to take the floor. "Some bases were controlled by unfriendly governments, which makes reaching out to other survivors a concern. None of those bases know of our existence, and I caution you about letting them learn we're here. It could be an invitation to disaster. Understand me. We're incredibly well-armed even though we are few in numbers. I also realize that any hostile camps are also small. However, it would only take a few trained men to do some actual damage with the right weapon.

"My concern is that any generosity will unintentionally invite hostiles into our midst. I'm skeptical about survivors. We've had radio silence for over three years. However, suppose McMurdo Naval Base is functional. In that case, they'll know the whereabouts of any surviving bases. Unlike Phoenix, which is locked in a mountain valley, they can use the old radio signals to communicate. Moving at least one satellite dish further out onto the plateau above our valley will increase our chances for better reception, but it also exposes EP-1.

"In the event that McMurdo Naval Base made it through the pandemic, I'm confident they've already tried to contact the other bases. I've been hoping since Doomsday that they had someone like Doctor Saunders advising them not to allow ships with the sick to take harbor there and that they, in turn, didn't get on a navy vessel and abandon the base, thinking that getting home would be better than staying. Backing up slightly, I'm not against contact and lending a helping hand to fellow humans, but in my stance, I'd proceed with utmost caution and let them earn our trust."

"Excellent points, Captain," Brad said, praising Bryan. "Does anyone have anything else to add?"

Tony raised his hand and Brad acknowledged it with a stern nod. "Before we go, I have additional updates on transportation, safety, and equipment. We have a six-wheeler, sir. It's an Arctic Truck." All the men in the room turned their attention to Tony. Connor noticed the Italian beauty transfixed Bryan. "We expected land-ice transportation machines to arrive for perimeter checks, upkeep, and maintenance runs before the Doomsday event. But unfortunately, those never made it here. Other than the six-wheeler, we have abandoned excavators, cranes, and heavy-duty construction vehicles used for the initial construction. All are in fine condition. They're in this area, located here." He pointed to a spot on the map where the Athletics Dome disappeared into the mountain. "Considering the concerns expressed by Mika about weather and increasing seismic events among the potential threats to Phoenix, I suggest that when not in use, all this equipment be stored in a dome, which will afford it much better protection."

"Excellent point. Thank you, Tony," Brad said, as he continued assigning responsibilities. "Captain, you'll work with Tony to assign a work detail to help achieve favorable end results."

Connor made eye contact with Mika, trying to encourage him to speak. He opened his eyes to baseball size as if to say, *Tell them! Tell them now! Tell them about the babies! B-A-B-I-E-S!* Instead, Mika just smiled at Connor, shaking his head discreetly, so no one else would pick up on their silent conversation. Thus, letting Connor know that now was not the time to talk about the Omega Project.

"Connor, how soon can you start trying to break the codes and take control of those government satellites?" Brad asked, unaware of the silent dialogue Connor and Mika were having.

"Yesterday, General," Connor said with a smile. "I started yesterday," he repeated.

Tony cleared his throat. "General, I'll draw up the plans and line up volunteers with Captain Howell's help. It should take no more than three days at the most to complete the adjustments on the dishes. The plan is, on the first day of decent weather, we'll engage the cranes, moving the dishes up onto the plateau."

Brad looked impressed with Tony's resourcefulness. "On a side note, Howell, you brought up a valid point about how well-armed we are, but that our soldiers are few. Draw up a mandate advising the civilians that they're all in the army now. They're all young and healthy, or they wouldn't be here. Just mention the unlikely possibility of an outside threat and how everyone should be prepared to defend Phoenix. I'm not thinking hardcore boot camp, but rather a Saturday every two weeks, where they'll be familiarized with basic combat skills, assembling and disassembling weapons, and a defense plan. I expect everyone will enjoy it. Tell them to see me personally if they have reason to believe they shouldn't have to do it. That Joshua Adams character is about the only one that I think will be resistant." Brad was making reference to the sour-faced Mormon, who was very solitary and by no means a team player. Both Brad and Connor wondered why he was chosen to be in their scientists' team.

"Yes, sir! Sounds like fun." Bryan smiled.

"Very well, men. I'm pretty interested in this, so keep me apprised of any pertinent developments. Dismissed!"

Once alone, Connor mentioned to Mika that he saw an emptiness in Brad. "The man projects loneliness. I'm worried about him, yelda. Simon confided to me he was worried about Brad's melancholy. My guess was that he may still be mourning the death of his wife and other family members. My suggestion was that we be supportive and available if he needed us for now. I promised Simon to intervene if his father's depression persists, to urge him to seek Dr. Longarrow's advice for his well-being and the good of Phoenix since we don't have any psychiatrists."

Mika whispered in his ear. "What better time than now?" He gestured to Connor that he would wait outside. When everyone left, Connor approached his friend. "May I have a word, Brad?"

"Of course, Connor. Have a seat and tell me what's on your mind," Brad answered, ever professional.

"Is everything okay? I mean, you just seem so unhappy. You're not the same upbeat and positive friend I knew," Connor noted with concern in his voice.

Brad appraised Connor emotionlessly. Then he took a deep breath and answered. "Of course, I'm unhappy. The world I knew is gone, my wife is dead, and I can only assume my parents are dead. I'm suddenly in complete charge of the lives of one thousand nine hundred and ninety-nine men. I tread unfamiliar waters each day, and my personal values have proven to be a joke in this new world. So perhaps I'm unhappy, or perhaps I'm not adjusting well. You tell me. Sounds like Simon talked to you."

Connor didn't validate Brad's suspicion of Simon talking to him, since the young man had spoken in confidence. "Brad, I'm your friend, but everyone here has suffered loss, some more than your own. You at least have a son safe here with you. Many men here lost loved ones but are adapting. You're admired by all those under you. The cost of your position and mine as second is the burden of exemplary leadership. None of us at Phoenix expects you to be infallible, but you're the best of the best, and we're grateful. Your values were not a joke, but based on old prejudices and misinterpretations. You seemed like you'd reconciled with them."

Brad laughed sarcastically. "Well, I had no actual choice. It turned out that my teenage son and his best friend had been jumping each other's bones for years. I sat in a meeting that let out just a few minutes ago where my two successors are lovers and my civil engineer and my head military officer are fucking, or at least I suspect they are."

"No shit!" Connor blurted out at the gossip.

"I don't know that for a fact, but did you see them looking at each other? I know they're workout buddies as well. It just seems odd. But keep that to yourself. My gaydar, as you guys call it, is obviously not very efficient. Simon and Paul, case in point." Brad seemed upset, but hid it jokingly. "But you're right. I'm blessed that my son and his friend are both here with me."

"Promise me one thing, Brad?" Connor asked respectfully. "If you continue to feel so down, please go see Dr. Longarrow. He's a professional, and mentioned at my appointments he had extensive psychiatric training, not that you need a psychiatrist. We can all use someone impartial to talk to occasionally and who doesn't know a lot about us." Connor got up, slapping his friend gently on his back. "I'm leaving to work on hacking into the Chinese government's satellite. I've given up on trying to reach the International Space Station for more than a year now. Maybe jumping from orbiting satellite to satellite will work. Who the fuck knows?"

"I'll consider Longarrow, and that's also between you and me. Didn't know you knew Chinese," Brad joked.

"I don't, but Mika does, and those codes will be mathematical, anyway. Not that I'll tell Mika that. I have to make him think he's useful."

"Why does that not surprise me?" Brad smiled at his friend.

"One more quick question?" Connor asked with a tremble in his voice.

"What is it, Connor?"

"Given no religious hierarchy, can you, as the highest-ranking man at Phoenix, perform marriages?" Connor asked.

"Why does that not surprise me, either? Yes, I suppose I can. Need I ask why?"

"Well, I've convinced Mika to say he'd marry me. I don't want the mood to disappear. I'll see about having the chapel opened and dusted," Connor said as he left.

\*\*\*

Brad stood there shaking his head and feeling more alone than ever. Connor didn't say as much, but he was pretty sure Simon had talked to him. Connor was someone Simon had always trusted and looked up to. But he knew Paul was concerned about him as well. He did like that boy even though he was dicking his son on the regular. Don't think about that. Perhaps he should give consideration to seeing Longarrow. He knew he could trust that it would be kept confidential, and he wouldn't see it as a sign of weakness. He decided he would make an appointment, but only to talk.

# Chapter Twelve

*"Good morning, Phoenix residents.*

*It is I, Lasitor, wishing you a happy morning. It is now six a.m.*

*Did you know that men in their twenties to forties are the most frequently afflicted with Temporomandibular Joint Disorders? This chronic temporomandibular joint problem is caused by the jaw's connection to the temporal bones of the skull, which are located behind each ear. It enables you to speak, chew, and yawn by allowing you to move your jaw up and down and side to side.*

*To alleviate symptoms, moist heat or cold packs can be applied for approximately ten minutes three times a day to the side of your face and temple area. Additionally, avoid hard, crunchy, chewy, and most importantly, thick or large bites that require you to open wide.*

*Breakfast is served until eight a.m.*

*Thank you, and have a day filled with stillness and tranquility."*

# We'll just chalk this up as part of our sexual resume

**Paul Chevalier**

"Come on, you'll be doing us a big favor, and I promise you will enjoy it," Amir said.

"Yeah, I don't think that's something the two of us would want to experience. What if Father found out? We don't want to push him too far," Simon told Amir.

Dylan and Amir were close friends with Simon and Paul. The four often had lunch and worked out together. Paul and Simon provided math and physics tutoring to them, since they'd enrolled at Phoenix University and found those subjects challenging.

"Yeah, you never know who's going to show up, and they never know who you are," Dylan agreed.

"Simon and I are committed to each other," Paul said.

"I know you are, and this won't change that. You'll be doing it together. How many other men have you two experienced?" Amir asked.

"No one. We're each other's first," Simon said.

"You won't believe how hot it is to watch your boyfriend doing another guy. Making another man cum will make you wild for each other," Dylan said.

"I don't know if either Paul or I would be comfortable with that. I can get a little jealous," Simon said as he sat back in his chair. "What are your feelings, Paul?"

"I don't want to screw up a good thing, and that's what I think we have."

Amir looked back and forth between them. "But I'm telling you. When you're done, you get up and walk away, and the guy you sucked off will never be able to tell whose mouth worked on him," Amir insisted.

"You two nerds don't have a hair on your ass if you don't try this at least once." Dylan chided. "It would be a big favor for us. You'd only have to do it for an hour, and we'll come in and relieve you. We didn't realize we had an evening watch and wouldn't get off duty until midnight. It's not that busy on a Monday night," Dylan pleaded.

"It'll save us from getting in trouble with Captain Howell and maybe even Doctor O'Hara. The entire program is based on being dependable," Amir added.

"Let's flip a coin," Simon proposed. Paul gave him a this-is-a-mistake look. Simon still carried a quarter around with him. Paul didn't know why, since money was of no use at Phoenix. Simon flipped the coin into the air, and of course, it landed on heads.

"Yes!" Amir yipped, high-fiving Dylan.

"Okay, you'll show us where to go. This is how it's going to work," Paul said. "We'll stay for one hour. Then, if you're not there, we give it five minutes and walk even if people are waiting for service. You don't want us to leave it unattended since your numbers will be on the sign-up sheet. You understand?"

"Understood," Amir said, smiling, looking scarier than Batman's Joker. All he needed was face paint and a green hair job.

"I also want to clarify that from now on, you guys book according to the calendar. This is a onetime thing we're doing for friends," Simon said sternly. But as with most young men throughout history, these two geniuses didn't concede to intellect or gut instinct. The decision was based more on a desire to be accepted by new friends than anything else.

Dutifully, Simon and Paul followed Amir and Dylan down the little-known corridor, through the unmarked fire door to a stairwell with a sign saying allowed personnel only. It was between shifts, and Amir opened the heavy metal door, ushering them through first. "It'll probably only be the two of you. At least, that's all who had signed up the last time I looked. You simply sit in the middle seat or the one on the right. Those are the seats Dylan and I signed up for," Amir explained, stepping forward and sitting down. He slid the latch aside on the little round door and swung it in. The room beyond was empty, as expected. "The rest is self-explanatory; a man will step up, take his cock out, and stick it through here. I don't have to tell you how to suck dick. So, enjoy. Oh, one other thing. You can peep through this little gage hole up above each door if you want to see who's waiting or coming up to your window. Please, be on time, guys, at eleven tonight. We'll be here to relieve you at midnight." After the brief tour, the guys went back to class.

That evening while they were working out before dinner, Paul nudged Simon every time he saw a man casually walk over to what had been the women's locker room and go through the door leading to Quik-Fix Hall. "Why did we let them talk us into this?" Paul whispered to Simon.

"No point in questioning it. We've already given our word," Simon replied. "I suggest we do it for the experience and never talk about it again. We'll be there with each other, and it's only an hour."

They were so nervous that they arrived twenty minutes before the service center of Quik-Fix Hall was due to open.

They slipped inside the room and looked at each other. Then both stepped forward to pull the other into a kiss. "I wish I hadn't agreed to this," Simon said, shaking his head.

"Hey, it wasn't only you. I went along with it, too. Do you think they drugged our soda with some secret military drug?" Paul asked, trying to put a humorous slant on it.

"That's what we can claim if my dad catches us," Simon said.

"I don't even want to think about that. The main thing for us to remember when we see each other doing this is that we're supporting the Phoenix Code program by doing our part this one time. But, most importantly, we must remember how much we love each other. In an hour and a half, we'll be back in our apartment making love, and we'll never bring this up to each other, ever," Simon said, kissing Paul lightly on the lips one more time before sitting in the chair on the far right.

"We'll just chalk this up as part of our sexual resume. We'll be able to say that we have had multiple sex partners. Like we've had lots of experience," Paul added, following his lover and taking the middle seat.

"It'll probably mean we service more men, but in a way, I hope no one signed up for that third spot. That way, we'll be the only ones knowing what we did, except for Amir and Dylan, who won't have any idea if we did any men or not," Simon advised quietly. He proceeded to peek out the tiny peephole to see if anyone was out there. Sure enough, two men were leaning against the back wall, waiting for the little doors to open.

"I'm afraid to look," Paul said. "Do you recognize anyone we know?"

"Well, that's a stupid question. Who wouldn't we know?" Simon rolled his eyes. "But there are two out there so far. I would get up and leave if it wouldn't get Amir and Dylan in trouble. The more I think about it, the more I realize it's only you I want to be with. To hell with not having experience or broadening my horizons," Simon said.

"We promised. Maybe Amir was right, and not many will show up. It's only for an hour. We'll do it and go. But from now on, the only cock that goes in our mouths is each other's." Paul made the vow. Simon nodded eagerly in agreement. "So who's out there?"

"Ronnie Kerrigan and Bryce Richards," Simon answered. "Should I open the little door yet?"

"Nah, still five more minutes. I want to put this off as long as we can," Paul said nervously.

Ronnie Kerrigan was a reticent twenty-four-year-old young man with dark brown hair. He had sharp but pleasant features. Paul and Simon had met him once or twice at some function or other. Paul remembered him because he was so quiet, almost withdrawn. Maybe it was the loss of his wife and two young children or his regular demeanor. Ronnie was part of Howell's military group and was a sniper SPC Class 1. Paul remembered discussing with Simon why Phoenix would have needed a sniper.

Bryce Richards was a thirty-two-year-old Australian, standing five feet ten. He was a head-turner in the pre-Doomsday world and now at Phoenix. With sandy blond hair curling over the ears and striking emerald green eyes, Bryce presented a ready smile and was always the first to volunteer when a need was announced. His function was directly under Tony Bonillo as maintenance head. He seemed to have every manual for all the diverse scientific instruments stored in his handsome head. Simon remembered when first meeting him that not five minutes had passed before he'd pulled out pictures of his wife and three children to share. Even though he knew chances were slim that they still lived, he loved talking about them as if they did. His Aussie accent was heavy and engaging.

Minutes before time to open the little glory-hole doors, Bryce and Ronnie, who'd been whispering about a storm that seemed to brew, were joined by Juan Martinez and Joshua Adams. Paul and Simon exchanged glances. "I hope they don't start filling up that room with only two of us here," Paul whispered. "I'm surprised to see Joshua Adams, aren't you?"

Joshua's presence was a real surprise. Dr. Saunders had gone to great lengths to draft the world-renowned quantum proteins biodiversity specialist, who was a devout Mormon. No one knew what the negotiated contract had included. Still, it was common knowledge that it must have been substantial to convince

Joshua to leave his position as Alderman in Salt Lake City, not to mention leaving his wife and six children behind for three years. Adams was five feet eight with a receding hairline. At thirty-two, he had a plumper belly than any of the well-toned men who made up the Phoenix population.

"Hopefully, we get only two each, and they'll be quick cummers," Simon said softly. "I'm surprised to see Joshua, but not so much Juan. I'm surprised he's not back here with us. Juan was a shameless and provocative little fucker."

"Who knows, but I heard he's in a serious relationship with Drew, another cook who works with him," Paul replied, grinning. Both had suspected Juan and Drew were gay. Simon had mentioned his surprise at Juan getting past his father's scrutiny. The cook had effeminate traits as he sashayed around Phoenix's large kitchen. He had a great butt and wore his chef's clothes tight, to his buttocks' advantage. He was a second-generation American. Although well-spoken, he possessed a slippery and sharp tongue with a distinct Latino accent. His complexion was light brown, and he had coal-black hair, dark brown eyes, and the longest curly lashes that he liked to flutter for attention. Paul had only spoken to him on one occasion when they'd been working out and had later seen him in the common shower area. He'd been surprised that with the light café latte complexion, his uncut cock was a shade darker in pigmentation.

"Time to open for business," Paul announced with an air of confidence he didn't possess. Simon acknowledged him, and Paul hoped now that a third person would show up to service, even if late.

The doors opened, and the four men in the waiting room became silent. Ronnie and Bryce, being there first, walked forward to take their positions. Their bodies blocked the peepholes and the glory-hole openings. The boys swallowed in unison as they saw the flash movement of hands in front of their assigned glory-hole. The only sound now was the pop of snaps on trousers and the unmistakable buzz of zippers being lowered.

Paul, who'd been looking unobserved by the client through his minute peep-hole, knew that it was the sniper, Ronnie Kerrigan, who had chosen his space. Paul looked over at his lover. Bryce slid this thick and veiny eight and a half inches of uncut cock through the hole where it hung over the ledge waiting for

Simon to do his work. Great, thought Paul, I'm certainly never going to be able to satisfy him again.

Simon stared at the huge cock hanging in front of him. He'd never seen an uncut cock up close before, and it seemed he wasn't exactly sure what to do with it. He reached out, bent forward, and sucked that monster into his mouth. As it grew, Simon continued sucking, looking like he was about to dislocate his jaw. Eyes closed, breathing like a locomotive downhill. All speed and a lot of noise.

Bryce, apparently liking what he felt, moaned and pushed his pelvis tightly against the glory-hole.

Paul turned his attention to his customer who had a rock-hard, throbbing penis. Unlike Simon's client, Ronnie was cut. The soldier had a very thick cock of about six inches. It had an unyielding upward curve that made Paul wonder how it would feel going in. He gripped the man's shaft and stroked it a few times before going down on it to the base. Initially, the upward curve caught Paul's somewhat practiced gag reflex by surprise, and he had to back off. After a few tries, though, he had a good rhythm going that had the young soldier giving out little gasps of pleasure. This guy was seriously leaking, and the way he was trying to thrust through the hole into Paul's mouth, Paul knew he wouldn't last long.

The thought suddenly ran through Paul's mind that he and Simon hadn't even discussed what to do when the men climaxed. He'd swallowed no one's cum other than his own and his lover's. Too late to ask now. He could only hope that his decision would be good with Simon. Since Phoenix was ultimately disease-free, he decided he would swallow whatever his efforts produced. Besides, he liked the taste of cum. The taste of Simon's and his own, anyway. He was sure he and Simon would agree on the delicacy, as they usually did on most things.

The Aussie was more vocal than the sniper and gave muffled instructions to Simon. "Right on... suck it deeper and faster! Lick the slit. That's it... feels good... aww... pull back and wash that head again, mate. You got it, keep doing that," Bryce instructed Simon in his heavy, down under accent.

"Ow! Watch yer fuckin teeth, mate," Bryce said with a roar. Like an anaconda swallowing a hippopotamus, Simon opened wider. The scientist was in no hurry to finish; he just settled into enjoying Simon's mouth.

Paul watched Simon's deep-throating Bryce from the corner of his eye.

A series of grunts came from the other side of the wall and then he was swallowing the ejaculate. Ronnie pulled out of Paul's mouth abruptly, zipped up, and left without a word. Paul shrugged, shaking his head.

After Ronnie's hasty retreat, Paul looked through his peephole in time to see Joshua Adams step forward. Paul, who always made it a point to get along with everybody, was not fond of Joshua. He and Simon both considered the man somewhat of an elitist and noticed a very obvious coldness from the man once it was announced that Paul and Simon were mates. Paul reasoned he was there to serve, not be judgmental, and put his distaste for the short, pompous scholar aside. He looked straight ahead through the hole while Joshua fumbled with his belt and slid the zipper down. Paul glanced at the man's eager dick. The base was fringed by a scant growth of dark, wiry hair above a wrinkled scrotum. Paul watched the slender five inches slide through the hole. He closed his eyes and encapsulated the man's cock in its entirety.

Joshua emitted hiss-like sounds. Paul picked up on the fact that the religious zealot liked it when he made loud sucking noises around his cock. It throbbed a little more intensely every time the Australian made a deep, erotic sound while standing next to him. Paul had intentionally detached himself from what he was doing when suddenly, ninety seconds into servicing the condescending man, he felt his mouth filled with volley after volley of shooting sperm. Wondering where the short man kept all that stored when just as suddenly it stopped, he kept it in Paul's mouth for about ten seconds, pulled out, hitched up his pants, and with a soft, "I'll be back," made his exit. Not while I'm here, thought Paul, who'd turned his head aside and for this man reneged on his earlier decision to swallow, exorcizing the mouthful of liquid into a towel he'd brought with him. Paul looked over at Simon, who was still diligently sucking the big cock. He seemed to have found a more comfortable situation in which Bryce was doing all the work. Simon was simply providing a tight humid orifice for the Aussie to fuck, and he seemed pleased if the noises coming through the wall were any indication.

Just then, Paul's cheek was punched by an incoming dark cock. Juan Martinez presented the first uncut dick Paul had ever seen up close and personal. The fully erect seven inches was encased by a pouting protrusion of skin. Unlike Simon, Paul grasped the penis and skinned the covering back from the head, which elicited a quick, "Be careful, man," from the handsome Latino. Paul soothed the shiny cock head with his tongue and supple lips. Juan was in no hurry, and Paul enjoyed the easy deep thrusts he delivered rhythmically. The only problem was, it wasn't Simon's big erection sliding in and out; he hoped he had the energy to take Simon when they got back to their apartment.

Simon looked exhausted; the Aussie knew no end.

"Ah, fuckin cripes! Hold my head in yer mouth and roll your tongue. Yer about to drink Australia's best," Bryce yelled, not caring that he was sharing his ecstasy with everyone in the room.

Paul counted fire one! Simon swallowed and gulped audibly. Fire two! Simon pulled a face as if a second explosion of bitter, rich sperm grazed his tongue.

Six more spasms and cum streamed down his chin. Finally finished, Bryce pulled out of Simon's mouth.

"Ah, mother fuck! Look at the size of your cock!" Juan yelled, obviously looking over at the Australian standing next to him for the first time. Juan came in rich spurts, filling Paul's mouth. The cock sucking accompanied by the visual of Bryce's cannon had pushed the gay Latino over the edge. Paul swallowed. "If you're interested in planting that, you're always welcome to join me and Drew. We won't tell anyone."

Bryce chuckled. "May have to take you up on that, mate."

When both men were out of the guest room, Simon slumped back in his chair, rubbing his jaw and sweat coming off his forehead. "I'm fucking whipped."

"I bet. Man, I didn't think Doctor Richards was ever going to cum for you. I wonder if all cocks that size last so long?" Paul asked.

"I imagine they all vary, but I'll never look at Richards again without feeling some respect for him." Simon reached out to take Paul's hand.

"Neither will I. I'll also never view Doctor Adams the same," Paul quipped. "Did you see how little his gonads were, and he'd fathered six kids?"

"Just goes to show you only need to get it in, I guess."

"He came in buckets, though. Didn't you see me spitting it out?"

"Yes. I don't blame you." Simon grinned. "What time is it, anyway?"

"We have twenty more minutes, and the room beyond is empty," Paul answered. "Come here and kiss me. I'll share a little aftertaste of Juan if you share some of Bryce."

"Gross! Okay," Simon said, and Paul bent toward the guy he knew was his true love. Their kiss was long, deep, and sincere.

"I hope those two assholes are on time. Promise me we'll stop each other from ever agreeing to do something like this again. I don't want to get used to doing this sort of thing," Paul said, pleading.

"Same here. You can't miss what you've never had. I'm sure I'll never miss this, but I wish I hadn't done it. It's like being unfaithful," Simon lamented.

"Well, sweetheart, we did it together, so we can't say we cheated on each other. Let's think of it as a lesson learned early in our relationship. We can reminisce about this wild moment when we're old," Paul said, kissing Simon once more.

"Talk about something wild. Connor told me that my dad was going to officiate at his and Mika's wedding. That hasn't been officially announced, so it's just between you and me," Simon warned his lover, knowing he need not fear betrayal of the confidence.

"How cool. I have to admire your dad for putting aside his principles about gays and supporting them," Paul replied. "We're too young, and it would be foolish to get married now, but until we are older, what do you think about officially being engaged?"

"What a strange time and place, after you've just blown three men, to ask me to marry you," Simon said with that serious look that only his father's son could manage.

Paul looked down at the floor. "I'm sorry."

"You're so fucking easy, Paul! I can think of nothing more I could want than the prospect of being officially yours for life." Simon hugged and kissed Paul until Paul didn't think he'd be able to get enough air.

They just had ten minutes to go, then Amir and Dylan should be there, and they could get the hell out and go to their apartment and fuck all night with the person they felt they should be doing it with.

They heard footsteps in the other room. "Oh, fuck no!" Simon whispered. Paul looked at his watch and then looked exasperated. "Let's close the doors and leave. Amir will be here in five or ten minutes. They can wait that long." He stood up and tried to pull Paul with him.

"No, we can't. We gave our word, and it could get them in trouble if it were reported," Paul said. Then, both boys looked through their respective peepholes to see who was there. Just as they focused, Dr. Broderick Longarrow came around the corner. His blue-black hair lay on his shoulders, glistening in the low light of the lineup room. He stood still, one hand stretched back as if halting someone while he was doing a scan of the waiting area. Stepping into full view, he turned and lifted his right hand like a traffic controller, motioning someone forward. Light footsteps, and then a very nervous General Bradley McCormick, came into view.

Simon's and Paul's mouths dropped open, and each jerked their head toward the other. "Tell me this isn't happening!" Simon whispered hoarsely.

Paul, at a loss for words, didn't say anything. Then, finally, "I'm out of here," Simon said firmly. Still not saying anything, Paul shook his head and pulled Simon back into his seat. The doctor was talking to Brad in a low whisper like Brad would be the only one to hear, but the room's acoustics were such that almost anything said funneled right to the open holes, even if a server wasn't trying to listen.

"Brad, I think this will be good for you. It's been well over three years since you've had any intimacy with anyone but yourself." Longarrow coaxed.

"This isn't exactly what I call intimate, Rick," Brad replied cynically.

"It's a start. I need it, too," Longarrow replied, laying his hand softly on Brad's shoulder. Paul noticed the doctor had his left hand over his crotch and was subtly rubbing.

"What do you mean, a start?" Brad asked in a louder whisper.

"I mean, this may loosen you up enough to have a meaningful sexual relationship with—"

"Don't even say it, Rick! I'm the highest-ranking person in this facility. What would my men think of me? What would my son think of me if he found out?"

"Ask me in the morning," Simon mouthed to Paul. "I'm going to kill Amir for getting us into this predicament. If they keep talking for five more minutes, those two jerks should be here, and I'll get out of here and pretend this was a nightmare."

"All I'm asking is that you take one step at a time. Do this and then give yourself some time." Dr. Longarrow said with a calm, soothing tone. "Actually, Brad, this is off the record, but I would very much like to be the one to take you to that next step."

Shit, my dad and my doctor? Simon didn't have to speak the words as Paul looked over at him, eyes wide.

"Not you, too," Brad said, shaking his head.

"I always liked both, but you're the only person since getting here that I've propositioned, if that helps." Rick's eyes were black and glistening, even in the dim light. His smile showed perfect ivory white teeth. He unzipped his pants and pulled a long and already hard cock out. He held it in his hand, looking at Brad. "Come on, Brad, you've come this far." Brad looked from his new friend's face to his cock and then back to his face.

Slowly, like in a daze, Brad stepped forward toward the waiting holes, the doctor close by his side. Of all the holes to choose, Brad got in front of the one Simon was manning. Simon, in a panic, grabbed for anything and everything to get out of the way of his father's approaching manhood. Paul gripped his arms, stopping him and frantically motioning for him to switch chairs. Simon and Paul moved fast without making a sound.

As soon as Simon sat in Paul's former seat, Longarrow pushed his cock through the hole. Simon's already well fucked throat was about to swallow another thick and long one. The girth was impressive. Paul quickly checked his hole. No cock yet. He turned his attention back to Simon, opening his mouth to receive what looked like a nine inch cock. Perhaps his last name is indicative of a family trait shared with his ancestors.

Dr. Longarrow threw his balls in as well. The bag hung low and had large nuts weighing it down and was completely smooth. At the base of the cock was long silky soft public hair, not wiry, not curly, just perfectly straight and in an abundant supply. Holy shit! Simon and Paul were shocked, looking over at each other.

Paul focused on the opening in front of him. He dreaded seeing his adopted father or future father-in-law, whatever he was to him, sticking his manhood through that hole. On the other hand, he knew it was better him than Simon, who was looking completely traumatized. He doubted Simon had ever seen his dad naked, let alone with a boner. Paul had never seen his father hard either, but his family was much more liberal when it came to nudity around the house, so that part didn't bother him.

Paul nodded to Simon to get started on the doctor, thinking that it would distract him a little. Brad, hearing some more encouragement from Rick, unzipped his pants but didn't undo his belt. Instead, he fumbled in the opening and finally brought out a soft cock that could only be described as massive.

"Nice," Paul thought he heard the doctor whisper. Brad cleared his throat and stuck it through the opening where it hung against the wall. It had more girth than Paul would ever have imagined and a huge head like his son's. Maybe he's a general for a reason, thought Paul, who then silently chastised himself for thinking such thoughts about his lover's father.

At Paul's prodding, Simon looked away from the opening in front of Paul and took Longarrow's cock in both hands, and started stretching his dry cracked lips over the head. His tongue swirled and licked the slit where he played with the opening. "Ah," Rick sighed, letting out his breath. It looked like Simon was going to take that all down his throat. In the small space, Paul smelled clean soap and aftershave wafting from Rick's balls and pubic hair. "Ohm, yeah. This feels so good. It's been way too long," Rick breathed out. Paul noticed Brad standing to the side with Rick's long arm reaching over, rubbing Brad's lower back. Paul almost fell out of his chair sneaking a look at Brad's face as they looked at each other with smoldering gazes. It was intimate and it was beautiful to Paul. He saw the vulnerability Brad never showed to anyone else.

Paul closed his eyes and vigorously laved it in his saliva. He used his full lips to provide friction around the large cap. It felt like less than a second when Brad's large penis became engorged with blood. He thrust gently in and out of Paul's mouth. Paul noted that lengthways Brad and Simon were similar. He hoped his lover never grew to match his dad's width. The thought of Simon impaling his tight ass and fucking him with that sent an involuntary shiver up his back.

Thoughts swirled round Paul's mind. How had Simon ever handled Bryce's demon dick? Opening his mouth as wide as possible, Paul gave his best effort to get this job done as soon as possible. To his credit, he managed to get about seven thick inches in his throat with the head a little past his tonsils without gagging. He was sure he'd heard soft gasps coming from his future father-in-law, and he was being rewarded with sweet-tasting semen, very reminiscent of his son's.

"Oh, that's it. It's been so long I'm going to cum, Brad. I can't hold out," Rick said. He withdrew a few inches after every ejaculation only to ram it back into Simon's waiting mouth, shooting load after load.

Simon had no more finished swallowing the doctor still lodged in his mouth when he heard the door behind them open. Amir and Dylan had finally made it back to replace them. The doctor pulled out of the glory-hole, and Simon was up out of the chair with lightning speed. "Where the fuck have you been?" he whispered directly into Amir's ear.

"We're only five minutes late. Sorry," Amir whispered.

"Just take over for Paul... that's my dad he's blowing!" Simon looked almost beside himself miming in silence so his father didn't recognize his voice. Amir's eyes went big. He turned and wanted to leave, too, but Simon wielded him around, shoved Paul with his mouth wide and trying to suckle his dad away, and pushed Amir into the chair. The exchange was successful. Much more experienced at sucking a whole gamut of dick, Amir had Brad sighing louder than before.

Dylan had taken the seat where Simon had been sitting and watched his buddy sucking off their commander. Simon grabbed Paul's hand and headed for the exit when he heard his father's distinctive voice. "Oh! What are you doing?" Brad's cock jerked out of the hole and Amir's mouth with a pop. Simon, trying to find out what was happening, ran back to the peephole over Dylan's head and looked through. Paul heard the gasp coming from Simon and went to the spy hole over Amir's head and looked through it. Dr. Longarrow had turned Brad sideways, fallen to his knees, his cock still hard and pointing at the ceiling and sucking on Brad's cock. Paul thought for a second that Simon's dad was going to push the doctor away, but instead, he'd locked his hands into Rick's long silky hair and held his head in place. His knees were slightly bent, and absolute pleasure was written over his face.

Simon pulled away from the peephole, grabbed Paul, who was glued to the opening, and pulled him toward the door. "We're getting the fuck out of here," he said as low as he could in Paul's ear. Before going, he bent over to Amir. "We're still friends, but I won't be responsible for my actions if you ever ask us here again or breathe a word of what just happened!" Amir, never taking life too seriously, nodded and gave him a thumbs up.

Simon and Paul were gone and up the stairs. They didn't stop until they were safely locked in their apartment. Paul didn't know what to say to his man. Was Simon going to cry or be angry? He'd never been in a situation like this. They stood frozen, looking at each other. Simon's face widened into a grin that grew into a laugh. He was laughing so hard that he couldn't utter a word. The laughter was contagious. Paul doubled over, thinking about what a night they'd been through. This went on until they were both crying from the laughter.

"Wonder if Dad will invite the doctor to spend the night with him?" Simon wondered aloud. "What a complete hypocrite. It'll be fun to see how he acts over the next few days. I hope I can keep a straight face around him."

"I hope your cock never gets as big as his," Paul said.

"Are you saying I'm small?"

"I'm saying you'd never be topping me if you were as big as your dad. But I'm also saying you fit and feel just right," Paul added. "Come on, let's go to bed, and I'll show you."

# Chapter Thirteen

*"Good morning, Phoenix residents.*

*It is I, Lasitor, wishing you a happy morning. It is now six a.m.*

*Did you know that if you fill a cup with boiling water and step outside, and then throw the water into the air, it will fall to the earth as snow? Yes, that's how cold it is outside today. That means other than the joy of seeing water turned to snow, galivanting outside will be an unproductive endeavor.*

*Why not bring the snow inside and look at it under your microscopes? Did you know it is a myth that no two snowflakes are exactly the same? In 1988, Nancy Knight, a scientist at the National Center for Atmosphere Research in Colorado, USA, found two identical snowflakes that came from a storm out of Wisconsin, USA.*

*Visit our community news page to find more interesting facts about snow.*

*Breakfast is served until eight a.m.*

*Thank you, and have a joyful day."*

# *J'm still tripping hard*

## Juandre

J uandre was determined to entertain and make others happy, as Ish had suggested. He had an idea and wanted to run it by Andrew. Their apartment was in the ghetto of Phoenix. The side opposite Brad and his family and friends. The city of Phoenix seemed divided into two zones by the prime meridian of the world, the Greenwich. A boring straight and narrow-minded side versus the *be-yourself* and be comfortable side. The side where cis-gender and transgender melded together and didn't fit into Brad's little box of rules anymore. Something Juandre wanted to re-mold from the inside out. News and entertainment were scarce. Gossip about their leader meeting up with Dr. Longarrow was making its rounds. Bets were placed, and some even suggested drugging Brad so he could snap that straight stick up his ass and enjoy the life they had left.

They had been partying for two days nonstop. The Canadian scientist, whose name was not to be divulged, had mixed up a savage batch of microdots. Partying and letting loose monthly had become an essential source of escaping their doomed existence. Juandre hinted things would be fine, without revealing their time-traveling friend. This acid was so potent, they partied for over fifty hours. It was a wonderful, colorful, chaotic mess, but so much fun and laughs. Sex was in abundance, and it seemed he had worn his husband out. Juandre sat cross-legged and naked on their bed. In front of him lay his beautiful vampire. They had just showered, fallen into bed, and fed each other. The last sheen of water was evaporating from his marble-white skin. They were finally coming down and Andrew was passed out and asleep first, as usual.

Wide awake Juandre's eyes roamed around the room, testing the acid remaining in his system. Dammit, all the colors continued to pop a bright neon. Leftover sparkles and light distortions fell on the furniture, making it wobble and move, proving that the acid hadn't been fully digested yet. So, he waited. Being here with Andrew was what made this place special to him. He wished he could unroll his pretty little butterfly wings, have a stage, and perform his favorite 1920s drag. Dressing up and walking the hallways no long scratched the need to entertain. He needed to breathe life back into the rainbow of humans who'd defied conformity during the conservative revolution of 2039. Juandre was born in 1983 and Andrew was born in a Nazi camp in the 1940s. This made him much younger than Andrew. More optimistic. More zest and flair, he guessed. Their small apartment was cozy and homey. They'd decorated their abode with beautiful forgotten and found furniture. Like the neon green sofa they moved from the abandoned children's daycare. Juandre smiled, remembering Drew carrying it for him all the way to their new two-bedroom apartment. From there, the color scheme grew to embrace a bright purple shaggy carpet, yellow vase, and red plastic plates and cutlery. They'd found all of it at the children's place.

"My bear, are you asleep?"

"Hmmm."

Juandre poked him in the ribs a few times. He bit his lip to prevent himself from laughing. He was super annoying and enjoyed it.

"Stop it. Juandre, no, I don't have the strength for a fourth round of sex. Please, we haven't slept in two days."

"I know, but do we really need sleep? I have all these ideas and want to talk to you."

Andrew rocked sideways in answer.

"Was that a yes or a no?"

"Talk, I will listen," Andrew mumbled into the pillow.

"Okay. So, you know how Ish said to cheer the men up and entertain them?"

"Hmm."

"I've been thinking. The Blue Ballroom is empty, and no one is using it. Why not make it an entertainment ballroom? There is already a stage and a sound system. All it needs is performers and an audience."

"I'm not performing," Andrew muttered.

"I know silly. You'd be terrible at it. I was thinking you might organize the food and drinks. Like a cocktail lounge."

Andrew lay with one arm supporting a folded pillow beneath his head, the other arm lay along his side. He snored contentedly. Juandre poked him in the ribs again.

"Juandre, we can talk, t–tomor–row."

"Okay, you sleep, my bear. I will go for a walk and plan my new ballroom." He uncrossed his legs and scooted off the bed.

"Hmm," Drew replied and snored away. Juandre slipped on his red chiffon gown and silk slippers. He thought better of it and dressed in snow boots and arctic gear. He wanted to go outside to breathe fresh air.

The shiny silver titanium and plexiglass corridor blinded him. The hallway felt cooler than usual. As he turned the last corner to the exit, he noticed someone had left it open. A pen was stuck between the door and frame. Strange, he thought, stooping to pick it up and inspect it. A small hand covered his. Like they had both gone for it at the same time. Juandre looked up and frowned. A small boy with wild blond curly hair standing in all directions looked at him with the strangest eyes.

"Dear lord, where did you come from?" Juandre asked, clutching his pearls. The boy gasped. He looked like he wanted to bolt.

"Stop, I'm just saying hello. I won't hurt you. Come inside. It's cold out in the snow. Where are your shoes and why are you only wearing a shirt? You will lose your toes and what will you use to walk on?" Juandre asked. He spoke in a childlike manner. He guessed the boy to be about ten years of age.

The boy tilted his head from side to side. Never taking his inhuman gazing eyes off Juandre. A look of recognition. Of understanding. He smiled back at him. *Such an odd little face*, Juandre thought. The boy blinked and said in a sweet voice, "I don't need shoes; I wear only this." He pointed to the oversized dirty white t-shirt that hung like a dress on him.

Before Juandre could ask, the boy said, "People believe in lies without seeking the truth."

"I know. We call those people ostriches," Juandre answered, amused, and taking an instant liking to the boy. The boy seemed to have read his mind. He briefly considered telling Brad about the boy but considered Ish's warning. Although Juandre's respect for the man had grown after observing him in Connor's class, he didn't want to overwhelm Brad. He'd only just accepted the facts about his sexuality and gender identification. *How will I explain vampires and now this small boy that seems to be a goblin? God, I'm still tripping hard.*

The boy chuckled. Hiding his mouth behind both his cupped hands, his eyes glinted with amusement. He didn't look emaciated or underweight. His fingernails were clean and cut short. Other than the rag he had on, he looked healthy.

"What's so funny, little man?"

"Nothing? I like you, too."

Dull footsteps approaching from behind Juandre distracted him. He turned to see who was about to be rounding the corner. They could call someone while Juandre lured the boy inside. He needed shelter. The little man was walking barefoot outside.

"Are you a survivor? Where do you live? Where are your parents?" Juandre asked as he turned back to look at the boy, but the boy was gone.

"Hello, Juandre. Are you going for a walk?" Joshua Adams asked. Dressed in his arctic suit, he had a look of urgency about him.

"Joshua, you won't believe it! Hold on," Juandre said as he jumped to go searching for the boy.

"What won't I believe?" Joshua asked. Joshua frowned and seemed nervous.

*Is he hiding something from me?* Juandre dove into his psyche to listen to his thoughts. *Eryn, was it Eryn he saw?* "Who is Eryn, Joshua?" he asked.

Joshua's whole body stiffened. His face froze mid-smile in shock. Eyes wide and bewildered, he said, "No-no one, Eryn. Hmm, Eryn is my friend from the grain lab. Have you seen him?"

"No, but I saw a little—"

Joshua interrupted. "Sorry, I must go. I remembered. Eryn said he would meet me tomorrow night. Tomorrow night," Joshua repeated louder than necessary. "Stupid me. Okay, goodnight," Joshua rambled, then turned and scurried away. His snow boots squeaked on the titanium floors as he disappeared around the corner and out of sight.

Juandre dove through the exit door, hoping to find the boy, but he was gone. The cold air slammed him so hard he couldn't take a breath. He swore each time he came outside it was colder than the previous fucking time. The wind blew snow in all directions, obscuring his view. He clung to the open door and surveyed the white backdrop a few feet away. Searching for footprints, anything that moved. But he saw nothing. The blizzard howled. He would get lost if he went searching. The ground tilted and elongated. Fleetingly, he thought he was hallucinating and imagining the boy. It could be the acid. *Maybe I should come the fuck down and go to bed*, he mused. But was it possible that Joshua knew the boy? He was acting strange, but he was his usual elusive self. Juandre made a mental note to visit the grain lab and ask for Eryn. He closed the door with a bang as he moved back inside, bringing the pen for evidence.

"The pen's real, so the boy must be too," he muttered and made his way back to his apartment.

# Chapter Fourteen

*"Good morning, Phoenix residents.*

*It is I, Lasitor, wishing you a happy morning. It is now six a.m.*

*Are you aware that nuts are packed with vitamins and minerals, including magnesium and vitamin E, and provide nutritious fiber, fats, and protein? Most of the fat in nuts is monounsaturated fat, as well as omega-6 and omega-3 polyunsaturated fat. They do, however, contain a small amount of saturated fat.*

*Did you know that healthy fat is required for the formation of cell membranes within sperm cells? Also, by boosting blood flow to the testicles, omega-3 fatty acids contribute to sperm production. Not excluding the arginine content in walnuts, which contributes to the increase in sperm count.*

*Visit our community news page to book a tour of our very own Hydroponics Dome and its nut plantation; it may be more than it's cracked up to be.*

*Who knows, you may get a* nutsack *of samples to take home.*

*Breakfast is served until eight a.m.*

*Thank you, and have a nutty day."*

# This is how it happened

**General Brad McCormick**

B rad had to admit he felt a ton lighter after meeting with the young doctor. There was an extra hop noticeable in his step. It had been a long time since he felt so revitalized, even before Doomsday. He smiled, recognizing the truth of emotional release through ejaculation. He's not saying he was gay or in love, but he felt like pounding his chest like a proud mountain gorilla.

\*\*\*

Earlier that morning

"So, General McCormick, there's no way I can convince you to take a mild antidepressant? It wouldn't be for life. I don't have that big of a supply," Dr. Longarrow asked Brad, who was sitting across from him in his office.

"No! Absolutely not! I want all decisions I make, right or wrong, to have come from my reasoning ability and not artificially produced by an abnormal increase in my serotonin level," Brad firmly answered. "Call me Brad, please," he blurted as his heart rate was speeding up. They often passed each other in the hallways or communal dining area and he was always jittery around the stunning doctor. "The general title makes me feel even more weighted down, I'm afraid."

Dr. Longarrow nodded and scribbled something on an electronic notepad. "Do you work out regularly? Do you make time for leisure activities with friends or family?" He put the pen and tablet down. "Do you realize you're the only person in the entire community I can ask that question?"

Brad gulped as the doctor's gaze bore into him. The truth stung. He should be thankful to have Simon and Paul with him. No other man in Phoenix had any family alive or here with them.

"Do you find you drink more alcohol than you used to?" He asked more personal questions than Brad was comfortable answering.

Brad's initial nervousness turned into anger. "I work out daily before break-fast, and before you ask, my nutrition is excellent and on an almost perfect schedule. I'm responsible for one thousand nine hundred and ninety-nine men and running a vast complex in an inhospitable environment, so my social ac-tivities are limited. However, I do try to have at least Sunday dinner with my son and his... partner. I neither drink more nor less than pre-Doomsday. I have a glass of wine with my dinner and the occasional rare whisky late in the evening before reading a book and going to bed."

"How about sex?" Longarrow asked.

"What about it?"

"Do you have sex?" the doctor pursued, undaunted by Brad's dismissive tone.

"Dr. Longarrow, how in the hell would I have sex? My wife is no longer alive, and there may be no other women within a five-thousand-mile radius."

"If you want me to call you Brad, please call me Broderick." He impressed Brad as he diverted his cynicism effortlessly.

"Broderick, that has three syllables like your last name. Saying one is like saying the other," Brad retorted with a hint of a smile. He sat back in his chair. Longarrow mirrored him, his gaze not leaving Brad's.

"True. My fiancé and some close friends used to call me Rick. I'd be fine if you also did." His gaze smoldered. "What about masturbation? How often?"

"What? That's very personal. I won't lie and say never, but I can honestly answer, seldom," Brad mumbled a response, annoyed.

"How often would you say?" Rick broke the stare and reached for his pen and tablet.

"Oh, my god! Probably once a month. Are you taking notes?"

"What do you fantasize about?" Rick asked and smiled with a glint in his eye.

"Okay. This is enough for one day," Brad said dismissively. He scowled and crossed his arms.

"Very well, but you need to do it more. To be quite honest, it would probably be good if you took part in your Phoenix Code and had an occasional partner yourself," Rick told Brad.

"Rick, let's get one thing straight. I know you're trying to help me, I guess, but that code is certainly none of my doing. I went with it for personal reasons," Brad said, getting more agitated.

"Well, talking to you has made me realize that I probably should follow my own advice. I've denied myself sexually too. So between now and next week, think about some fantasies and try living them in your mind," Rick told him.

"I'll think about it." Brad got up and turned to leave the office.

"Brad," Rick called after him. Brad stopped, looked back at him, and listened.

"Would you consider meeting me tonight around ten and having a drink with me? Of course, it's therapy-related, but I haven't had a drink and shot the bull since I got here," Rick asked.

He was at least ten years younger than Brad, but he seemed sincere. Brad thought for a minute. He liked this young Native American, whose intellect and interest in his profession, Brad suspected, matched his own.

"Okay. Sundowners at ten," Brad said, referring to the shared lounge area that for right now was well stocked with about any spirit a man could want. "But no questions about my masturbation habits."

"You have my word. We won't be discussing masturbation," Rick replied.

Brad answered with a silly snorting laugh as he turned and left.

***

Later that evening

Brad was two martinis into his planned drink with Dr. Broderick Longarrow when Rick brought up the possibility of sex to cure Brad's depression and avoid taking antidepressants. Rick had suggested that he was suffering the same depression from sexual deprivation. As the discussion went on, Brad became more open to the idea that Quik-Fix Hall could have medical benefits but pointed out that he had to be aware of how his own activities might be perceived in his position.

Rick countered, "As the medical director responsible for all residents, I am in the same situation. That's the beauty of Quik-Fix Hall. Everybody's there for the same thing, and anonymity is assured, under threat of punishment. Despite differing opinions, Quik-Fix Hall therapy is helping my patients recover from loneliness and depression."

After two more martinis, he felt like he was in a dream state and had reluctantly agreed to follow Rick, pleased when no one seemed to be out at that hour. Entering the former ladies' locker room, Brad could smell the muskiness of male sex, and it excited him. He knew he wanted what he was following the doctor down there to do. When they got closer to the area, which was just around the corner, as he'd promised, Rick went around first to ensure there was no line. Brad had told his doctor he didn't want to stand in line for a BJ. In fact, when they'd entered the locker room, Brad had locked the door with his master key. No one else would be following behind him, and they couldn't complain to Connor until morning. He felt relatively secure except for wondering whose mouth might be on the other side of the glory-hole.

A few feet from the glory-holes, Brad had been surprised to see Rick pulling out a very long, erect penis, giving Brad ample time to peruse its length and girth before smiling at him and going toward the hole. Brad gathered up the nerve to walk up to the only other open glory-hole and fumbled with his zipper. He'd heard some rustling on the other side of the wall but thought little about it. His cock was far from erect, but he blushed when Rick looked and complimented his penis, of all things. That's a first!

Rick was obviously enjoying his decision to put his cock into that dark hole and by some of his sounds, whoever was licking him must have felt pretty good too. He could feel his cock getting bigger and damned if it hadn't jumped from an involuntary throb when Rick had placed his hand on his shoulder. They hadn't been there long when it was apparent that Rick was blowing his wad into the darkness. As for Brad, whoever was sucking him knew what he was doing. It felt so nice to let someone give him the pleasure that his own hand had gotten used to doing.

He hoped Rick wouldn't leave him alone now that he'd finished. He even thought about pulling out of that soft, moist mouth and leaving with him sans orgasm, but he couldn't make himself pull back and end the exquisite, long forgotten warm wetness of a mouth on him. Suddenly he was pulled back from the hole and swung around so he was face-to-face with Rick, those penetrating black-brown eyes looking deeply into his own. Brad's breath hitched, and he couldn't seem to move.

Rick whispered, "No one will drink from your cock but me tonight." Then he slid to his knees in front of Brad and grasped his hips, pulling him forward. Brad's cock was still sticking through his zipper; the pants remained buttoned at the top. Rick took the enormous cock deep into his throat without gagging, but he was clearly unable to breathe. His throat muscles massaged the head, and his tongue danced on the underside of the throbbing shaft. Sooner than Brad wanted, Rick had to pull back to get a breath of air. Instead of pushing him away, Brad placed his hands behind Rick's head, weaved his fingers through his mane, and guided Rick to work the top third of his cock with his mouth and tongue. Groaning escaped from Brad as he rhythmically fucked Rick's mouth, then he reached the precipice.

"Rick, I'm... ah... going to come!" He pulled out of Rick's mouth just as his ejaculation started. Long ropes of sperm shot over Rick's nose, in his eyes, in his open mouth, and long shiny strings of pearlescent strings glistened like spiderwebs in Rick's black hair. Having never lost his grip on Brad's cock, Rick pulled it back into his mouth, catching the remaining globs on his tongue.

Rick pulled off, wiped some cum out of his eye, and said, "Wow!" Then he smiled. Brad regained his composure and tucked himself back into his pants. "Rick, I'm so sorry. I rarely drink, and it had hit me hard."

"You did this because you were drunk?" Rick asked.

"Yes. Again, I apologize, and it won't happen again," Brad stated as firmly as he could under the circumstances.

"Yes, yes, of course. The two beers had me drunk, too," Rick lied, standing to face Brad.

"What do you propose we do about this?" Brad asked Rick while thick strings of cum dripped on his forehead then ran down his cheeks and chin.

"Well, General McCormick, I think we need to talk at length"—Rick reached up and swabbed a finger up his cheek, gathering cum on it and sucking it into his mouth. Brad followed every move; his eyes were locked on that finger being sucked clean. He found the filthy act revving his motor on all cylinders as Rick seductively pulled his finger out of his mouth with a wet plop—"about the next step in your recovery. I don't want any headway you've gained tonight to lose momentum."

"What do you say we go straight to my apartment where we can actually make love like I know you want?" Brad said surprising himself. Rick smiled and smeared a small drop of cum across Brad's lips. For a second they stood still, their lust-filled gazes locked. Brad did a quick flit of his tongue across his lips and said, "Let's do it, doctor."

\*\*\*

"Mother fuck!" Amir exclaimed. Standing up, he stepped over to Dylan, sliding his pants down his hairy thighs. They exchanged no words as Amir slid his cock into his friend's mouth.

\*\*\*

The Present

As Brad walked the corridors, he thought about the past twenty-four hours. He recognized that he'd done something totally out of character; he'd let himself go. Not worrying about the past or the future.

Strange how fast life can change direction. Just last week, he'd felt like picking up a gun and swallowing a bullet. It wasn't even impossible to imagine a future. The men they afforded him to lead were all doing much better than himself. They were the personification of resilience, and Brad realized they didn't need him at all. They were well-equipped to survive and make Phoenix a success. Phoenix didn't require a general. His rank was only a meaningless bureaucratic stamp on a paper.

*For fuck's sake. How sorry for myself I'd felt.* He dismissed all feelings of self-doubt. He was General Brad McCormick, the unquestioned leader of Phoenix.

"Oh, my god!" Brad roared aloud as he realized how much time and energy he had wasted. His wife had often told him to simplify his complicated thought pattern to a simple A and B.

"A, I was just stressed. And B, Rick had sucked my cock and unscrambled my brain. Dear god, I'm fucking losing it." He laughed at himself.

# Chapter Fifteen

*"Good morning, Phoenix residents.*

*It is I, Lasitor, wishing you a happy morning. It is now six a.m.*

*Do you get motion sick, dizzy, or have trouble following a moving target? Can't remember when you last had an eye exam?*

*You're definitely overdue if it's been more than a year. Our community news page has a self-assessment application if you are experiencing symptoms like red, dry, itchy eyes or have spots, flashes of light, or floaters in your vision. Take advantage of it while you can still see what you are doing.*

*Keep in mind that Lasitor provides information only for informational purposes and does not provide any kind of medical advice, medical recommendation, diagnosis, or treatment. Always seek the advice of your eye doctor, physician, or another qualified health provider for any questions you may have.*

*Breakfast is served until eight a.m.*

*Thank you, and have an aesthetic day."*

# Orange, you glad to see me

### General Brad McCormick

"Morning, General," Rick greeted him. He was all smiles standing next to the dining hall entrance and looking all kinds of sexy. He had his left leg crooked backward against the wall for support. Before Rick had slipped out of Brad's bed to find fresh clothes, have a shower, and a shave, they'd agreed to meet for breakfast. Rick had his white lab coat on, and as always, around his neck was his stethoscope. He hooked his thumbs into the pockets of his lab coat, and he was wearing those comfy white medical shoes.

He looked delicious, like a bar of double-dipped chocolate, and Brad wanted to eat him. Maybe ruffle him up so he didn't look so perfect and so bloody sure of himself.

Why do I still wear my military boots daily? Brad wondered. He was jealous of the medical shoes, so he made a mental note to discuss clothing options at their next meeting. *This place was never meant to be a military institution, and I want to wear comfy white shoes, too.*

He stopped in front of Rick and just looked at him; his hair was still wet, braided tightly, but some dry hair stuck out at the sides. Still, he looked perfect, and Brad could smell the fresh scent of shampoo and cedar body wash he'd used. Brad wanted to push those strings of black hair back over his ear, but had enough self-control to resist. So instead, he greeted him.

"Morning, doctor, shall we go have breakfast?" He held his hand out to activate the automatic sliding door of the mess hall. As soon as they stepped inside, silence greeted them. The place was empty. No one. No dirty plates or cups. No sticky messes on the floor in the juice self-serve area. Only one server stood waiting and greeted them.

"Good morning, sir. Morning, Doctor Longarrow, welcome to breakfast," he said as he opened the trays of food on the warmers. The nameplate on his left upper chest said *Andrew Cunningham, Food and Nutrition Management Services*. "My name is Drew. Just Drew, please. I'll be your server for this lovely morning."

Drew was a big hunk of a man, one that would look very comfortable on a motorcycle, dressed in black leather chaps and black boots. Even now, while working, he wore his outfitted white kitchen uniform with his black biker boots. Brad knew him in passing and had spoken to him occasionally. A friendly teddy bear, some might say of him. He wore his blond hair braided back neatly, and while working, he kept it hidden under his hairnet. His tummy wasn't big, but it was on the soft side. He had a friendly, open face, one that Brad enjoyed greeting in the mornings, either when he helped to serve breakfast or during staff meetings. He liked the comfortable, colorful aura Drew emitted. It felt like he was someone you could tell all your secrets to and get a hug afterward.

"Morning, Drew," Rick greeted him. "Usually, I hear you talking and laughing in the back. Now you are serving food. What's going on?"

"Morning, Andrew. Where is everyone?" Brad asked. He had a big smile on his face. He had woken up with it and it seemed stuck on.

"They were all in for early breakfast. The men were called outside for a special operation today," Drew answered. Brad stood gob-smacked and blinking at the six-foot, happy giant teddy with his glinting green eyes.

"All of them?" he asked, surprised. "Why wasn't I informed of this?"

"Sir, last night, Captain Howell sent out an announcement. He requested volunteers to help go outside and move ground satellite dishes to contact the outside world. So, shortly after we arrived at four this morning to prepare breakfast, most of the men were already up and falling in line for coffee and toast, ready to jump into arctic suits. They were so rowdy it sounded like a party when I entered the dining area. I think it's a toss-up between just getting fresh air and exercise, doing something exciting and different, or helping to reach the outside world, sir."

Just then, Juan, one of the cooks, entered through the swinging doors that connected the kitchen area with the dining area. Behind him, the kitchen staff were boisterous; Brad could hear the plates and pots clanging.

"Good morning, General McCormick. A splendid day isn't it, sir?" Juan asked with an effeminate lilt in his voice.

"Yes, morning, Juan." *Phoenix has an automated, artificially controlled environment. What would make today any more splendid than any other day?* Brad wondered. He had spoken with the Hispanic chef frequently but hadn't given him much thought except for his flamboyant, sleek appearance. He liked him. He was friendly, open, and very approachable. Simon and Paul had also mentioned that he was resourceful and always willing to lend a helping hand, no matter what the situation. Today, however, there was something different about Juan. Thinking back, Brad recalled a man good-naturedly mentioned that he was roguish and should be supervised. Today his eyes were more snake-like, and Brad didn't like the cunning vibe he projected toward them. *Almost like a fucking spider, waiting to entrap Rick and me. Maybe he knows what we were doing a last night. Let it go, Brad. You're acting like a guilty boy... afraid everyone knows he just rubbed one out in the men's room.*

Both Brad and Rick grabbed their breakfast trays, chose the closest table, and sat down.

"Where's my pager?" Brad asked as he realized no one had contacted him since he woke up this morning. "Dear god, Rick, what in the ever-fucking hell did we do to my pager?" Usually, a missing pager would've freaked Brad out, but he found himself to be mischievous and not nervous. Just as Rick wanted to give an answer, they were interrupted. Brad lifted his hand and showed Rick should wait.

"Ah, thank you, Drew, thank you, guys, this is stellar. I can't remember when last I had freshly squeezed orange juice." Brad and Rick held their glasses as the server walked a pitcher over and offered them the juice. *Again, even Drew's acting weird. What the fuck is going on?* Brad hunched over and followed Drew's rounded backside, checking the cook was out of earshot as he disappeared behind the swinging doors to the kitchen's food preparation area. Then he leaned in and whispered, "Rick, what's going on? And where did we lose my pager?" He continued his whispering, "If we lost it in Quik-Fix, I'm going to wring your neck." Brad was joking and he chuckled as he realized the humor of the situation.

"Don't know, don't worry. I'm sure it'll turn up somewhere. Wait, I think you switched it off yesterday afternoon when you came to see me," Rick whispered back.

"Jesus, Mary, and Joseph, you're right!" Brad said excitedly. He felt like a naughty boy who skipped school as they laughed together.

Brad and Rick both inhaled their food. Brad especially felt the need to see what the volunteers were doing so enthusiastically. Brad knew about the plans, but he didn't expect it would happen the very next day. He was sure he'd told Connor to keep him updated.

"Don't worry, I'm sure your council has it under control," Rick told him as if he could read Brad's mind. The two of them were like peas in a pod. Like old friends who thought the same.

"Well, in all fairness, I did okay with it. But I should've been informed about when it would have been executed. I'm supposed to be kept in the loop," Brad repeated as he threw the last of his orange juice down his throat. "Let's go!"

Rick swallowed the last of his cheese omelet and also downed his juice. Then, he jumped up, put his tray away, and followed the somewhat disgruntled Brad into the corridor.

\*\*\*

Andrew Cunningham

Drew shook his head in disbelief. "You gave both of them some of our special orange juice? You are such a cock slut. You want everyone in Phoenix to be one, too."

With the sass and drama of a proper queen, Juan spun around, tapping himself on his ass, holding an imaginary rein, and pretending to ride a pony. He gave a long and loud, "Hee-ha! Ride me, cowboy!" Drew chuckled and joined him in the silliness, rubbing his hands all over Juan's delicious ass.

"I love doing the naughties with you, especially when we play naughty monkey business. Feel how hard you make me." Drew took Juan's hand and rubbed it over the bulge in his pants.

"Ooooh, orange you glad to see me?" Juan joked.

"But you do realize if we get caught, I'm throwing you under the bus."

"Nah, we won't get caught. Anyway, it's all harmless. If we didn't play these little jokes, our days would be extremely long and boring, my big teddy bear," Juan replied with all kinds of suggestive devilry in his voice.

"Let's just hope those two don't have heart attacks from bonking like rabbits." Drew snickered at his own joke as he grabbed Juan's arm to pull him closer for a deep kiss.

"At least they'll die happy, orgasming like geysers," Juan said into Drew's mouth.

"Lacing the *Rooster Booster Juice* is sadistic, especially if they don't know what's happening," Drew said, kissing Juan down the side of his neck.

"No, it's not."

"We better get to work on lunch. I'm sure we're going to get a blow-by-blow description later. I just hope we don't get court-martialed. Brad isn't known for his sense of humor."

\*\*\*

General Brad McCormick

The murmuring of men's voices became louder. "This way!" Brad called as he swung into a stairwell marked *Emergency Exit*. Rick kept up, and after a few flights of stairs, Brad pushed a door open and burst onto the platform where Connor, Bryan, Tony, and Mika stood, all wide-eyed at his unexpected entrance. "Why the fuck wasn't I told about this?"

"Sir, I tried contacting you, but you never answered the pager."

"Bryan, excuses are never acceptable. On the rare occasion you can't reach me, you should physically track me down."

"My apologies, sir. Tony said it would be advisable to execute the mission as soon as the weather permitted. I relayed this to Mika, who told me the winds had abated, and the weather would likely be clear today and most probably for the next day or two. So, I contacted Tony, and told him Mika's guess on the weather," Bryan said. "I asked him about getting the cranes out to move the satellite dishes. We thought requesting volunteers to show up at sunrise would be a good idea to help thaw the bolts, disassemble the foundations, move them, and reassemble them in their assigned positions. But the whole of Phoenix wants to go outside and help, General, sir. So, to prevent an incident, we called the council and, of course, you as well." The rest of the men looked at the doctor with Brad.

"Is something wrong, sir? Were you down at Medical all this time? Is that why you didn't respond to my pages? Why didn't you let us know you had a medical problem?"

"And now the spotlight is on me," Brad said nonchalantly. "Sorry, men, I lost my mind. I mean my pager. Maybe it's at the gym. No, gentleman, don't you worry about my health. I'm as healthy as an ox. Doctor Longarrow can attest to that fact."

Connor cocked his head to the side. "Who is this man in front of us? Did you just make a poor joke?" Connor asked.

Brad waved him off and strutted with his hands on his hips to assess the crowd awaiting them. He felt like a fucking proud peacock or something.

"Are you bloody preening, my friend?" Connor asked, baffled. Brad slapped him hard on the shoulder.

"Yes, my man, I certainly am! The best advice ever is to go see the doctor. He fixed me right up!" He popped his 'p' loudly. "You know what popping p's means, right?"

Connor looked flabbergasted. "If I didn't know my friend better, it looks like you two are tripping. Are you sure you're okay?"

"Yes, yes, let's get the ball on the road, or the spikes on the ice, ha-ha!" He laughed at his own joke. "So, I hear we're going on an adventure, and all the bloody men of Phoenix, too! Ha-ha! Not to worry, I'll sort this out because that's what I do... I sort things!"

"Dear god, General," Connor exclaimed. Mika pushed him back. "He is acting totally bonkers."

"Leave him," Mika mumbled.

Brad ignored them and continued, "I already knew this was all Bryan's and most definitely all Tony's doing." Brad joked and felt excellent, almost invincible. He noticed every sunbeam through the glass of the domed roof had different colors. *So pretty.* "Maybe Mika, yes, Mika?" He swung around, searching for Mika. When he found him and focused, he pointed at him. "Yes, you, my Russian c-o-m-r-a-d-e!"

Bryan and Tony looked taken aback, but Mika stepped up. "I'm sure you are joking?" He pulled Brad closer for a man hug as if they were long-time friends. "Morning, Brad, I mean, General. All this is just a demonstration of how much men value teamwork. Connor and I were looking at the latest local weather data from the weather balloon we sent up a few days ago, and we saw blue open skies for miles. So, we forecasted perfect weather for the next day or so. We contacted Captain Howell, and we thought sending out an invitation for volunteers would be the thing to do. You know, for moving the ground equipment."

"Ah-ha! I knew it was you, Mika." Brad said and looked up at the dome's ceiling. He never knew it was so beautiful. It felt like seeing it for the first time.

"Sir, this is a good thing. We can complete the project in one day instead of three. You know, more hands, lighter work, and all that. The men are all eager to get outside to lend a hand," Mika continued explaining, hoping to defuse the situation.

Connor had sidled up to Rick and said in a whisper, "What the bloody fuck did you give him?"

"Color, lots and lots of color," Rick responded with a sly smile.

Brad was vibrating. All his gears clicked into place. He winked at Rick, who straightened his back and gave him a *go-get-them-tiger* look. Brad kept it together. He stood tall and gave Rick an *I-got-this* look. Epiphany just struck. He decided he was going to take his *General hat* off and instead manage these men as Dr. Saunders intended. He'd manage these men like a fraternity—a brotherhood with common goals and aspirations. These men made a commitment to each other for life. Together, they would learn, grow, and make Phoenix stronger.

Pumped up, happy, and so horny he could drill a few holes in the snow, he stepped onto the podium. In front of him stood brilliant men, but probably waiting for him to spoil the day for them. He felt the closeness of Rick behind him, and he saw the worry in his leadership team's eyes. He knew this decision would mark him as a leader or as a dismal failure. No matter how giddy he felt, he had to keep it together.

"I was chosen for this exact reason," he said. "Doctor Saunders and the WHPSS chose me because they were divinely inspired," he quipped to them with bravado and confidence. Connor, Mika, Bryan, Tony, and Rick stood aghast. "The early morning breakfast show has started," he said, as boisterous as the master of ceremonies. Taking the microphone in hand, he faced the crowd of men and spoke. "Gooooood moooorning, men of Phoenix!"

"Jesus, did he just copy that dude from that old movie, *Good Morning, Vietnam*?" Bryan asked under his breath to anyone in earshot. Brad gave him a look and a smile, then continued.

"Yes, I'm sure he did. I still watch the original with Robin Williams, though. I don't like the series. It's kind of lame without Robin Williams," Connor whispered.

Brad spun back to reprimand the spoil-sports behind him. He put his pointer finger on his lips and shushed them, "Shh!" and then returned all his attention to his men. "Men, I'm impressed by the enthusiastic reaction to Captain Howell's call for volunteers last night." The men erupted in jubilation, and as soon as it happened, Brad knew he had made the correct call. *Yes, absolutely a bunch of cooped-up university geniuses, can't blame them, let's go with the flow.* "I know it's been a tough three years, and I've been informed by my leadership team that we may contact... well, who the fuck ever if we reposition the ground satellite dishes."

"Hooray!" the men cheered.

"Thank you for coming out to assist while the weather permits. I'm proud of you all, and I'm humbled by your willingness to persevere and succeed with whatever life throws at you. Have fun!"

"Hooray, hip-hip-hooray!" They roared their approval of Brad. Brad gestured to Bryan and Tony to take the floor. They both stepped up and organized the men into teams.

As Brad stepped backward, he listened to how the men of Phoenix planned to work miracles in one day. *A splendid day indeed.*

\*\*\*

Dr. Broderick Longarrow

While Brad's attention was on his men, Rick was busy with a lustful trip of his own in the background. At that moment, he realized he was in love and so happy he wanted to walk to the podium and declare to all that he loved Brad and that he was the one he'd been searching for. Falling in love was a magnificent feeling and he was convinced Brad has a halo around his head. And it sparkled. *Brad didn't turn asshole, because he didn't feel in charge or inadequate when his men had taken the initiative. Instead, he spoke to the masses. He'd not only supported his leadership team, but he also cemented Phoenix's group's cohesion into an unbreakable bond for success.*

Rick had to reposition his cock a few times as it grew like it had a mind of its own. He'd discreetly moved it from his underwear so it could grow alongside his left pants leg. Brad, in all his gloriousness, a demigod with a sparkling halo, managed to give him an embarrassingly hard erection in front of nearly two thousand men. He couldn't wait to get Brad alone to show him how proud of him he was.

Connor, Mika, and Brad were hugging, then Brad grabbed Tony, Bryan, and Rick around their waists to pull them in closer for a group hug; all of them were embracing and slapping each other's shoulders.

Another celebratory roar came from the crowd as the colossal electric doors started to roll and retract into the roof as they all marched outside onto the ice.

Longarrow couldn't tame his libido for another second. He leaned over to whisper in Brad's ear and gestured to the crowd. "I'm going to go back to Medical. I think I need to prepare for anything from a smashed thumb to a total leg amputation."

With that said, he turned around and left by the emergency exit doors, the same ones from which he and Brad had entered the platform. He was halfway through the tunnel when someone slammed into his back and pinned him to the wall. It was so unexpected that the air left his lungs and he couldn't draw another breath due to the pressure on his back.

"Where do you think you're going?" Brad's deep voice rumbled through him. His hot breath on his ear gave him goose bumps.

"Dear ancestors!"

"Don't talk. Just listen!" Brad hissed. Rick felt spittle hitting his neck as he spat out the words. Brad pushed Rick's face against the cold steel wall of the stairwell landing with the flat of his large right hand. His groin pushed intrusively into his buttocks, while he forced his left hand between the wall and Rick's groin, roughly groping it.

"Brad! What the fuck are you doing? We're not alone!"

"I ordered you to fucking listen," Brad repeated. "I've got to... I can't help it... I... I... don't have the strength to resist. I'm so fucking horny. I don't know what's come over me," Brad continued, relaxing his hold on him. Rick turned to face Brad, prepared to hear him out. "I've relived it and relived it. Since you left me in the early morning hours, I've wondered if my personal code has always been fake or just too much pressure from my position. I've even wondered if you put some kind of Native American curse on me that zapped my moral compass. Okay, okay, I didn't really take that thought too far. I am a rational man most of the time. Why I—" Brad blubbered as his thoughts seemed to race through his mind.

"Hold on, Brad. I'm at a loss. Seems to me you thoroughly enjoyed last night! Am I wrong? What are you expecting from me?" Rick interrupted.

"No! By god, you're not fucking wrong. That's what's wrong! A minute ago, when I saw the tent in your scrubs as you headed back inside... well, it just hit me that I had to have you again. Now! Not tonight! Now! Four stair flights up, there's a landing with enough room for us to fuck each other right out of our systems." Brad pointed at a damp spot on the front of his crisp uniform pants. "I need your cock, I need your mouth, I need your ass, I need you now!"

"I bet I can beat the old general up those four flights," Rick said, breaking free from Brad's hold, springing toward the stairs and taking two steps at a time.

"Old!" Brad yelled, chasing after him.

They reached the targeted stair landing in record time. Brad first brought Rick's face to his. From the moment their lips touched, Brad's tongue breached Brad's mouth. The kiss was deep, long, sensual but abruptly ended when Brad grasped him roughly by his shoulders, turned him a hundred eighty degrees, and without fanfare jerked Rick's scrub pants and briefs below his knees. "Bend over! Grab hold of the rail," Brad commanded. Rick complied without question. Brad was instantly on his knees behind Rick. He freed Rick from one leg of the scrubs but did not bother to take the other foot out. "Spread your legs."

"Good god! Motherfucking, fuck, fuck, fuck!" Rick almost shouted as he felt Brad's tongue penetrate his ass. Brad was wild with lust, eating him out as if to devour him. Like he'd been doing this his whole life.

"Hmm, your masculine musk arouses the fuck out of me. My cock is painfully hard for you." Brad stood and Rick watched over his shoulder as he undid his belt and trousers before pushing them midway down his hairy thighs. "This isn't what I would have planned, but it's going to have to do. That was foreplay!" With those words, Brad grasped his thick leaking cock and painted pre-cum around his pucker. Rick felt him push against his entrance, then he heard Brad spitting saliva onto his cock. More smearing and pressure on his hole and then Brad breached him. Quivering with lust, just like a virgin Rick withstood the pain as Brad forced his massive cock head through Rick's sphincter.

"Mother fucking gods," Rick screamed; those words echoed repeatedly throughout the stairwell. Brad had a tight purchase with his big hands on his hips. Rick heard him spit another gob for smoother lubrication.

"Oh my god, the heat of your ass," Brad whispered.

Despite the pain, Rick hadn't pulled away from him. "Fuck! Oh, fuck! Please don't move, Brad! Let me adjust... don't want you to tear me... please!" Brad didn't reply but obeyed his plea. Rick closed his eyes and tried to relax, heaving breaths of cool air. Eventually, he relaxed, and then he pushed back, taking more of Brad in.

"Dear fucking god, you feel so fucking good," Brad exclaimed through clenched teeth. He slowly rocked, bumping into Rick's prostate, sending excruciating volts of pleasure throughout his body.

"Mother-fuuuck! God, you feel good, you sadistic asshole! Fuck! Fuck! Fuck! Keep doing that!" Rick begged. He was shivering; he took pleasure in every drop of sweat that fell from Brad's body onto his back. He was hammering his ass with relentless speed. Miraculously, Rick came, his cum hitting the railing he was hanging onto. Brad gave no notice and continued fucking that sweet ass without slowing down. Rick couldn't believe this was happening. Never had he been fucked like this before.

Brad grunted, "I'm coming," and just fucked his way through his orgasm, like a runaway freight train, passing the station, not being able to stop. With his cock never softening, he just continued like the sex-hungry maniac he was. "I'm not stopping, baby. I want more," Brad murmured. His cum was leaking and sloshing sounds mingled with their moans. The juices ran down Rick's ball sack and inner thighs. The wetness combined with the continuous tapping on his prostate, pushed Rick toward another orgasm.

"I'm going to cum, god yeah! I'm going to fucking cum!"

"Fuck you are," Brad contradicted, moving a hand from Rick's waist and grabbing his cock. Brad squeezed its base. "I have plans for that. Do not cum until I tell you to." All Rick could do was suck in a breath and nod his head in acquiescence.

Brad slowed his rhythm to a pace that allowed Rick to feel every sensory nerve in his cock tingle. Brad bent over Rick, his hands clenched on the steel rails, interlacing Rick's fingers. "Stand up for me, baby," Brad asked, and Rick did so slowly, his ass still full of Brad's dick. Rick waited to see what delightful madness was next.

"Try not to move. I want to be like this for just another minute. Inside you, holding you, I have to return to reality." Brad rubbed his thumb along the Rick's cheekbone and then followed that line with feather-lite kisses. "Give me your mouth, Rick." He turned his neck as far as he could to the side. Their mouths and tongues awkwardly met, dueling until Brad pulled away from the kiss. "This is for you." Brad pulled his throbbing cock to where only the head remained inside. Shoving the entire length of his shaft back inside, he hissed, "fuck yes," as he ejaculated. It was intimate and passionate. Brad's arms clenched around Rick's abdomen until well after the contractions stopped. Slowly Brad withdrew his length. His flaccid, thick cock glistened in the low light of the stairwell.

"I don't think I can walk," was all the well-bred Rick could say.

Brad smiled as he got on his knees behind him. "Turn around and feed me! I've worked for it."

Rick turned to face his general. His scrubs, down around the ankle of one leg, were dragged through the semen accumulating on the floor as it continued to run down his legs and drip from his low-hanging sack. His dick arched up and out toward Brad. "I'd never seen such a long cock, and the head does indeed resemble a wicked-looking arrowhead," he said, and Rick chuckled at the silly remark.

"Ahh fuck!" Rick hissed out, grabbing onto the rails that had supported him for the last thirty minutes. After getting his balance back, he found more pleasure with his fingers combing through Brad's hair as they fell into a comfortable face-fuck. "Feels so damned fucking good! Oh god, I've never... never... ah!" Rick blasted cum down Brad's throat. Brad swallowed, but some escaped his mouth and dribbled down his chin.

"Is everything alright up there?" a familiar voice asked. Brad was on his feet in a flash, tucking his spent cock into his trousers and desperately signaling Rick to get his scrubs back up.

"I repeat, is someone hurt?" The words were coming closer. Then Connor appeared, halting the climb just as he saw what waited on the landing.

"Everything's fine, Connor! Just fine! Indeed, just fine. I was just giving Doctor Longarrow a highly confidential briefing."

"I see," Connor replied as he studied the scene before him. Rick was barely standing, with his white scrubs wet and wrinkled, a pronounced outline of a cock beneath the fabric and going down his thigh. Brad, always immaculately dressed, was now in a rumpled, half open shirt which was missing a few buttons, his trousers damp at the crotch and wrinkled. He stood wide-eyed and his hair scrunched up like a bird's nest. He looked at Connor like the cat who ate the bird, too. Connor cleared his throat. "I can't help but notice your roughed-up hair, and what's that pearly substance on your chin, General?"

Brad and Rick didn't say a word. Brad wiped his chin and straightened his back. "That will be all, Connor."

"Well then, I'll just be on my way." Connor snickered as he turned to leave.

"This was confidential, Connor," Brad repeated.

"Yes, sir! I'll inform the others at the base of the stairs of the confidential nature of this meeting."

# Chapter Sixteen

*"Good morning, Phoenix residents.*

*It is I, Lasitor, wishing you a beautiful morning. It is now six a.m.*

*How ready is your emergency preparedness kit? Preparation means en-suring that you have the supplies you might need in case of an emergency or disaster. All Phoenix residents must ensure they have the supplies they may need in an easy-to-carry emergency preparedness kit. This kit can be used at home or taken with you if you must evacuate.*

*On our community news page, take the short quiz to test your readiness. Then scroll down for our full list of recommended supplies.*

*There is also a sign-up sheet to participate as an emergency preparedness team member. Not only would you be the first to know of any pending disasters, but you would know precisely how to help those who were not signed up or ready to go.*

*Breakfast is served until eight a.m.*

*Thank you, and have a fruitful day."*

# Our descendants would all be princes

**Dr. Connor O'Hara**

Tony Bonillo and the men had successfully, with no incident, repositioned the dishes in the valley within one day. As per Mika's weather forecast, the day was perfect, sunny with blue skies and no crosswinds. They'd placed the satellite dishes as best they could for optimal wind resistance, since dish replacements were a finite number. Therefore, it was critical to keep the ones in use functioning for as long as possible.

It had taken Connor a total of ten, twelve-hour days to break the codes of the government satellites. Without Mika's help, it would've taken months, if ever, to break into the sophisticated Chinese orbiter. The biggest help was the fact there was no government authority on the other end to detect and thwart his hacking attempts. He'd repositioned six satellites and programmed them to take close-up pictures of virtually every square mile of the Earth's surface and much of the oceans. The project would take many months, and the study would be time-consuming. Photos would start coming in a matter of hours.

The next project for Connor was to try to dual program these same satellites to chart weather patterns and develop models for storm tracking. Understanding the long-term global situation is important beyond just the critical situation in Antarctica. One of Phoenix's initial delegations was to monitor the rate of global warming to prepare the world's populations for severe climate change. While that reason no longer existed, what they learned could be definitive in their future survival. That would be especially true if Mika was correct in his theory that the men of Phoenix would be able to reproduce artificially. That thought both frightened and delighted him.

It amazed Connor, Mika, and Bryan how relaxed Brad had become in the last few weeks. He was much calmer about problems that would've agitated him in their meetings not too long ago. While always fair about his final decisions, Brad no longer tried to bear the weight of Phoenix on just his shoulders. Instead, he delegated to his council and weighed their feedback on more critical concerns.

Mika had mentioned several times that he'd seen Brad and his boys working out together. Connor and Mika were competitive tennis players and frequently would see the boys playing opposite Brad and Rick Longarrow. If you saw one in the dining hall, you would likely see all four sharing a table. Connor thought it was terrific to hear Brad laughing again.

Besides striving for monogamy, Mika worked in secret on artificial embryonic growth with Peter von Leutzendorf. They'd named it Project Omega because it was mankind's last hope. Mika was determined to present Connor with a child within two years. He was also working on something that would be an additional benefit from the project. Mika thought of it as a surprise bonus. It never ceased to amaze Connor that his partner could stay focused on so many projects at the same time. Mika had never slept over two to three hours a night before meeting Connor. With all of their respective responsibilities, the two men had very little alone time. Both men knew that a healthy relationship required quality hours enjoying each other's company. Conner became a stickler that they spent eight hours each night in bed; if they got that much sleep was another matter.

Connor's schedule was as busy as his partner's. The men were still in the *learning about each other* stage. It was usually in the darkness of their bedroom that they would discuss concerns or simply ask questions of the other. One such night, while lying on the bed with Mika, who'd just extracted his prick from him, Connor said quietly, "Mika, I need to ask you some questions."

"You can ask me anything, except for how many lovers I've had... things like that"—Mika creased his brow—"that is personal history involving others that are best left in pre-Doomsday world."

"I would never do that. I would never expect you to ask me about my past lovers," Connor assured him.

"But I need to know about your past lovers so that I can profile the type of man you are attracted to, and then I'll better be able to steer you away from them," Mika joked and slapped Connor on his exposed buttocks.

"Seriously, I need to know some things. I'm sharing my life with someone I've only known a little over a year."

"Are all the Irish as nosy and paranoid as you? A year can be a lifetime. I knew you for thirty minutes, and I knew I would spend my life with you. My parents knew each other for over thirty years and knew very little about each other. But I know I will not get any sleep until you have the answers you need. I will answer your questions honestly and fully unless I decide not to do so," Mika said, intent on finding out what was on Connor's mind. "But make this a mutual talk... one that's worthy of my time."

"When have I ever not answered you honestly and fully? You can ask me anything you want. I daresay I have nothing to be ashamed—" Connor was interrupted by Mika flipping him to his side, facing away, lifting his smooth muscular thigh, and reinserting his cock in the still moist orifice, his spent cum lubricating his return.

"This is all I meant by mutual, and you go off on a tangent," Mika chided him.

Connor gave a quick ragged intake of breath on the intrusion. Once he adjusted to the fullness he said, "What am I to do with you, yelda? The way you dominate and throw me around while taking pleasures from me, one would think your name referred to more than the old Imperial Russia."

"Are you referring to the fact that my family name is Romanov? If you ask me if I am a tsarist, I will have to answer that I am not. If you are asking me if my ancestors were Tsars, I would have to answer yes, they were."

"That wasn't one of my questions... are you serious?" Connor, a history lover, asked in disbelief. "How did you survive? I thought they'd killed all the aristocracy they could get to."

"Certainly a dark time in my country. Probably no bleaker than life under the Tsars, who tried to maintain starving people under a feudal system and refused to change with the times. My part of the family made it out of Russia at the beginning of the revolution to France. We were cousins to the last Tsar, but shared a Tsar as a common grandfather. In the 1960s, using the surname of family servants, my great-grandfather and family immigrated back to Russia as Tsitzkosky, a huge mistake. Once they got there, they were unable to leave. It wasn't until I defected while on an educational tour hosted by your mentor, Doctor John Saunders, that I proved my name and inheritance in France, and I elected to keep that name. True story, my love," Mika said while sliding his cock in and out of Connor.

"I didn't know."

"Doctor Saunders knew. I believe it's in the files you downloaded. I'm surprised that you haven't read them," Mika said.

"I would never read files about you. I'm not asking you to tell me confidential matters. I've only looked at a small number of files for the people in this complex. Although I will add their contents have gone no further," Connor replied, pushing back against Mika for deeper penetration.

"Well, now that you have stumbled on to that little-known truth, do you still want to marry me? We have a ruthless history, you know."

"I'll deal with it. Does that mean you come with a title that I'll share?" Connor asked as an afterthought.

"See, already you are getting grandiose. If I was a tsarist and used the title, then yes, I would be a prince. In further response to your question, it would be the first time in history, but you may be my prince as my legal spouse. Our descendants would all be princes." Mika laughed in his deep timbre. Still moving in and out of Connor, rubbing his prostate. Connor let his head roll from side to side, enjoying the torturous closeness with Mika.

"So, you have a reason to blush when I refer to you as my prince among our friends," Connor teased, feeling Mika's hairy legs tickling the backs of his thighs.

"I'm blushing now," Mika replied. "What did you really want to ask me about?"

"Nothing that illuminating, I'm afraid. I just wanted to know how you keep up with everything you have going on without having a *meltdown*, as the Americans call it. I mean, how smart are you really?" Connor asked.

"I like to think I'm brilliant, and then something will confound me, such as you, and I will think I'm not very intelligent at all. How smart are you, my noisy little leprechaun?" Mika asked, giving three rapid thrusts.

Connor grabbed the bedding to hold on, eliciting three grunts in answer. "You're probably the smartest man I've ever met or even read about. I know you earned your MD barely out of high school before obtaining doctorates in three fields that I know of, and you studied and mastered multiple languages as electives," Connor said, recounting Mika's accomplishments with each deep thrust.

"It's not important. But I guess it is critical that you know. First, tell me how smart my Connor is?"

"I believe the intelligent quotient number was one-seventy-eight, genius-level, I'm told. Which is high, but there are people with higher. I know I could never do what you do, and that doesn't bother me. I'm quite proud of you, actually." Connor sighed a faint exhale as his seed spilled on the bed from Mika's rhythmic prostate massage.

"The truthful answer is that I don't know. I'm telling the truth. I don't know because they did not have tests that would adequately measure my intelligence. That's the truth, but if you feel better if I tell you a lie, I'll give you the number one-eighty-one... still three more than you!"

Connor laughed. "No, I don't want you to lie. I believe you, and I'm astounded that someone with an IQ as high as you would give me the time of day."

"You have a tight ass that milks me without even having to do anything but insert my cock while I work out mathematical equations in my head. You were a logical decision," Mika teased.

"Why, you arrogant..." Connor started, but then stopped, relishing in the final six thrusts and feeling Mika's immense organ pushed in him, swelling and filling his insides for the second time in an hour.

"Do you have more questions? I need to sleep," Mika asked as he pulled Connor tightly against him, leaving him impaled as he started snoring softly.

So, my Mika is a prince. I'm going to marry a prince. Connor smiled as happy thoughts carried him off into a deep sleep.

# Chapter Seventeen

*"Good morning, men of Phoenix.*

*It is I, Lasitor, wishing you a glorious morning. It is now six a.m.*

*Have you ever woken up and wondered what happened to the contents of your bowels or bladder and where it all goes?*

*Have you ever wondered why the Phoenix wastewater system never froze and what sewage breakdown treatment and method is being used to benefit the ecosystem while reducing environmental pollution?*

*Visit our community news page to book a tour to learn more about Phoenix's underground pipe and tunnel system and the fascinating transportation of your sewage to the treatment plant.*

*Also, learn about Phoenix's architecture and how all the types of man-made systems work in harmony with Antarctica's environment while promoting health and well-being: enriching your lives aesthetically and creating a legacy that reflects and symbolizes your culture and traditions.*

*Breakfast is served until eight a.m.*

*Thank you, and have a sparkling bright day."*

# The Omega Project

**Dr. Connor O'Hara**

C onnor had an ingenious thought that even impressed him after he had downloaded several thousand more photos, specifically capturing weather patterns in the southern hemisphere. So far, findings showed that Earth was heading into a nuclear winter. After he'd punched in a series of codes at lightning speed, his computer accepted and transmitted the data. In less than a minute, the object of his once highly illegal assault began to answer him. In two minutes, he had a visual of the Earth being sent to him from the low orbiting International Space Station. It had been the last human inhabited-crewed Space Station. Since 2035, governments had ceased sending humans. The training and upkeep of one human was a waste of money, was what the politicians had told the public. But Saunders and Todd worked at Huston HQ, and on highly secretive projects. Connor knew the space stations were manned, but uncertain if they were during the crisis of Doomsday. If they were, those people couldn't come home and that would be a lonely way to die.

He believed that communicating with the International Space Station would enable communication with other inhabited stations in Antarctica and other environment projects by Saunders.

Wanting to see Mika's face when he shared the information, he headed for his lover's lab. It has multiple large rooms for his diverse projects and meetings with his scientists. He entered quietly through the waiting area to not interrupt a possible scheduled conference. The door to the central lab was open, so he snuck inside to have a look. Seeing no one, he proceeded to the next room. As eager as he was, he came to a dead halt, hearing an emotional exchange of words. Connor peeked through the door, out of sight of the two men talking. He could see them. His heart raced at the visual of Mika unlocking from an embrace with Dr. Peter fucking von Leutzendorf.

"You know how much this means to me. But we must be careful and not say anything. If the timing isn't right, it could break Connor's heart, and he doesn't deserve that," Mika told the arrogantly beautiful Peter.

"I respectfully disagree, Mika. I think you should tell Connor before we go further with this. He's very loyal to you, and you owe him that much respect. However, you do him a disservice by not telling him what we've done. You are engaged, aren't you?" Peter asked Mika and laughed, putting his hand on Mika's side affectionately. *Motherfucking snake!*

"I just have to find the right time to tell him," Mika said. The two hugged again. Connor crushed the printed photos and data in his arms against him. He turned and was out of the lab, running down the passageways, with tears streaming down his cheeks toward their apartment.

*The cheating bastard! That's why he wandered in at two in the mornings. Too tired to kiss me goodnight. I fucking trusted him. Why did Mika go along with the marriage plans? I thought he loved me and would always tell me the truth. He lied to me. He fucking played me. I'm such a fool.*

Connor passed several people who spoke, but he didn't want to talk to anyone. The humiliation. How will he face anyone in Phoenix again? Everyone probably knew about Mika and Peter, and he was the last to know. Once in his apartment, he slammed the door, thew the armful of good news on the floor and fell on the bed, although it was only three in the afternoon.

\*\*\*

Dr. Mika Romanov

Mika tried several times to reach Connor regarding dinner plans they'd discussed earlier. It was out of the norm for Connor to forget dinner arrangements, so Mika grew concerned and went home. Oddly, the bedroom door was shut, and the apartment was in darkness. Opening the bedroom door as quietly as possible, he switched on the low-light switch. He could see Connor lying across the bed sideways and facedown. Mika rushed to him. "Connor, are you okay, my love?"

Groggily, Connor responded without opening his eyes, "I'm fine. I just want to be left alone right now."

"Okay, but do you want something to eat or drink? I will get for you anything you want," Mika said, nuzzling his ear and putting a slight accent into his speech. He'd never seen his little leprechaun act like this.

"I said leave me alone! What I want... you're incapable of giving me. Now get out... go eat or something." Connor turned his head away.

Mika got up from their bed, speechless for the first time in his adult life. He walked out of the bedroom, shut the door behind him, and walked out of the apartment. Mika had never been in a situation like this and with Connor, of all people. He needed to think. The more he thought, the angrier he became at the rude rejection without an explanation. Finally, Mika tore back toward the apartment, entered, and burst into their bedroom.

"Look here, you fucking little leprechaun, you have no right and no cause to speak to me like this. I thought we had a relationship based on honesty and trust. If we're unhappy about something the other has done, did we not promise to be open with each other? When we agreed we would marry, we promised the other that we would never have secrets and we would discuss anything at all that troubled us. If I have done something, I need to know it before addressing it or fixing it. You owe me that much respect. If someone has hurt you, then you better fucking tell me, and we will get it set right if I have to throw them out into the Antarctica winter buck naked!" Mika yelled at Connor in anger for the first time since they'd known each other.

His booming voice echoed off the walls. Connor made himself smaller, lying in a fetal position. "But by god, you are going to sit up like a fucking man and tell me what's wrong, or I'm going to rip your pants off, spank your Irish ass like the child you're acting, and I won't be back in this room until you beg me... and you will beg me to come back!"

Connor was an intelligent young man, and while he flinched at Mika's wrath, he also listened and would know what Mika was saying was true. They'd promised each other to always talk before reacting. Connor had been the first to breach that agreement—he'd reacted to something before talking. Connor sat up on the edge of the bed and directed his bloodshot eyes at Mika.

"That's better," Mika said sarcastically. Connor's bloodshot and teary eyes looked up at him. "My god, you've been crying. Who hurt you?" he asked, seething with anger.

"You did," Connor replied, eyes downcast and looking at his feet.

"I did? What exactly did I do besides love you with all my heart?" Mika asked, pointing a finger at himself.

"You were unfaithful to me!" Connor cried. His luscious bottom lip quivering.

Mika's mouth dropped open in disbelief. "Who in the fuck told you that? And why in the fuck did you believe them? You give me a name, and I will bring him in here, and he will recant his lie to you."

"Oh, Mika, I saw and heard for myself. I'm just more upset that you didn't tell me your feelings, ha—"

"You saw and heard what yourself? Are you hallucinating? Are you taking that fucking acid that's been going around?"

"I had some exciting news I wanted to share with you. You're always achieving so many things, and I wanted you to be proud of me," Connor blubbered.

"I wanted to show the photos and data. And tell you, we may have a way to communicate with others if we take control of the ISS."

"That's superb. That's wonderful. But for your information, everything you've ever done has made me proud of you. I find you to be the most amazing man I have ever met and the most attractive as well. I thought that the first day I met you... on the plane coming here. Now, tell me what happened, that you did not share the discovery with me?"

"I wanted to deliver it in person. It sounds stupid now, but I wanted to see your expression when I told you I'd finally cracked the NASA ISS program. Then I walked in and saw you and Peter von Leutzendorf hugging and breaking up from a kiss."

Mika's eyes lit up. "Ahh, you saw me and Peter hugging?"

"Yes."

"You saw, without doubt, Peter and me kissing?"

"No, but you were breaking up from a hug, and then I saw you hug him again."

"Did you see me kiss Peter when we hugged for a second time?"

"No, because that's when I decided I'd seen and heard enough."

"So, you don't know if we kissed or not? You're just assuming that we did. Is that not a little unscientific?" Mika was playing with him now, and Connor knew it.

"But what I heard would support my assumption," Connor replied.

"What did you hear?" Mika asked calmly.

"I heard you say that you didn't want to break my heart and that you would tell me about what you'd done when the time was right. I heard Peter disagree with you and tell you that since we were engaged, I should know, and I could handle it."

"Did you hear anything about illicit affair? Did we say anything about our feelings for each other or what we'd done that you overheard?"

"No, Mika, but what was I to think?"

"If I had been in your place and saw or overheard the same conversation, let's say between you and Amir, I would have walked right in the room and confronted both of you. I would not be a respected scientist like you and turn into a teenage girl carrying on like she'd just lost her first crush." Mika could see Connor knew what he was saying was true. The situation would have been resolved by now if he had confronted it head-on.

"You're right, Mika. I mishandled it, but what's done is done. There's nothing I can do. There's an Irish saying that words set loose in anger wound the hearts of all."

"What the fuck is that supposed to mean? An old Irish quote will not set you free of what you've accused me of doing," Mika stated, getting off the bed where he'd been sitting next to Connor.

"Where are you going? What can I do?"

"Get your little fairy leprechaun ass off the bed. You're coming with me to the lab to confront Peter now about our affair, like any good Russian worth his salt would do. I know you're not Russian, but you have enough of my blood in you, so get up... now! Or so help me I will carry you there for everyone in Phoenix to see." Connor got up wearily, put on his shoes, and walked meekly beside the blond giant toward the labs.

Peter was busily jotting notes as he stood in front of a battery of plasma screens that had a plethora of graphs and changing calculations appearing and recalculating every so many seconds. The handsome scientist saw them peripherally and turned to face them. "Hello, Connor. I haven't had the pleasure of speaking with you for some time. But, of course, Mika fills me in on you often."

"I bet he does," Connor replied. "He doesn't fill me in on you at all."

Peter seemed taken aback by Connor's demeanor.

"My husband-to-be or to-have-been"—Mika began sarcastically—"came to the lab a few hours ago and caught us in an embrace. As a result, he knows that I have been unfaithful to him. I suggested that since he has confronted me, he should also confront the new man in my life. I would appreciate it, Peter, if you would reflect on the situation and tell Connor truthfully what I didn't want to tell him for fear of possible heartbreak, but what you encouraged me to confess to him."

"You want me to tell him the truth, Mika? For me to tell the other man what he doesn't know seems out of line," Peter said nervously.

"Absolutely! You were so right in advising me to be honest with the little leprechaun here. So tell him truthfully everything," Mika encouraged Peter, but his words got an annoyed look from Connor.

"Very well. Connor, you saw Mika and me hugging. In fact, to be totally accurate, we hugged several times today."

"I've no doubt you have." Connor pouted petulantly.

"Believe what you want, but today was the first day. I swear that to you. We were ecstatic. Mika, admittedly, was more ecstatic than I, but I shared in his delight. We successfully blended sperm for the first time some weeks ago and..."

"Ha! I thought so, and yet you just hugged for the first time today. Started things a little backward, didn't you, Peter?" Connor's Irish blood boiled again, and Mika barely contained a laugh, but when Connor raised a fist and started toward Peter, he held him at bay until he calmed. "Think it's fuckin funny, do you?"

"As I was saying," Peter continued. "We successfully blended sperm." Peter walked behind the battery of screens, and Mika was guiding Connor along behind him. Peter stopped in front of a transparent cylindrical sphere full of a slightly yellow-tinged liquid with thousands of tiny bubbles moving about. The sphere had a translucent divider suspended mid-center. On each side of the separator was a minute deformed bean-shaped object that, while free-floating, was attached by a wavering straw-type hose to the translucent divider. Connor peered in quizzically, squinting his eyes, trying to make sense of what he was seeing.

"Congratulations, Connor, Mika. You are both the fathers of half Russian and half Irish twin boys," Peter said. "I hope I've exonerated myself." Peter walked out of the room, leaving them alone.

"Oh, Jesus, Joseph, and Mary! Was he serious? Those are mine? Ours? When did this happen? Why didn't you tell me? What does he mean they're half Irish and half Russian?" Connor was so beside himself with joy that he'd forgotten the earlier issues.

"Right now, Connor, I truly want to just share this moment with you. I want to be a part of the happiness that you feel becoming the father of a child that's biologically yours... at least one-third biologically yours. But in a bit, we need to talk about how you behaved and talked to me." Mika emphasized the last sentence, but then he smiled and stepped forward, placing his long arms around Connor's chest and his chin on the top of his lover's head. The two stared at the two tiny embryos.

"What a complete miracle. Given even artificial opportunity, life tries to flourish," Connor said with wonder as the tiny embryos swayed about in the bubbling liquid. "Mika, let's speak about my foolishness later, like in twenty years or so or when you really tire of me or if I have another temper shenanigan down the road."

"I think you brought it after seeing the loneliness of the world outside of this complex, and how uncertain our lives are with the possibility of losing what little we have was compounded by me hugging another man and not you. It rocked your already shaken hope, so you regressed in perspective and instantly became insecure. You literally felt alone and seeing me, instead of getting the reassurance that I will be with you no matter what happens, you saw me in the arms of another man. So, I forgive you. I love you. Next time, just pause and ask yourself, is this what I perceive, or is this fact?" Mika drew Connor into an even tighter hug.

"I wouldn't ruin this for you for anything. I was hurt that you distrusted me so easily without confronting me immediately. I think we may have to agree on some rules regarding a code of conduct, just like we'll be teaching them to those two boys. They should never detect distrust between their two dads. They should also never have to witness the violence of seeing Russian dad spanking their Irish dad's ass for being stupid," Mika teased and kissed Connor's hair, which he was letting grow longer.

"One other thing." Mika arched his golden-white eyebrows in question. "Thank you for this wonderful gift and for being yelda," Connor said, as he placed his hand up behind Mika's head and pulled him down for a deep kiss.

Turning their attention back to the sphere, the two fathers stood side by side, each with an arm slung around the other's back. Connor was the first to speak. "Mika, I want to hear the details of how you did this. I want to know everything about our children."

Mika smiled. "It was the process that I explained to you, which had attracted Doctor Saunders' attention. When Peter and I started working on my embryo growth theories, we could provide solutions for most of the problems I'd encountered in earlier attempts. Unfortunately, I've not been able to find a solution to successfully keeping both X and Y-bearing sperm alive. The egg only carries the X-chromosome, while, as you know, the sperm carries either an X or Y. If the X-chromosome penetrates the egg, the result is a female. If the Y fertilizes the egg, a male is a result. Something in my fertilization process destroys X carrying sperm. The result is that, for the moment, only males will be produced. Hence, we have two sons," Mika shared proudly, gesturing toward the sphere and its two tiny inhabitants.

"It's amazing that you've achieved your process to the point you have," Connor marveled. "I'm still not totally clear about what you've been saying about them being half Irish, half Russian."

"Of everything I've done, this, to me, is truly the most amazing. In trying to determine the cause of the X-bearing sperm's mortality, it occurred to me that perhaps I could splice into the sperm so that it would carry both X and Y chromosomes. If the sperm bore both, there was a possibility that when the sperm penetrated the egg that one or the other would survive producing either a girl or boy or that the intrusion of the pair would be a catalyst for the egg to split, should both survive, the result being female and male twins. The third possibility was that both would fertilize the egg, and the end product would be a new human... both male and female. There could be many disastrous consequences if that happened. So for preliminary tests, we spliced in DNA. It took many attempts, but eventually, the sperm survived and was healthy. The sperm donor's DNA blended perfectly with another human male's DNA, thus taking on characteristics of both donors.

"To make a long story short, my love, the embryo on the right is the result of splicing your DNA into my sperm. The one on the left is the result of splicing my DNA into your sperm. In this case, I didn't want to fertilize the egg with two sperm and have identical twins... just too risky this early. Peter suggested we used two eggs from the same female donor, and while we're two separate beings, these boys are equally ours and share the same mother. Also, I think you'll be happy with the donor I chose for us."

"Absolutely amazing," Connor whispered. "So, the boys are Russian Irish in every sense?"

"Well, half Scandinavian... the donor egg contributed half of the DNA string," Mika said. "The egg donor was a five-foot-ten blonde, her eye color matched yours almost perfectly, extremely high IQ, a nearly perfect family health background, a doctorate in physics, and paid for it by modeling for some of the top agencies in the world."

"So now I'm definitely going to have sassy seven-foot-tall teenagers towering over me with both of our temperaments, who will probably blow the place up." Connor laughed.

"Peter warned me about the potential dangers of mixing a Cossack warrior with a little six-foot leprechaun... said I could do better mixing with his sperm." Connor gave Mika a look. "I am, of course, joking with you. But I hope the boys get my sense of humor."

"Two fuzzy blonds, huh?" Connor asked, reaching up and pulling some blond chest hair showing at Mika's collar.

"Not necessarily, love. Dark tends to dominate. They may be blond and smooth, beautiful black hair like yours and smooth, or hairy, a combination of both, or one could be more like you physically and the other like me. One or both may even take more characteristics from their maternal side. It's going to be fun to wait and see while they grow into men," Mika said, smiling and looking from Connor's glowing face back to the sphere.

"Mika, you and I love each other and wanted a family together. But the boys may be straight, and there are only men around. They'll grow up thinking something's missing no matter how much love we give them."

"My love, you worry too far in advance. Life takes care of itself. I think all men are potentially bisexual. They'll find someone they're content to share their lives with. Also, don't forget, we are very early in this new field. I'm sure there's a scientific explanation for the failure of X-chromosomes to survive the process. Peter and I will continue working on the solution," Mika assured the young Irish father-to-be.

"You're right. I'm becoming my sainted mother. I'll let you worry about bringing them into this world, and I'll worry about having twin boys out of wedlock. Speaking of my sainted mother, I'm sure she must be spinning in her grave," Connor said, sticking his bottom lip out and looking up at Mika.

"I'll never get the Catholic out of you, will I?" Mika asked, shaking his head. Connor shook his head in agreement, still pouting.

"I'm going to suck that luscious bottom lip right off your face," Mika said. "Very well. We will have what the Americans call a shotgun wedding as soon as you can arrange it. We wouldn't want the neighbors to talk about your virginity and how easy you were," Mika teased, then he remembered the night he showed up at Connor's quarters, vodka in hand, the goal in mind, and decided he should drop the subject.

"Speaking of having a wedding performed, Brad doesn't know anything about this project. How do you think he'll take all this?" Mika asked.

Connor thought for a minute. "Good question. If he was still like he was when we first got here, he wouldn't be thrilled at all. Brad must consider that two more lives will be supported and coming into the world encapsulated in an artificial environment in a hostile climate. He'll wonder if everyone wants children. He'll have to set up guidelines for permitting everyone to have children in a fair format. We only have a university, he'll have to think about setting up an entire education system, and the list goes on. "

Mika chuckled. "I think we're going to have him pretty stressed. The boys will be born in about eight months if all goes well. It gives us some time to think about how to tell him."

"Maybe we could approach Rick Longarrow and see what he thinks. I know he certainly seems to have some influence with Brad, since they've virtually moved in together. Simon is another possibility," Connor rambled, hands in his hair.

"This is crazy talk. I don't have to hide the birth of my two boys from anybody. They're more than a quiet little secret that has to wait to see if their existence is okay with the upper hierarchy, of which, by the way, I am one. What did I just scream at you a little while ago? The best way is always to confront a situation so that they can properly assess it. It is the Romanov way, just disregard the last Tsar," Mika said sternly as he picked up his communicator and watched in amusement as Connor's eyes grew very wide. Wisely, his Irish fiancé kept quiet and watched the scene unfold.

"General Brad, Mika Romanov here," Mika said into the handheld device.

"Brad McCormick here, Mika," Brad answered immediately.

"Brad, good to talk to you," Mika said, his voice wavering with nervous laughter. He swiped his hands through his hair and winked at Connor.

"Yes, Mika, same here, but you're the one who called me. How can I help you? Is everything okay? Is Connor okay?" Brad asked.

"Yes, he is fine. I'm fine. We're fantastic. Happy and bloody fantastic," Mika said, eager to tell his friend the news. He flicked his eyebrows at Connor. "And Connor is more than fantastic as well, Comrade General."

"What's going on, Mika?" Brad pressed, beginning to sound impatient.

Mika looked at Connor, who had placed his hands lovingly on the sphere. That was all Mika needed to see. "Brad, Connor and I would like to know if you will do us the honor of performing a marriage ceremony between us, say the night after tomorrow night."

"Ah, well, I thought that was a few months off, but I can clear my schedule to do that. Sure, I'd be happy to perform it for you," Brad said, enthused. Mika stared at Connor. Connor smiled and rolled his eyes. This was the shove that Mika needed.

"Thank you, Brad. Oh, and there's one more thing," Mika said rapidly and before Brad could respond. "Connor and I are growing embryos. So, we would be honored if you and Rick would be godfathers to our twin sons."

Connor's mouth dropped open in shock. "That's Russian bulldozing! Is that how you confront and get a handle on a situation? I don't believe you. No wonder there was a revolution," Connor said, grabbing the communicator from the flustered Mika.

"Brad, Connor here. Please don't ask any questions. Just trust me, and get Rick. Come to Mika's office, both of you, as soon as possible." Connor turned off the communicator as soon as Brad assented to the request. "We're growing embryos. What a thing to say."

"But it's true," Mika said defensively.

"It's bloody true that your dad stuck his cock in your mother in a fit of passion, came in her, and she got pregnant. But you don't bloody say that about your wee ones. Instead, you say you've been blessed, and you're expecting a baby or two, as the case may be. Good lord, Mika! You big, gigantic, beautiful man." Connor burst out laughing and punched Mika's shoulder. He couldn't stop laughing, and the more he did, the more amused Mika became.

"I don't understand all this Irish blarney. We're not expecting babies. We have them right there. To expect something means it has not arrived. These boys have arrived." He pointed at the sphere to back up his statement. Then he started roaring with laughter. "I would've loved to have seen the look on Brad's face when I said that. I guess I could have chosen my words more wisely."

"Mika, you did well. I'm just a nervous father-to-be. We'd better get out of here and into your office. I've no doubt Brad and Rick are both running over here."

When they went through the series of labs to Mika's office, Brad and Rick were indeed waiting for them.

Mika and Connor didn't explain, but invited their friend and leader, accompanied by Rick, inside the lab. The four men stood before the sphere with its yellowish-tinged bubbles. Connor had the proud look of a father looking at his most cherished possession. Mika was indeed in love with the dark-haired splendor holding his hand. He was grateful for the two tiny lives that were part of the two of them. Rick Longarrow looked at the sphere with a look of scientific amazement, and General Brad McCormick looked at the bubbling container of life with righteous concern.

"I want you to both know that I'm truly happy for the two of you. Even as a student, Connor often wished for a family he thought he would never have. At the time, I thought he was referring to his career and that he wouldn't have time for a family and marriage. But somehow, out of the chaos of Doomsday, he has the life he wants with a man he loves, and somehow that man has given him two children that are biologically theirs. I'm happy for you. Just don't go giving Simon and Paul any ideas until they have their degrees. That said, I want to know why I wasn't told of this study and the tens of thousands of eggs sent here. I would be directing that to you, Mika," Brad said, appearing highly annoyed at this breach of conduct. "I remember vaguely that Doctor Saunders told me to ask you, but I could swear it was about something else. So much happened that day."

"Comrade General Brad, you never asked me, and you always seemed happy with whatever Peter and I worked on. Your interest was in the present, not in the continuation of mankind, so I could see no reason that I couldn't work on present projects and my little sideline here. It's not like you were paying me for one thing, and I was doing another," Mika said in his most charming way of speaking. Seeing the annoyed expression still on Brad's face, Mika continued. "Seriously, Brad, you understand that this is why I was recruited by Doctor Saunders. He could see much of what was going to happen on the planet ecologically. I'm not so sure that he didn't see the outbreak coming. That we will never know unless Connor finds reference to it hidden in his files. He knew that men and women would be here, and there would undoubtedly be births. Still, he wanted a huge genetic base to draw from, not one that would be limited to relatives in a few generations. My process would have pleased Doctor Saunders. I truly think it would have. For the present, we can only have male births, but I'm optimistic I can find out why and probably remedy that. If I cannot, perhaps my sons will find an answer or someone else's son. The point is that because of this, humankind will go on." Mika paused as he pointed to his embryo babies. He couldn't help but preen as fatherly fondness overcame him when seeing the cute bean-sized boys drifting while growing. They were so small, and he already loved them.

He turned back to Brad, who was also standing in awe looking at their babies. "Hopefully, after the upcoming nuclear winter, we'll go back into the world, and this time we'll know how to treat it. That will probably not be in our lifetime, but now there's hope that we can make it our legacy to our descendants. The only other option I can see is the eventual extinction of our kind. Suppose you don't allow future births, and I say future births because I know you'll let our sons be born. In that case, we'll grow old, die one by one, until there are only my sons and perhaps Simon or Paul left alive in this entire complex. Then they will grow old and die alone on this frigid continent. And that, comrade, will be the end of everything we represented. The death of your son, Paul, and our sons will be a lonely one. Phoenix would heat its vast rooms and send light out into space for who knows how long..."

"Jesus Christ, Mika, you've sold me!" Brad snapped. Rick jumped to place a hand on his shoulder. He looked at Rick and then back at Connor, and lastly at Mika. "Did you also get a doctorate in method acting?"

Connor straightened, undoubtedly impressed by Mika's performance. Rick smiled, shaking his head.

"I considered it, comrade, but there is only so much time yet so much to do," Mika said humbly with a hand over his heart and followed that up with a dramatic bow.

"Well, guess that's settled then," Rick said. He moved closer to Brad, placing his arm around his lover's waist. "I think Brad and I might want to talk to you about giving Simon a little brother."

"Don't even start, Rick," Brad retorted. "Thank you, Mika. Now you've planted that idea and I probably have little to say about it."

Rick chuckled and nodded affirmatively, agreeing with Brad. "What I don't understand is how the embryo is nourished. I understand you've created an artificial placenta, and the embryo is attached to it by an umbilical cord. It's very complex how the fluids are taken in by the placenta and filtered to nourish it. But can you elaborate just a little, Mika?" Rick asked.

"Anytime," Mika replied. "Let me introduce Project Omega, the first of its kind and the last hope of humanity. A very simple explanation—even a child could understand it.

"As you know, six to ten days after fertilization, the embryo attaches, or implants, itself into the lining of the uterus. Then, a week or so later, the embryo starts receiving its nourishment and oxygen from the cells that make up the lining of the uterus. This is the same with my system. During this first trimester, my artificial placenta, which is artificial only in the sense that I created the organic makeup that clings to this divider. In this case, I've used packed red cell plasma and very complex proteins and lab-created vitamins in the liquid you see. Doctor Peter von Leutzendorf can tell you more about the vitamins. He's running his own research project as well, Brad." Mika stretched his eyes as big as saucers, and his eyebrows almost disappeared into his hairline. "You should ask him about that, and by that, I mean, please ask him as soon as you are able." Mika hoped Brad got the message loud and clear. He continued explaining the process of placental adaptive nutritional support.

"Note the tinge of the liquid caused by the packed red cell plasma being yellow in color. The artificial placenta sustains its life-giving equilibrium by balancing nutrients through positive osmotic pressure. It delivers the enriched formula to the fetus while simultaneously exchanging the fetus's waste products collected via artificial siphoning, almost like human kidneys or liver. But instead of recycling it back to the placenta, we discard it. Oxygen, of course, is infused much the same way. I hoped, Rick, that you would share the birth with us since I know your birthing skills are much more up-to-date than my own. The first few births I anticipate will be high risk. And considering I'm the father, I can see where Peter could use a cool head working with him, delivering the babies."

"I hoped you would ask me. It'll be my pleasure. Hopefully, you'll do the same for me when we have ours." Brad shot Rick a look, but before he could speak, Rick continued, "I look forward to your wedding. Let me know if you need help with the arrangements. Come, Brad, we need to leave these two alone, and you and I need to go to dinner and talk." He hooked Brad's arm in his and led him out.

"I think we may have started something," Connor told Mika.

"Probably, but little Ivan and Cian will need playmates," Mika said.

"I don't think those would be their names. A son of yours would soon be known as Ivan the Terrible throughout Phoenix, and you know how things went for him. I'm thinking Shawn and Patrick," Connor responded.

"We have a few months to decide and for me to talk some sense into you. But I can tell you right now, Shawn and Patrick Romanov sound really weird."

"Who said they were going to be Romanov?" Connor asked.

"Well, whoever heard of any boy called Ivan and Sergei O'Hara? Besides, you are marrying me, so I think you should take my name."

"Connor Romanov, that's weird, but I guess Mika Ivan Nicolai Peter O'Hara doesn't sound good either," Connor said, referring to Mika's royal birth name by an insistent grandfather. "How about we compromise? Romanov-O'Hara for legal purposes, and we'll just go by Romanov. I mean, we rarely go by last names around here anyway."

"You are learning, my little Irishman. That sounds like the way to go. But what about the boys? Is it fair to stick them with a name like Ivan Patrick Romanov-O'Hara and Sergei Shawn Romanov-O'Hara?" Mika teased.

"Let's think about it. I'm hungry and drained after all that's happened today," Connor said. "But I hate leaving the boys here unattended."

"They won't be. I'll call Peter. That's why I've been coming in so late. I stayed with them, or Peter was with them, and most of the time, we were both present. Now that the cat's out of the bag, as you people say, this area will have to be on lockdown and off-limits, just so nothing gets accidentally changed on the sphere controls. I'm sure Bryan Howell will be more than happy to supply us with soldiers for around-the-clock guard duty as well."

"I'm impressed with the care you've taken. No wonder you were pissed off with me. Here you were working and taking care of the boys. Thank you. But don't you think round-the-clock soldiers might overdo it?"

"Connor, these are Romanov twin boys. The first in over four hundred years, I might add. Round-the-clock soldiers are not overdoing it," Mika countered, fatherly pride bubbling up from his insides.

"I understand. I'd like to spend time with them as well. I'm sure you could teach me the controls not to tamper with. I'd like to be familiar enough with the readings that I'd know if anything was heading in the wrong direction. We can bring a desk here. I could definitely work remotely from here."

"I think that's an excellent idea. I could have a bed moved in here so when we watch together, we would not have to be bored," Mika said in a deep sultry murmur as he nibbled Connor's neck.

"In front of the boys? Really, Mika? Maybe, if the bed isn't within direct view," Connor replied, leaning into Mika's kisses.

"Little leprechaun, these boys are Romanov. Seeing lovemaking will give them a sense of self."

"I hope I'm not interrupting," Peter said.

"Ah, Peter, thanks for coming so soon. We're going to have dinner and such, and I will be back to relieve you," Mika told him.

"The *and such* part of your statement causes me to doubt how soon you'll be back," Peter said, looking at the two of them and winking. "Just be careful. Two children are enough to handle."

Mika chuckled and then explained that General McCormick and Dr. Longarrow were now in the baby loop of knowledge. He also told him the plans to make the lab off-limits to absolutely everyone unless they had clearance. Bryan would be selecting armed guards just as a precaution. "I hope Brad will also ask you about your Enriched Vitamin Project. I did not elaborate on it. I felt it's your project, and you may have the floor, dear friend. I would appreciate it, Peter, if you would help me make a schedule of qualified people to be in here, so we don't wear ourselves out. Please include Connor on that schedule," Mika asked his lab partner and friend.

"Not a problem. I'm happy to help any way I can," Peter assured the two fathers.

Once out of earshot of anyone, Mika bent down to Connor's ear. "First, we eat in the dining room. Then we get a bottle of champagne to celebrate as I had planned to do earlier today before being chewed up and spit out."

"Said I was sorry, and that sounds like a plan," Connor replied.

"I wasn't finished yet. After the champagne, we're going to our bedroom, where I'm going to spank your ass for the way you acted and then I'm going to fuck you so long and hard that you'll have to wheel yourself down the aisle."

"Christ, the wedding—I forgot. I've got to get with Simon and Paul to help me plan it all out," Connor said in a panic.

"First, we eat, drink champagne, get your ass spanked, and Mika gets rewarded with a piece of Irish bottom! Then you can call Simon and make all the plans you want while I go back to the lab, my cock drained, and babysit your sons." They both laughed and headed into their apartment.

\*\*\*

Dr. Peter von Leutzendorf

The financial backing provided by Dr. Saunders and his benefactors at the WHPSS, helped Peter expand and continue his research by solving one of humankind's oldest dilemmas: The quest for longer life spans without disease. The Eden Bean Project branched off the DNA gene manipulation, which coincided with the Omega Project, not the artificial wombs, but their synthetic amniotic fluid and the DNA string code manipulation. The placental nutrients originally developed for optimal fetal growth and development were structurally adjusted slightly to be injected as a slow-release gel bullet, almost the size of a kidney bean. The capsule would dissolve and slowly release its magic over ten years.

Peter thought of a simple, easily replaceable solution, depending on each person's preference. Some people do, and others don't want to live forever. The working mechanism is an antigen for chromosomal structural damage. Aging would cease completely while the new genome sequence deprogrammed cells from breaking down. This also included fending off disease, for example, cancer, which was ultimately nothing more than abnormal growth of cells.

Mika and Peter were able to create a molecular hook made from the mitochondrial DNA of Connor's DNA that captured DNA fragments that most resembled itself in Mika's DNA creating a new strand of both fathers. Since they were splicing, Peter decided what the hell, he could remove the human SIRT6 gene and spliced it with a shorter linked but identically SIRT6 gene from the bowhead whale, which was easy enough to get. Animal specimens, including eggs and sperm, were frozen and stored in the freezers behind him for precisely these purposes. Bowhead whales were one of the few whale species that live almost only in Antarctic waters. Of all large whales, the bowhead was the most adapted to life in icy waters, and they lived over two hundred years. And while he was already splicing bowhead genes and humans, he might as well strengthen it with the string code he's been carrying around and working on for many-many years. Peter felt giddy. He talked to himself as usual when alone in his lab.

"I fucking did it, Ish. I just hope Brad and the men of Phoenix appreciate it for what it is."

"What do you have there, Peter?" He pretended he was with his imaginary lover.

"Oh, this, I isolated the bowhead SIRT6 gene. I replaced and then reprogrammed the structure signaling with our string code, to repair and rejuvenate broken down strands on the human DNA."

"Oh my, whatever do you mean, Peter, you brilliant and wonderful, beautiful man?" he said in the voice of his make-believe lover.

"I just created this little old thing that would increase human health and their lifespan."

"Wow, Peter, you are a genius."

"I know, right? Thank you very much and guess what?"

"What, you sexy scientist? Tell me, or I'll pull you over my lap and spank your Bavarian buns?"

"Oh my. Okay, Daddy, I'll tell you."

"That's a good boy," he said with a deep baritone.

"Yes, Daddy. I bypassed the defective degenerative qualities on the human DNA strands to increase their lifespans by hundreds of years," Peter monologued like a crazy scientist, the side effect of being lonely and left alone with frozen dead people for a little too long.

His Cryonics Laboratory was a gigantic frozen zoo, human and animal. The men of Phoenix didn't know that some of the rich and famous celebrities were frozen inside those freezers. After all, they paid billions of dollars to be there. Waiting to be thawed and cured of whatever disease they had. Of course, Peter was apprehensive about all that, but they paid for his laboratory, so for now, he just talked to them and used the equipment they'd paid for.

Peter had already injected himself with his Eden Bean, although he doesn't need it. He felt the best spot would be four fingers below the clavicle, in line with the nipple. Then, with a small nick of the skin, he'd slipped it in, and stapled it closed just between the muscle layers. That was one of the immobile spots, padded with muscle, and easily accessible so the person could feel and monitor their Eden Bean's size and position.

He was excited about going to the wedding. "They're going to shit their pants when they open my gift. Especially after they've made their vows for as long as we both shall live." He chuckled at that, wrapping Mika and Connor's wedding gift inside a ten-inch square black box with a big red bow.

# Chapter Eighteen

"Good morning, citizens of Phoenix.

It is I, Lasitor, informing you it's time to rise and shine. It is now six a.m.

Did you know humans need to surround themselves with family and friends to receive or give support and comfort at both happy and sad moments of their lives? Many studies have demonstrated that having supportive connections is an essential component in reducing your risk *of developing mental illness and helping to improve your overall mental well-being.*

*Visit our local community news page to search for friends to become your family because they always have your best interests at heart. You never have to be concerned about their motives or mistrust their advice.*

*Breakfast is served until eight a.m.*

*Thank you, and have a productive day."*

# Family Time

**General Brad McCormick**

"I just am not sure about your moving into my apartment, Rick," Brad told his lover.

"Why? I've spent every night here since Quik-Fix Hall. I have to get up at an ungodly hour to get back to my apartment. If I stayed here, it would give us both a couple of extra hours of needed sleep," Rick argued.

"Like you would really let me sleep," Brad teased. He'd become very comfortable with Rick and the sex life they shared. He'd learned that he trusted the man entirely. Yet, when he gazed at the doctor while the young man slept, he couldn't understand why anyone so beautiful and good would want to settle for a man who'd just turned forty-two years of age. "I just don't know if Simon is ready for it or if the men of Phoenix will understand."

"You're afraid! My commander fears the opinions others have about his personal life. You have to grasp the truth of things, Brad. The life that you and I would share here is the new normal. It's what we have to work with in a post-Doomsday world populated only by men. The truth is, I would have fallen for you anyway, even though I could never have had you. But you and I have each other, and that's saying a lot. The second thing is I think you underestimate your son and his partner. They both want you to be happy. Think about it, Brad. Your son and Paul have been dicking each other for some years. You found that out not too long ago, and you've accepted it. Why don't you give them the credit they deserve? I'm willing to bet you that they have us figured out. If they don't have that much intuition, I'll be very disappointed in them. As for the men of Phoenix, what can they say? You're the commander. Your top three men are gay. Two are in a committed relationship looking forward to marriage. One is the captain of the guards, who fucks anyone willing to have fun with him, or at least he was until Tony. Just think about it, okay? I really am falling in love with you."

The truth was Brad was falling hard and fast for him as well. "I'll think about it. In fact, you're probably right about Simon and Paul. I'll talk to Simon about our situation."

"Baby, that's all I can ask of you. I have to get to my office. I'm doing some routine physicals today, and for some reason, every second man in Phoenix wants an eye exam lately." Rick got up, put his shoes back on, walked over to Brad, leaned over, kissed him, and squeezed his crotch.

Brad playfully smacked his hand away. "Okay. I will ask the boys to meet me for dinner."

"Sounds good. I get tired of the dining room, even though Juan's cooking doesn't disappoint. We can work out later... here... in bed," Rick said over his shoulder on his way out of Brad's apartment.

Brad smiled, thinking about how happy he had been lately.

\*\*\*

His day had been busy and productive as usual. This was the last and most important issue on his list to tick off as completed, done and shelved. His heart-to-heart discussion with his boys. Better to get it over and done with, he thought, as flashes of his beautiful Apache's features with his intelligent, quick-witted remarks hovered in the back of his mind. He'd agreed with Rick just that morning that he would speak to his son, and he was eager to get his young lover officially and permanently moved into his apartment. Rick was convinced that Simon and Paul would have no objections. But in a way, asking for their blessing was like asking his dead wife if it's okay. He knew it was silly, but if they had objections, he preferred to know before Rick moved in.

He raked his hair with his fingers just after knocking on the doorframe of their apartment. Seconds later, his time of truth arrived. "Thank you for seeing me," Brad blurted nervously as the titanium steel door swooshed open. He'd paged them earlier to inquire about their whereabouts; luckily, they were home. They'd planned to eat in, so they'd invited him over for dinner, and insisted that he invite Rick as well.

"Hello, Son, thank you for seeing me. So... well... I need to talk to you, and Paul, about something that has come about," Brad said, mouth dry and hands in his pockets. Simon gleamed and seemed glad to see him, and motioned for Brad to come sit in a chair opposite him. Brad was impressed by the immaculate, cozy home the boys were running. Paul was busy cooking dinner, which smelled mouthwatering and hopefully would be delicious, considering the cacophony of clanging pans coming from the kitchen.

"What is it, Dad? Is there a problem?" Simon leaned forward, giving Brad his full attention.

"Not a problem... no, not necessarily a problem by any means." Brad stroked the itchy stubble of his beard. He was not usually at a loss for words but found himself extremely nervous about what Simon was going to say. He had grown into a handsome, responsible young man and his disapproval of Rick moving in with him would hurt deeply, and Brad wasn't sure who's side he would choose. Simon was his only family and his happiness had to come first before Brad's attraction to a much younger man. The workouts at the gym had turned he and

Paul into well-chiseled hunks. Brad heard nothing but glowing reports from their various teachers at the small Phoenix University. They were well on their way to becoming elite members of the scientific community.

"I'm sure you've noticed that Rick Longarrow and I take part in a lot of different functions here at Phoenix."

"I guess that's one way of putting it," said Simon with a smirk, making Brad super uncomfortable so he shifted in his seat. Realizing what he'd done, he sat back and crossed his arms. "He seems to be involved in many aspects of your personal life, Dad. The two of you are kind of cute. You are inseparable. So why do you bring it up? Paul and I think it is great that you have a lover who can keep up with your energy level," Simon said.

Brad's face heated. He knew he was blushing. He rubbed the sweaty palms of his hands on his upper legs. Most men had seen Rick and him together by now, but he worried someone saw them entering Quik-Fix Hall and had told Simon. How will he explain they went for mutual blowjobs while looking longingly at each other while being sucked off by a stranger on the other side of the wall?"

"Dad?"

"Well... now... how did you know?" Brad sputtered and had just noticed the silence from the kitchen, and a smiling Paul standing in its doorway.

"Oh, come on, Dad! Paul and I have been lovers for almost five years. We aren't as naïve as our age may lead you to believe."

"Then you are okay with it? With his age? I came to ask your blessing and if it would be all right for Rick to move in with me. We are kind of together all the time when we are off duty," Brad said nervously.

"Pop"—as Paul had been calling Brad in recent months—"Simon and I are happy for both you and Rick. He's a nice man and seems to have made you very happy. That's what's important to us."

"He's much younger than me," Brad said, making sure they were onboard with this. It was one of the big worries on his list for tonight.

"Twelve years difference isn't a lot. Unless you were my age, and that would make him eight," Simon said and moved over to hug his dad. Paul walked over and gave Brad an embrace as well. There was a knock on the door.

"That would be Rick," Brad said with a big smile on his face.

"Dinner's almost ready," Paul said. Then to Simon, "Sweetheart, will you help me set the table?"

"Sure thing, babe," Simon replied, bounding youthfully over to the kitchen. Brad got up to answer the door when Simon stuck his head out of the kitchen. "Should we call him Rick or daddy?"

"One crack like that out of you, and you're grounded, young man!" Brad teased. He saw Paul's hand reach out and grab his son's shoulder, pulling him back into the kitchen.

As always, Brad was stunned by the gorgeous doctor's sexy look when he opened the door. Rick had a bottle of red wine in his hand. His smile showed brilliant white teeth against his permanently tanned skin. His blue-black hair hung long and straight and favored hanging over his left shoulder. There were essentially three styles of dress among the men in Phoenix. Brown and white camo pants and t-shirts, lab coats and scrubs, or gym warm-up suits. However, Rick had chosen a pre-Doomsday civilian tonight. He was wearing a black and white plaid shirt with an open collar and a thin gold chain around his neck with a gold eagle pendant showing against his smooth chest. The shirt was complemented by a tight pair of black jeans that discreetly displayed a prominent basket and snugly encased butt. His belt was woven black leather with a moderately sized buckle studded with a beautiful array of turquoise. Brad ushered his man into the room, and once the door shut, he hugged him, whispering in his ear, "My god, you are perfection. I don't think I can wait to take those pants off you tonight."

Rick stepped back from the embrace, eyeing Brad with surprise, his eyes quickly surveying the living area for witnesses to the hug. "Apparently, my optimism for bringing my two hosts wine is not in vain."

Brad shook his head in the affirmative. "How soon can you pack and move into my apartment?"

"Went well then?" Rick asked, his face full of love and his smile growing even more.

"I should've listened to you all along. They knew, just like you thought. I just didn't want resentment to play any part in our family dynamics," Brad said. Rick looked as delighted as he felt. They were two delighted men, moving in with each other, Brad thought. He was more than delighted, he was ecstatic.

"Welcome to our family! Dad is very smart as a leader but sometimes clueless in matters of family," Simon said, as he entered the room with Paul. Then he gave Rick a warm, sincere smile while stepping forward to hug him. Paul followed with a welcoming embrace and a light kiss on Rick's cheek. Then, for the first time in his life, Brad shed a tear in front of his son.

"Well, unless we're going to break out in Kumbaya, the table is set, and it's serve-yourself. Rick, I can only assume the wine is for us. Would you do us the pleasure of opening and pouring it?" Simon asked, leading the three men to the small but cozy dining area. Brad's heart swelled, loving the warm welcome Rick had been given by his boys. Rick never ceased to amaze him, and it seemed his boys were just as impressed.

Having opened the wine, Rick took a seat next to Brad. "Your table looks beautiful," Rick said. "I love the plain white dinnerware and blue napkins. It highlights the tiny blue LED candles, simplistic and yet stylish."

As Rick poured four stemmed glasses with the wine, Simon added, "I think Paul's culinary skills will impress you. I hope you can cook because Dad certainly can't. Tell us about that wine. It looks quite aged if judging by the state of the scratched bottle and the label."

"I'm glad you asked. I chose the wine carefully for tonight. This is one of my favorite bottles from Bollevich Vineyard. I've kept it for a special time, and this is, indeed, a special occasion. This wine was known for its unique microclimate, and 2039 was a solid year for grapes. This Cabernet Sauvignon was noted to be the best of that year. Being known for its aroma of bay leaf, mint, anise, dark chocolate, and distinctive palate.

"Interestingly, it was aged three years in new French oak barrels, one in neutral oak, and an additional ten years in bottle before being released on the market. If you sip and savor it, you'll taste the robust flavors of sweet black fruit, fresh red plum, and a touch of warm vanilla, very smooth and hopefully a true pleasure to your taste buds. It'll go perfectly with Paul's dinner. The garlic and the savory pasta salad will enhance the crispness of the fruity orange peel."

"I didn't know that besides being a brilliant physician, you're also a wine connoisseur." Brad leaned over and kissed Rick. It didn't feel awkward to show his affection in front of the boys. The boys were yipping, oohing and ahhing, like two happy meerkats. They seemed overjoyed that their dad was happy and in love. Brad's heart swelled with humble appreciation as he looked around the table. He wondered what he had done to deserve this level of happiness. This unique and beautiful bond his family had, made him the happiest and luckiest man alive. And it was all because of Rick and his boys accepting and loving him. Unconditionally. He stood up, lifting his glass. "I wish to thank you Paul, Simon, and Rick. Thank you for your unfailing support and love. I realize I am blessed beyond measure to have you here with me. I want you to know how much I appreciate you. Thank you for inviting me over on a minute's notice and accepting me and my new boyfriend." His breath hitched, the raw emotion cutting the armour he'd been wearing all his life. He gulped around the thickness in his throat. "Your mother would have been so proud of you, how you have adapted and grown into strong and steadfast men. I want you to know how deeply proud of you I am. Thank you for listening to me. For allowing me to find happiness in this unlikely situation at the bottom of the world. This is the one place where I can be myself, I realize. Here with you. Around this table. I've found the thing that matters most in life."

# Chapter Nineteen

*"Good morning, Phoenix residents.*

*It is I, Lasitor, urging you to wake up and face the day. It's now six a.m.*

*Have you ever woken up in the middle of the night fearing or dreading pending doom while you experience physical signs of anxiety, such as a pounding heart and sweating? Those are nightmares and aren't usually a cause for concern. But if you develop a fear of going to sleep or having difficulty functioning during the daytime, especially while putting everyone else at risk, Lasitor urges you to visit the community news page to book a consultation with a doctor or a faith healer if you can find one.*

*Breakfast is served until eight a.m.*

*Thank you, and have a productive day."*

# Triggers

## Tony Bonillo

Tony Bonillo had been working late in his office preparing the schematics for a pipe system that would tap into the steam of the volcanically heated water running far beneath Phoenix's dry valley floor. The end purpose of this project was to turn turbines that would augment the solar batteries. They weren't designed to last indefinitely or provide the energy needs of the growing Phoenix complex. In the not-too-distant future, the volcanic steam would have to provide all the energy needs of Phoenix if Dr. Romanov's prediction of a nuclear winter darkened the sky.

As Tony completed the final notations on the blueprints and prepared to have dinner with Bryan and some of his engineers, he was grabbed from behind and enveloped in darkness. He opened his mouth to yell, but something hard and spherical was forced into his mouth and then taped in place. Strong, solid hands roughly bound his wrists behind him and then he was lifted by what felt like two or possibly three men and placed in some sort of rectangular container. Cloth articles were thrown on top of him, and he felt movement. He instinctively knew that he was in one of the facility's laundry carts and being rapidly transported as he heard the accelerated squeak-squeak from the wheels and multiple boots hitting the floor as whoever pushed the cart along.

*Where the fuck to?* He didn't have a clue. The unknown destination seemed far as the running felt like it took forever. At one point, he could hear the howling of the wind as it buffeted one of the passageways. He felt a significant temperature change. He knew he was being carted to one of the vacant domes off-limits to save energy expenditure. But why? Was someone trying to sabotage his volcanic power plans? That made no sense. It was possibly the only chance Phoenix had of surviving a nuclear winter.

*God, maybe that was it, a group suicide plan. Some of the residents who couldn't tolerate the feeling of desolation... of being one of the world's few human survivors... they'd decided everyone must die? Maybe my murder? Are they going to chuck me out to freeze to death?*

Many thoughts, some practical, some pure fantasy, ran through his mind as the prison cart on wheels continued on its journey to a forbidden area of Phoenix.

After what felt like ten to fifteen minutes, the cart came to a stop. He heard knocking, then what sounded like a steel door move on its cold hinges. Muffled whispers and low murmuring reminded him he was one man against many and they would soon overpower him again. If only he could reach his fucking communicator. He always carried it. He could feel it pressing against his chest from a pocket even now. If only he could contact Bryan. The captain would send his whole militia after him if he could just turn on the damn communicator so that someone could hear that things weren't right. The steel hinge sounded again, and the temperature got warmer. There shouldn't be an area this warm in the forbidden sector. What's going on?

Ruffled movement of the linen, and then air started to circulate around him. Thank god, he hated being enclosed. He'd almost panicked from not being able to move his arms from behind his back or straighten his legs because of the cart's restrictive size. Even worse, he was having trouble breathing through his nose, and the ball gag made it impossible to catch a breath through his mouth. Verging on a full-blown panic attack, it felt like he would die from suffocation.

Not knowing if it was a good thing or a bad thing, several hands hoisted Tony from the cart. He felt himself being placed on a cold metal surface face down. He continued struggling desperately to breathe. The tape was ripped from his mouth in a stinging swish, and the ball was removed. Finally, he was free to suck in deeply and feel fresh air filling his lungs. No longer in fear of smothering, Tony began to yell for help. He felt the ball being placed against his mouth. It was obviously a threat. Be quiet, or they would gag him. He held still and immediately became silent. Why was no one saying anything? He could sense the presence of several men around him. He could try to identify the voices and turn them in to Captain Howell if they would just say something. Of course! That was why they weren't making any sounds. He must know them. But what had he done to them that they would want to hurt him?

Still, Tony could hear only the sound of breathing and the occasional roar of the wind outside as it blew down from the ice-covered mountains to tease Phoenix with its strength. At least it was warm in this isolated place where he was the captive of men with unknown intentions.

He heard feet shuffling away, followed by whispers, some laughter, and a loud shush from someone cautioning for silence. He heard a rustling of cloth and a couple of thuds. Then he felt the binding around his eyes being loosened and pulled from his head.

*Oh no, they're going to let me see them. They'll have to kill me.*

The light, while not bright, blinded him for a few seconds. He tried to focus so he would at least see who and how they would kill him.

He had to be hallucinating! Standing in front of him was a beaming Bryan. Behind the captain stood four gorgeous men dressed only in black leather harnesses. Juan, Drew, Amir, and Dylan were holding a cake with twenty-eight candles flaming. "Happy Birthday, sweet boy!" Bryan said.

The four naked men, their cocks beginning to chub, yelled, "Happy Birthday, Tony," and then began to sing the birthday song.

Tony wanted to cry, overwhelmed by all kinds of emotions. Being so busy with the turbine designs, Tony totally forgot it was his birthday. Then he remembered Bryan asking him what he wanted for his birthday the previous week, and him telling Bryan he longed for a playroom where they could play out their fantasies.

"Thank you, sir," Tony said as he regained his composure. His voice was hoarse from yelling. He chuckled. "Even if we live another hundred years, you'll never be able to top this one."

Bryan stood proud; arms stretched out. "That's not all. A bunch of guys pitched in to build this playroom." He turned back to Tony's abductors. "It's for everyone's use, but it's called the Tony Bonillo Dungeon, and there's a plaque over the door to prove it." Grinning, he turned back to Tony. "Are you ready to break it in?"

*Of course, I am, sir. I've got to be the luckiest man in Phoenix.*

"Yes, sir, my lights are green!"

\*\*\*

Juandre

Standing in the background while helping Bryan surprise Tony with his birthday gift, Juandre felt a sudden constricting feeling in his chest. Like an elephant was sitting on it and he couldn't take a breath. His knees wanted to buckle and fold in under him. He wanted to run, and he wanted to sit down on his heels. The sounds, and the urgency Tony experienced, had ripped him from this reality and placed him in a dark and musty cavernous room. Many men with cloaked faces surrounded him. They were chanting.

\*\*\*

**2014 A.D.**

**Disciples of the Anunnaki compound**

**Lexington, Kentucky**

**United States of America Chapter**

Creepy Gregorian chanting woke Juandre. *We must be underground.* It's humid, cold, and musty. His thoughts rushed, trying to make sense of where he was. He thought he was in Rome for a moment, hearing the Latin plainsong he grew up with. Men dressed in black robes surrounded him, on their knees, chanting the medieval musical notes. On his right side was an altar adorned with all kinds of relics and papyrus rolls. On his left was a small table and one chair. High on the wall behind them, tapestries hung. *It must be an underground church.* Embroidery of a white dove sat on a robed figure's shoulder as the man pointed his hands up to the sky, to the moon. A gigantic hand reached down; fingers open as if reaching to pick the figure up.

Juandre watched the leader, puzzled and afraid for his life. The leader wore a black robe with golden lapels on the back of his neck and draped over his shoulders. He'd been chanting Latin, then speaking in English with a Middle Eastern accent. As he continued, the men repeated what he said, sounding like a mindless cult.

*Am I an offering? What the fuck do they want from me?* He searched for clues. His gaze fell on that table to his left again. He squinted to see through the hazy fog. He knew they'd drugged him. Shaking his head to clear the cobwebs and sober up, upon clearer inspection he noticed the apparatus.

*Fucking torture devices!*

They looked ancient and rusted and designed to inflict maximum pain. He was panic-stricken. If they used that on him, and he wasn't dying of blood loss, he was definitely checking out with tetanus—spastic and never-ending seizures. The sight of them horrified him, and he screamed. A piece of cloth was in his mouth—so he made lots of hmm-hmm sounds but no words.

The horrid chanting continued. Either they couldn't hear him, or they ignored him. A helmet with a lock, a weird corkscrew hand drilling thing for bones, pliers, and hammers had been laid out on the farthest end of the table. Juandre strained his neck to see. Oh, and six-inch nails. Also rusted.

Sweat beaded on Juandre's hairline and ran in rivulets down his temples. His groin itched and burned. It was damp and reeked of urine.

Two of them grabbed him, hauled him into the air, and carried him to the back of the cavern. One struggled with his belt but was too slow. The other men ripped his pants and pulled them down, then took off his underwear.

"You pissed yourself." They laughed.

"Put him in the swing and tie him up."

***

Juandre's mind returned to the present. He was outside with a towel draped over him. Drew sat on his haunches next to him, a big, white, terry cloth towel wrapped around his hips, still wearing the harness.

"Breathe, baby. Breathe in, one, two, three, four, five, and out one, two, three, four, five." He counted while rubbing Juandre's back.

"I remembered, Andrew. It was horrible. It was like I was there. I could smell and feel them on me," Juandre whimpered.

"I saw you freeze. You almost let the cake fall. You were turning paler and paler, and I knew that is where your mind went. I'm so sorry, I did not do a good enough job of wiping it from your mind. It was my first time trying. I'm so sorry, baby."

Disorientated and infuriated by years of suppressed anger, Juandre yelled at Andrew. "Then, do it again and this time do a better fucking job!" He trembled from fright, and he hated it. He was never scared of anything. "Delete it!" he shouted at Andrew.

With a concerned and empathetic look, his husband pulled him up and lifted him into his powerful arms. "Come, I'll take you home and help you. I'm so sorry, baby."

Juandre struggled to catch another breath as sobs escaped and air refused to return to his constricted lungs. He wanted to scream and hit something, but all he could do was hang his arms around Andrew's neck while sobbing as more memories of that day flashed in and out of his conscious mind.

"This is why you said you've taken care of everything."

"Yes, they were dealt with. Every single one of them. You were so happy not knowing."

"Maybe I should know. Maybe I'm supposed to know."

"It's your choice, whatever you think you can handle."

"Many people have been through worse. Maybe I should work through this." Juandre sniffled. He felt ashamed and so stupid. So belittled, as if it had just happened to him. He was trembling. "The bastards, I wish I could kill them with my bare hands," Juandre said as they entered their apartment.

"I will run you a bath and then we can talk about it." Andrew activated the door with his foot to close it and carried him inside. "Just know that I love you, and I did kill them with my bare hands."

"I know. I'm remembering it now." After Andrew had removed his harness, Juandre plopped himself in the half-filled bathtub.

"Maybe it's a good thing," Andrew said, pouring his favorite bubble bath for him. The delicious pink rose aroma filled Juandre's senses, and he calmed instantly. He lay back, looking up at his husband. "I think let me remember. Is that the only memory you've taken from me?"

"Yes, and you did ask for it to go away. When you fell asleep that night, I entered your mind and erased that day as best I could. I'm so sorry I did a shitty job. I'm a shitty husband and a shitty vampire." Andrew said and climbed into the bath behind Juandre.

"No. You are not. How were you supposed to know? Ish turned you into a vampire and left you to your own devices. For fuck's sake, you didn't even believe you were a vampire until you almost killed yourself in the sun."

"That was your fault. I was so in love with you. I watched you and forgot about the sun," Andrew joked and took the washcloth, soaping it up. He said, "I love you, talking about what happened is a good thing," and then started washing Juandre's back in rhythmic circles.

Tears streamed down Juandre's face. "I love you more," he said, sobbing.

# Chapter Twenty

"Good morning, citizens of Phoenix.

It is I, Lasitor, wishing you a happy morning. It's now six a.m.

Are you stuck with a boring partner? Do you think it's time for a change?

You might borrow this fantastic idea from Queen Marie Antoinette, who mastered this trickery back in her time. By all accounts, the king *was quite dull and always retired to bed at twenty-three-hundred. However, in her party chateau called the le Petit Trianon, the queen was known to set the ballroom clock ahead by a couple of hours. Shocked at how late it was, King Louis would rush back to Versailles and to his bed, leaving the poor queen to find her own entertainment.*

*Visit our community news page for more trivia and other tips and ideas on getting rid of or dumping a guy.*

*Breakfast is served until eight a.m.*

*Cheers, and have a wonderful day."*

# Never put all your eggs in one basket

**General Brad McCormick**

Not far from Connor and Mika's apartment, Brad's large apartment was situated in the living area close to Phoenix's eye, physically making him more available in the event of an emergency. Brad was flopping down on one of his favorite recliners. He had one brought in for Rick as well. The two of them had their shoes kicked off, relaxing while enjoying a cup of tea together. They had amazing long discussions, and he appreciated Rick being someone he could talk to, someone to bounce ideas off, but most of all, someone he could hold and who held him back.

Brad was curious to see pictures of the post-Doomsday world and also dreaded seeing firsthand the devastation that would be revealed. The orbiting satellites of both friendly and not-so-friendly governments had been commandeered for use by Phoenix. Mika never ceased to astound him. Such brilliance encased in an extraordinarily beautiful body. The man's knowledge seemed to rival that of a computer. Combined with his ability to reason, it made the man awesome—to use one of Simon's favorite words.

The amazing thing was that Mika also possessed profound humanity. Brad had seen the tenderness and caring he directed to Connor, always putting him first, despite his bravado with most people. He was happy for Connor; the Irishman had grown up with few advantages and many hard knocks but was still mainly all heart. His communicator beeped on the side table next to him just as he relaxed deeper into the recliner.

"Brad, Connor here. I think you may want to see some photos that came through."

"Interesting?" Brad asked into the handheld communicator.

"Depressing," Connor responded. "Come to our apartment. It'll be more private."

"That's what we expected. I'm on my way. Please have some coffee for me," Brad told his Irish friend, clicking off the communicator.

He walked briskly through the corridors, saluting the few military men he passed, smiling and speaking to civilian members of the community; he made a point of not showing his emotions on his face. Still, he could feel the tenderness in his ass with every step he took. His lover had pummeled him hard, long, and deep during the night. It felt like he'd chaffed his cheeks from the relentless in and out movements. But at least he no longer bled from the man's penetration as he had at first. Rick, on the other hand, had met the entry of Brad's thick cock stoically. Knowing that he wanted Brad regardless of pain, the physician was gifted at relaxing his own ass enough for Brad to make deep penetration before taking back control and tightening his ass on Brad's lengthy thickness.

As Brad approached the door to Connor and Mika's apartment, he couldn't help but smile, knowing that deep in his guts, Rick's sperm still lived. Rick and

Brad changed their positions regularly, but Brad had to admit that he preferred to be fucked by the young doctor more often than to be the one inside Rick.

Connor opened the door, a grim look on his face changing to a smile for his old friend, and then gestured him into the cozy common room. "Please have a seat, Brad. Your coffee is ready. I just need to fill your cup... black, right?"

"Yes, please," Brad said, looking forward to coffee for a change. "Where's Mika?"

"He's showering. We were up late studying some of the photos. I have it set up to project on the wall for you. It's depressing, as I already told to you, but there are some interesting developments as well," Connor said as he set the cup of steaming coffee on the coffee table in front of Brad. "Would you like some cookies with your coffee? Mika actually had a strange outcropping of domesticity last evening and baked these himself."

"Then how could I refuse?" Brad replied. "I never would've suspected that among his many talents he would be gifted in the culinary arts as well," Brad said, setting his coffee cup down.

"He's got many hidden talents; he surprises me every day." Connor smiled dreamily. Then he cleared his throat as he took a seat opposite Brad.

"Remember the last correspondence we had with Saunders at HQ? He was telling you to prepare to be more open. He also said the situation was closer to home than you might think," Connor reminded him.

"Yes, he'd completed psychological profiles on everyone. I assumed he meant I'd need to adjust to the fact that my son, Simon, is gay."

"Perhaps," Connor agreed. "However, Saunders was a man who left no stone unturned. For instance, he was able to access some of Mika's work. Along with a psychological profile, Saunders tested genetics, specifically chromosomal makeup. Not only for abnormalities because of that vaccine shite of 2038, but he was obsessed with why his son was gay, why I was gay, why anyone would be gay. Mika had discovered a gene that seems to appear at random in people. If they possess that gene, they're almost guaranteed to be homosexual or bi-sexual. Mika had little interest in that, since his work had much more important implications. But while this gene seems to run in the family line, there's no predicting when or where it'll show up."

"That's fantastic!" Brad exclaimed. "Why haven't I learned of this before now?"

"Because it had nothing to do with our survival here. I didn't know about it either. When I was downloading files in those last hours, I included Doctor Saunders' personal records on the possibility they might apply to us somehow. I wasn't prying, but it intrigued me when I discovered this phase of Saunders' work. Even Mika, who found the process for identifying the gene, has never read the files," Connor said.

"Was Saunders aware of Simon and Paul being gay?" Brad asked.

"Yes, and also of you. Hence the *much closer to home than you expect* statement," Connor explained.

"My god! So my phobia and intolerance were probably an effort on my part to suppress homosexual desires. Fascinating."

"Probably, but we'll never know for sure. The important piece of information to be gained is that you have the gene, your son has the gene, and you've learned to love and accept that part of him, and you're accepting yourself," Connor told Brad with a gentle smile.

"Well, comrades, now that we've shared all of our secrets, shall we look at what the world has become?" the boisterous Russian asked as he entered the living area, dismissive of their mundane conversation. "Brad, did you try my cookies?"

"Yes, thank you, Mika."

Brad got up to look at the photos Connor had turned his attention to. The world Brad was being made privy to was not the world he'd both hated and loved. A kaleidoscope of memories created visuals that ran through his mind, overlapping the reality of what was before him. The magnification and clarity of detail from the government satellites were outstanding. Mika and Connor took day and night photos of Earth to confirm no lights were visible at night. Initially they mistook burning buildings for a man-made light source, which may have resulted from lightning strikes or spontaneous combustion. In the Gulf of Mexico, several oil rigs were in flames. Those could burn for years or until a strategic hurricane put an end to the blaze. Only then would the oil end up oozing into the world's oceans until the pressure releasing it abated. Also noticeable in the night were active volcanoes, which Brad didn't remember having been active just three years ago.

"That was one of the first things that attracted my attention. There seem to be many that were not active before. I cannot explain why this is happening. Still, I suspect that a volcano was the initiator of our earthquake here last year," Mika said and programmed in a photo. "This photo is of a volcano here in Antarctica on Ross Island just off the west coast. It's been active before and recent enough that the ground has been too warm to support ice-covering for hundreds of years. The combination of oil fires, forest fires, and volcanic activity necessitates re-evaluation of global warming trends projection equations. Suppose this is a chain reaction and the so-called *Ring of Fire* becomes many active volcanoes. In that case, the world will be seriously affected for centuries. The sea levels are already rising, but I'm convinced that Phoenix is safe, at least from sea levels and earthquakes. My real concern is with the cubic tons of debris going into the atmosphere. Our solar backups will not receive the light necessary for charging them. It will jeopardize our ability to grow food. Another possibility is that the atmospheric debris might do one of two things. Trap heat around the Earth, which would expedite flooding and the associated climate change. Or the covering may allow heat to escape and stop heat from entering the atmosphere, thereby starting another ice age. Therefore, there are possibly two outcomes, and I could make a compelling argument supporting either one."

"My god," was all Brad could say. *I must assimilate this information and try to plan a course of action.*

"My theories need a team's assessment for validity. I may have over-imagined, or the Earth may self-correct. Let us show you more of our intriguing photo studies. But let me prepare you. There is some troubling material," Mika said as a caution.

"Might as well take in everything at once, I suppose. Connor, may I have some more of your delicious coffee and Mika's wonderful cookies?" Brad asked, situating himself more comfortably at the table. Connor smiled in the affirmative and went to get the pot of steaming coffee. He hurried back and took over the conversation.

"This is Houston Metro," Connor said, showing photos of the ground. "There has been a horrible hurricane in the past few months. The majority of buildings in this community were destroyed, some by fire. This is in the downtown area. Still pretty much intact, but not one sign of life. This is New York City. Again, no sign of life is clear, except for this pack of dogs. So, we know that at least some animals were immune to the plague. There are photos of birds, the rare cat which has probably gone nocturnal. There are cows and such in the more rural areas." Connor showed a photo of the earthquake-damaged Los Angeles and then the airport. The remains, or at least the remains of remains, lay strewn everywhere. Connor didn't dwell on that but instead flashed to images of London, Berlin, Paris, Rome, Sydney, Beijing, Bangkok, and city after city presented death. Wrecked vehicles, derailed trains, and a few crashed planes were all too common in the visuals.

"Connor, love, show the bases," Mika prompted him, and in a flash, Brad was looking at the continent of Antarctica. "Here are five of the bases that had survival possibilities. But unfortunately, we didn't get evidence of any living humans. On the upside, we don't have photos of human remains. And you'll notice the plane here, at McMurdo, is not iced over, and neither are two of the ships. They should be."

"You really think there are people there? Do we have the capability of reaching them?" Brad asked. The discovery excited him.

"Well, we can't jump to any conclusions. We don't see people. That base was enormous, and there should be activity going on twenty-four hours a day. We must keep quiet about this until we study further. It's possible that, if they *are* alive, they could be carrier survivors. If there were people there, McMurdo would be prepared to survive a few years with no problem. Not as well prepared as we are, but they will make it. Another possibility is that they prepared ships to leave but then, for some reason, took only one, and they're no longer there. Other bases along the coast may have gone to McMurdo for sanctuary, and we don't know if they were hostile or not." Mika covered as many probable possibilities as he could.

"I'll be damned. We may not be alone, at least not as alone as I feared. Keep me posted as your work progresses."

"Wait! There's a startling discovery we haven't even told you about," Connor chimed in. "Tell him, yelda."

"Yes. This confuses us." Mika excitedly backed up Connor's childlike enthusiasm to share a treasured discovery. "While we were studying the night skies, we found this."

Brad was dumbfounded. The photo he was being shown looked very familiar. Of course, the terrain was all wrong, but it had to be. Before he could ask questions, Mika signaled his lover to show other photos.

"We also found this and this and this," Mika said, jumping up and pointing at a specific position on each photo.

"But how? How would I, we not know?" Brad asked in an astonished whisper.

"Don't you see, comrade? All were top secret? If one failed, there was a possibility that the other might succeed. We may never know how many, but we know of four! Saunders, in his genius, did this intentionally. Somehow, he knew what was coming, not the plague, but the world climate change. It was his way of saving pieces of humanity and civilization." It made perfect sense that Dr. Saunders had built more facilities like EP-1. None were as monolithic as Phoenix, but all were enormous and architecturally constructed in the same fashion.

Brad interjected. "To avoid total loss, the man invested in multiple locations. Saunders is written all over this."

"More simply stated, never put all your eggs in one basket." Connor smiled.

"Where are they?" Brad inquired.

"So far, the Himalayas, the northern Rockies, the Alps, and the outback of Australia," Mika replied. "We would never have spotted them, but they cast amazing light into the darkness from *dead* earth, and the shapes of the facility reminded us of what we must look like from space. Surprisingly, however, there's no evidence that anyone besides my little hacker here has attempted to pirate the satellites."

"There could be thousands of humans housed in those facilities! This will be a boost for the residents' hope and morale." Brad was up and already heading for the door.

"Do as you will, Brad, but keep in mind Australia is the closest one, and it will be years before we can get there, if ever. Also, consider that those lights are solar like ours and maybe on automatic. That's doubtful, but worth considering. Another fact is that the climate will rapidly change with all that's being put in the atmosphere. So, some of those EP's may not make it. We have the advantage of volcanic heat to generate power. That's an advantage the other EP's most likely won't have." Mika's realism put a damper on the whole discovery, but Brad agreed with his logic.

"It's worth sharing, but visiting these places is a distant possibility. We need to continue working on communicating with them. I'll leave that to you, Connor. Thank you, gentlemen, for sharing this fantastic news." With that, Brad was off to his office to dictate an electronic notice to the men of Phoenix.

# Chapter Twenty-One

"*This is your wake-up call, Phoenix residents.*

*It is I, Lasitor. It's now six a.m.*

*Did you know not all animals urinate through their penis? Fish, for example, urinate either through their gills or through a*

*urinary pore. Scientists have found evidence to suggest that eating oily fish may help you live two years longer and extend your life.*

*And did you also know, in contrast to historical views on fellatio, it's revered as a spiritually fulfilling practice in Chinese Taoism, which regards it as having the ability to enhance longevity?*

*The point is whether you urinate through gills, a pore, or a penis, you can prolong someone's life.*

*Visit our community news page for the beginner's guide on instructions on the reverse wheelbarrow position. You can exercise and prolong your life. FYI, if I had a body, you'd frequently find me in this position.*

*Breakfast is served until eight a.m.*

*Cheers, and have a wonderful day."*

# Connor and Mika exchange vows

**General Brad McCormick**

The morning of the wedding, Brad and Rick were on their way to breakfast when caught so off guard they followed Juan and Drew like puppets into a broom closet without question.

"This way, please, sirs." The two cooks herded them into a small storage room and closed the door. The motion sensor lights flicked on just as the door shut, trapping four big men in a ten by five feet space, which was just big enough for floor mops and cleaning supplies, an emergency kit, and a firehose. Once inside, Juan started explaining with purpose like the queen he was before either Rick or Brad could ask a question. The two cooks couldn't let the first marriage in Phoenix go down without a celebration. *Juan and Drew had no respect for rank.*

"Sooory for catching you unannounced like thisss, but this is a secret operation of high importance." Juan looked back at Drew, making sure he had back-up, and continued. "Sirs, Drew and I are baking a wedding cake for the lucky lovers getting married tonight. But we've also organized a little entertainment, a small celebration of sortsss. But for this to happen, we need your help, sir," Juan said, just before Brad opened his mouth to speak and continued without giving Brad a chance to stop him. "We need you to divert Mika and Connor to the ballroom directly after the ceremony so we can all have a little get-together. Serve some cake, real cake, okaaay? Wedding cake and of course a classy showing of our asses." Juan flicked his hair for dramatic pause and then continued.

"We understand that only their closest friends were invited to the chapel, but we are a big family here, and we all wanted to celebrate the occasion with them. Both Connor and Mika are respected and loved by everyone," Juan explained. He truly wanted to create a memorable evening for the men. Of course, Juan being Juan had a hidden agenda. He knew from experience that the best way to realize what he'd planned was to get his illustrious leader to see things as if it was his idea.

"Uhm, that's not a good idea. The newlyweds want to keep it small and intimate."

"Yesss, but we have never had a wedding, and the ballroom is perrrrfect for the men to say their congratulations. We've prepared a special show for them." Juan flickered his gaze back and forth between Brad and Rick, preparing to stop the reply he didn't want and hoping for the words he wanted to hear from Brad's mouth.

"What... kind... of... show?" Brad asked, slowly, clearly not sure he wanted to hear the answer. "I know you two are always up to something, and you do have a reputation of being the two mischief-makers in Phoenix. But if this is a strip show... wait, wait. Wait a minute. To be honest, I still think you did something to Rick and me that one morning."

"Who me, nooooo, I... we would never. I mean, how, what do you mean, sir?" Juan sputtered, trying his best to feign innocence. Although mischievous, he was a horrible liar. "You mean, put something in your drink. Ah, forget about it, it's nothing. Okay, okay, we may have given you special energy orange juice."

"You little shits, the both of you! I knew it. I have never fucked..." Brad caught himself before he blurted out the events of that particular morning. Fucking Rick over the railing, coming twice without a softening dick, he'd drilled the poor doctor like a demolition hammer. It wasn't something the leader of Phoenix wanted to advertise. "What do you mean 'special'? If you drugged the food, you could kill someone!"

"Damn you, you are old enough to know giving someone drugs is never safe," Rick jumped in, not only to defend Brad but probably his honor too.

Aaand Juan lost his cool. He looked like a little salamander about to spit fire.

"Come on, Doctor! I knew what I was doing. It's not my first rodeo with chemistry. I'm not just a cook with style you know. I have a Ph.D. in chemistry. In fact, I think I have more degrees behind my name than you. So I know what I'm doing," Juan defended himself. "I'm not flaunting, I'm just making sure you know there are two doctors in the storage room."

"Dear god, what have you been doing in that kitchen? Have you been cooking up drugs and feeding them to the men? Juan, if I find out you've been drugging the men, you'll be the first person to be court-martialed. And you, Drew—" Brad pointed his finger to the two cooks, back and forth. He thought about Simon and Paul and worried about his kids getting drugged. "You're in this with him, too, so you're in just as much trouble." He pointed a finger at a wide-eyed Drew.

"No, sir. The men know about Juan's *Rooster Booster Juice*. They ask for it all the time."

"Are you saying the men of Phoenix are addicted to your what? *Rooster Booster Juice*?" Brad and Rick asked in unison. Brad looked at Rick, seeing the man wanted to laugh at the situation.

"Nooo, they can't be addicted, it's just vitamins, it's harmless, it just wakes the brain cells that signals you are aroused," Drew said like it was nothing. "Anyway, even if you overdose, it is just like edging someone for hours. No one's died from a bit of edging. At least not that I've heard off. If you take the person out of the situation, the horniness goes away, and they piss all the vitamins down the drain. It's all in the mind." He pointed to his head and then to his dick.

"All in the mind," Juan repeated. "You were just very hornyyyy for your doctor here."

"You should stop that immediately. It's not safe. Men might die," Rick said. looking back at forth between Juan and Drew, reprimanding them as if they were ten-year-old children.

Juan, batting his long eyelashes at Brad, feigned acquiescence. "Okay, you tell the men the *Rooster Booster Juice* is not safe. They've had the juice for almost five years, and it's not killed anyone. And when we have our shows, we have the liquid all the time. But tell them one of their few pleasures in life is now forbidden, and I can respectfully assure you there will be an outcry of cruel and unusual punishment. I'll bet you my dildo collection on that."

"Shows? What shows? Why haven't I heard of shows?" Brad asked, disregarding Juan's emotional outburst. He was getting increasingly irritated with the whole prisoner-in-the-closet game. It was stuffy in the small supply room, and Brad's enormous perimeter of personal space was not being respected, so the room was not working for him, at all. Drew took up most of the bloody space, and he's so sturdy, he can block an oil tanker from entering a harbor, Brad thought as he tried to conjure up an escape plan.

"Exactlyyyy, that's what we're saying. Wait! You didn't know about the shows? How were you not sent an invitation? Drew, darling, make a note to find out how Brad's many invitations fell through the cracks. Oh, well, sir, no worries. We'll fix the glitch. Come to the ballroom tonight, after the wedding. We'll organize the rest. I'll speak to sirs, after the celebration, only if you see what we can do, then you'll understand. Chop-chop!" He brazenly snapped his fingers at Brad and Rick.

Brad decided to respond with silence because he would either explode or pass out, so going with the flow was the fastest route out of the tiny room.

Spoiling this day was the last thing he wanted to do to Connor and Mika's day. *Anyway, this is not a military institution.* He had to remind himself of that often enough that it was a mantra he had on auto-play in his mind. He also knew Juan had never been in the military, so he didn't have the same reference of respect and discipline as a soldier. Also, there was something amiable, although feminine, about Juan, especially how he snapped his fingers and flicked his wrist at them. Brad found the pair was growing on him; the longer he spoke to the *Laurel and Hardy team*, the more they amused him. Both were colorful, weird creatures and so bloody, uniquely demanding, he doubted anyone ever said no to them.

"We have lots to do and a wedding cake to bake. Just let the men know it's a tux affair. We want to have a posh night for Mika and Connor. They should page two-four-four-five for a tuxedo, or if they want to wear a ball gown or something else, it doesn't matter, they will page, and we'll help them get ready for an astronomical night," Juan said with a lot of flair and pizzazz.

"What do you mean you'll supply them with tuxedos, a ball gown, or whatever?" Brad felt confused again; Juan was talking circles around him. At this stage, he just wanted to get out of the damn small room, but the two fuckers were blocking the entrance. So he caved. "Okay, I'll page general population, not including Mika and Connor, saying we have a wedding tonight and the reception would be in the ballroom. Anyone wanting to come and needing a tuxedo should page two-four-four-five, and they'll be assisted, right?"

"Riiiiight, I, Juan, and Drew will sort the rest. Don't forget to mention the ball gowns. Some of the soldiers love wearing the ball gowns."

"What time is the wedding?" the stunning teddy bear of a man asked in a deep baritone.

"It starts at six p.m. Unfortunately, I don't have a tuxedo. Can you help me?" Rick asked. "I realize now, I'd never planned on wearing something special for the wedding; I would have just arrived in smart casual street clothes."

"I have my formal Mess Dress, I did plan to perform the wedding wearing that, so I guess I won't be needing a tuxedo," Brad said as he started to understand the plainness of the wedding he'd planned. He began to feel guilty because he never thought of treating his best friend with a wedding to remember. He started to appreciate the two characters in front of him. "I see where you're going with this, thank you. Maybe we should tell Mika and Connor to postpone. That way, we can all be ready for what you envisioned for a wedding reception."

"Absolutely not, no, no, no, no, no, no!" Again, with the wrist flicking. But this time, there was a no with every flick that flew left, right, up, and down, making a cross over Brad. Like a holy cross, an exorcist fending off evil. Brad and Rick couldn't keep up with all the 'nos' being said. "We have lots of helpers." Finally, Juan stomped his feet and said very convincingly, "Yes, we have lots of tuxes. Just page us so we can give you directions. General, you just do that for us, and we'll sort the rest. We'll be ready at seven p.m. in the ballroom."

With that, he swung around and swooshed the door open, and with the flamboyance and happiness of a demon leaving hell, he chuckled at them.

Brad and Rick were stupefied. "Fuck me sideways, and swivel on it. I swear those two are incubi." Rick chuckled, grabbing his knees to prevent himself from falling over.

"Absolutely not, no, no, no, no, no, no!" Brad copied Juan as they laughed.

"I'll see you tonight, lover," Rick said and leaned in for a deep kiss. "We better go, or we'll never leave the closet." They laughed and excitedly decided to meet up for a shower before the wedding later that afternoon.

Brad felt like he was walking on air. But in the back of his mind, he knew this day of happy tidings would be short-lived. He was worried because he knew winter was coming.

"I, Connor Patrick Sullivan O'Hara, promise to love you, Mika, and take into serious consideration all that you ask me to do. I willingly give you my respect, my love, my loyalty, my body, and promise my fidelity to you alone for as long as we both shall love the other."

\*\*\*

"I, Mika Ivan Nicolai Peter Romanov, promise to love you, Connor, and take into consideration all that you ask me to do. I willingly give you my respect, my love, my loyalty, my honor, my body, and my family name, and promise my complete fidelity to you alone for as long as we both shall love the other."

"Mika and Connor, I pronounce you husband and husband," Brad said with a smile and a wink. "You may kiss your husband."

Mika put his arms around Connor, and the two kissed long and deep until Connor, glowing red from the neck up, forced Mika to let him come up for air. Laughter could be heard throughout the simple little chapel.

"Having heard both of these men speak soberly from their hearts and voicing their love and commitment each to the other in front of these witnesses, it's my pleasure to present to you Mika and Connor Romanov!"

Simon and Paul were tasked with taking pictures. Brad had asked them, and they eagerly accepted. "Smile for the camera," Paul said while clicking away. While he was doing the photos for Mika and Connor, Simon was taking videos in the background. They already knew what Juan and his minions had planned. They would leave ahead of the entourage so they'd have the best view of the newlyweds' faces when they entered the ballroom.

As soon as they were out of the chapel door, Connor turned to Mika. "That was a dirty trick you played, Mika."

"I don't know what you are talking about. Let's get to apartment before people think I'm happy to see them," Mika said, indicating his tented trousers and changing the subject.

"Don't pull that Russian accent on me, Mika. You changed your vows to say that you give me your family name. That wasn't there at rehearsal, and then Brad introduced us as only Romanov, not Romanov-O'Hara."

"I know, my gille-toine, but please understand I just want you to have my name. I don't want to share you with another family name. We are one family, not a hyphenated one. But if it upsets you, we can change it before Brad has it entered into his logs."

Connor seem to think about it, but reached a conclusion very quickly, "No, let's not change it if it means that much to you. It's a compliment to me that you want me to be yours alone and for everyone to know it. But you are going to have to quit calling me gille-toine. Calling the father of your sons a little fuck-buddy just won't do."

"But they won't know Gaelic unless you teach them. However, they'll learn Russian; it's their cultural obligation, so you must stop calling me yelda. They'll wonder why their father is always calling their father big cock. They might slip up and call me that in front of their teacher or something." They laughed and kissed. Before they could escape down the corridor, Brad and the guests sped past them.

"Gentlemen! The men of Phoenix have a surprise for you before you get any ideas about slipping away. We'll all now proceed to the ballroom," Brad said, very proud of his maneuvering with Phoenix's men today. They were all so excited, and Brad was happy to be part of the plan. He decided to let Juan and his vitamin *Rooster Booster Juice* go but would ask Mika to test a sample to ensure its safety. If it was found not to have any adverse effects over the last five years, why worry about it now? Nevertheless, he would call on Juan and Drew to discuss things that need council and medical approval before putting something into the residents' juice.

"What ballroom?" Connor and Mika asked.

"The Blue Ballroom," the crowd collecting around them answered. They looked like sugar starved kids in front of an ice cream truck, arms stretched out, trying to shake hands with the grooms to congratulate them.

Brad was acting as a traffic director. "Wait, please wait, men, let's move along. We might trample each other to death." Brad continued leading the crowd while he explained over his shoulder. "I know right? It was a secret affair room and now we're all privy to it. The Blue Ballroom is the one on the far side of the Communications Dome. Drew and Juan from Nutritional Services have a cake cutting and a little entertainment planned for you there. The men wanted to congratulate you and be part of your nuptial celebrations!"

They all followed Brad, Mika, and Connor. The boys, Simon and Paul, click-clicked as much as they could as the line behind them got longer and louder, like a gaggle of geese.

Juan, Drew, and their teams of busybodies had worked fast, hard, and efficiently. Juan had organized them into four groups of ten men to answer the pager and assist with clothing options at the clothing warehouse they'd discovered a year ago. Rows and rows of tuxedos, suits, and gowns of every style, size, and color, just hanging there waiting to disintegrate and be eaten by moths or whatever eats clothes in Antarctica. But, of course, a proper drag queen couldn't have that, so ever since then, they'd had their Blue Ballroom events on a weekly basis. Tonight, they would perform a Moulin Rouge early 1920 cabaret for the grooms.

To create an authentic City of Love, Paris, where lovers like to travel to when they go on a honeymoon, they'd constructed an eleven-foot Eiffel Tower on the left side of the stage, the tables were decorated with silver and blue trimmings, and for fun, each had chocolates in little Eiffel Tower shapes. For lights, tiny toy street lamps on Christmas LEDs decorated the tables and walkways. Ten massive flat-screen TVs had been installed on the walls every fifty feet for those who wouldn't be able to see the stage directly so they would have close-up views of the performances. When no one was on stage performing, scenes from the *City of Love*, the *Arc de Triomphe*, and people walking hand in hand in the streets at night would play to enhance the romantic ambiance.

On the stage was a gigantic red windmill, which had been constructed a while ago. This was one of Juan's favorite acts, therefore readily available for tonight as it was stored backstage with the other props, so had been easy enough to bring in.

As the humming noise of men grew closer, the guests jumped up to form a human tunnel or guard of honor, so the newly married couple could walk through and receive their congratulations.

It took the couple a good forty-five minutes to walk through, and when they finally sat down, Mika grabbed the bottle of champagne and downed it. When the show began, Connor was still talking to one of the last men, slapping him in a congratulatory man hug. Servers ran as Mika waved them on. "Bring me a bottle of vodka. If you can't find one, send Paul or Simon to get one in our apartment and another bottle of champagne for my husband. *Spasibo*." He thanked him in Russian.

"What's wrong, husband? Is the attention-getting too much for you?" Connor asked Mika. "I'm really enjoying the surprise. I would have been happy just going to our apartment and locking us away from everyone, but I admit, it feels good to see so many happy faces, just accepting us and our love."

"No, I'm just thirsty, very thirsty. And, hungry, for cock!" Brad heard him shouting and all those sitting close enough to hear, cheered.

As soon as the couple settled down, the show was underway. Connor moved his chair so he could sit-lie onto Mika's side.

Juan was on stage, in the highest heels Brad had ever seen.

"Look at those heels," Mika told Connor.

"He has damn beautiful legs," Connor replied.

Mika just laughed. "That was precisely what I thought my new husband would say."

Juan lip-synced while dressed in black fishnet stockings and a black and red corset. His hair was gelled to the side, making a slight wave and a curl at the end, so he looked the part of a 1920s lady of the night in Paris as he finished the first song from the *Moulin Rouge* soundtrack called "Your Song." Mika and Connor sang with the chorus to each other. "How wonderful life is while you're in the world."

Juan finished his performance, putting on a thick black faux fur, ankle-length coat. Then he congratulated the happy couple, thanked everyone for helping, and gave Brad an extra deep curtsy for helping and supporting the effort. Next, he announced the second act and that dinner was self-serve, starting with the newlywed's table. Thus, guests could grab their dinner during the performance. And, after dinner, the third act would be a surprise guest performance.

While finishing their dinner, one of the servers called Mika, saying he had a question about the vodka. Connor thought that odd looking questioningly at Brad who only pulled his shoulders up to his ears. Connor smiled and sat back to enjoyed the last bits of the show.

All went dark and quiet. Then, finally, Juan announced that the last surprise performance was about to get started. Connor looked around searching for Mika. Then, the lights shone on the stage, and there, bathed in white light, stood Mika. He was dressed in a traditional Russian wardrobe. He had a pair of bright blue narrow silky trousers on, an oversized traditional Russian *rubakha*, a black belt, and high black boots. Around his neck was a shiny gold chain with a medal-like piece of jewelry.

Connor was shocked speechless, hands covering his mouth. In front of him on the stage stood the last Romanov Tsar in all his glory. Not that he was advertising it, but Brad knew. "Fuck, he is beautiful," Connor said as the room roared with approval of his god of a man.

"Gentleman, the groom has prepared a special show for his husband. It's a traditional Russian warrior dance. Connor, we want you to come to sit right in front of the stage," Juan said.

Connor and his chair flew into the air as six men lifted him. Connor gripped his chair, tears rolling as he was overtaken by emotion. As soon as Mika saw his tears, he started crying. Then the whole room was teary. "God, what a beautiful night," Brad said. Then the room fell silent as Mika lifted the microphone and began to sing in Russian. You could hear a pin drop as his magnificently pure voice enthralled the whole of Phoenix as they listened to him serenading his husband. Connor spat snot, smiles, and tears left and right.

When the song was done, the room exploded with applause. Mika threw the microphone down to Juan, who caught it and switched it off. Then, all the lights went off, except for one spotlight on Mika and one on Connor. On the television screens, both men shared the screen, so those in the back could enjoy both reactions simultaneously. Paul and Simon were managing the lights and cameras like professionals.

Rhythmic clapping and feet stomping started on the stage. First Mika, and then Juan followed suit, and not long after the whole bloody Phoenix was clapping, while Mika went down on his haunches, shooting one leg after the other into the air. Connor pointed to Mika's tapping boots. His husband jumped up and tapped to the beat of the clapping crowd. It went on and on, until Mika was drenched in sweat. He ended his groom dance extravagantly as he jumped up in the air, tapped his boots, spun, and landed at the end of the stage an arm's length from Connor. Connor clutched his chest in awe.

"If Connor's not having a heart attack, tonight I'm sure he is going to make love to Mika until he does," Brad said laughing jovially. Overtaken by joy and happiness, he reached for Rick and kissed him.

Drew brought Mika a towel and a bottle of water. As Mika caught his breath and finished the water, he beckoned Juan closer for the microphone.

"Phew, what a night!" The crowd cheered, then Juan signaled them to shut the fuck up, or else. So they shut up.

"Connor, my husband, that was my way of blessing our marriage. I will fight for you and our family to my last breath. Thank you for taking my last name; you know my name has a big significance. I sang for you how much you mean to me, I danced for you to show you how hard I will fight for you, and with this last gift, I want to show you how precious you are to me. I want to present to you the double-headed eagle. The Romanov crest is a family heirloom. Created by Fabergé, a gift Nicholas II had made for the *czarina*. The last royal commission to Fabergé. But was never delivered and was retrieved by my great-grandfather at Fabergé in Paris." Connor got up and kissed Mika long and deep. He took the heirloom, inspecting the gold-encrusted sapphires and diamonds. He seemed overtaken by emotion, he had no words as he nodded up and down, mouthing thank you and kissing Mika again. Brad had seen the heirloom earlier when Mika asked him to hold onto it for him. Although Mika had planned this surprise for just them and their original small wedding guests, he had somehow found out about the wedding surprise, thanked Juan for the sentiment, and Juan worked Mika into the program for the night's festivities.

Mika was in the process of lifting his Irishman fireman style.

"No, no, no, no, no, no!" Juan stopped them before it went further. "Not now, come cut your cake, then you can go."

"Yes, please, I want coffee, too," Connor said. The cake was pushed closer on a small serving trolley. It was a plain white cake of three layers with two husbands on top. Connor and Mika cut and fed each other cake, then Mika grabbed Connor's hand and ran for the exit.

The two men made a hasty retreat to their apartment, where they remained for three days. Their meals were cooked by Juan and delivered to them, a gift from Brad and Rick, and General McCormick's orders were that no one was to bother the couple during their three-day retreat.

Bryan and Tony, as their gift, had set up a monitoring system in their apartment that had one camera focused on the bubbling sphere and another which gave constant readouts of all the graphs and recalculations.

Announcements about the couple's sons were not made before the ceremony so that the wedding would focus only on Mika and Connor. News about the impending births of Connor and Mika's sons was released to the population two days later, but only after guards were put in place and a schedule posted assuring that a qualified person would be monitoring the development of the boys at all times.

\*\*\*

Even the darkness that was enveloping the world didn't dampen the spirits of the men of Phoenix. Tony Bonillo's volcanic tap had been successful; the turbines turned to keep the batteries charged, the food growth lights lit, and the men warm. So far, the fossil fuel generators hadn't been used but made the men feel safe and secure if needed.

Over the next few months, the Romanov fetuses kept developing into healthy baby boys. Connor and Mika enjoyed standing by the large sphere and watching the boys kick and move to different positions. Connor was fascinated by the tiny hands that would make fists. Mika said he liked to see the movement of their eyes beneath lids so delicate that capillaries were visible. The time before they could hold their sons seemed like an eternity away, but it was set for less than two weeks.

Brad presented a set of rules pertaining to having children, which the council supported, as did the entire voting population. Several applications were already in and approved. After some convincing, Brad himself signed the approval for the birth his own future sons with Rick, stipulating that first, both parents need to be married.

Connor's photo gathering showed more volcanic activity, but the dreaded Ring of Fire hadn't had a chain reaction in eruptions so far. Mika was concerned about how much longer the powerful telescopic satellites would penetrate the growing debris in the atmosphere. Weather patterns were radically changing, and tidal waves indicated heavy seismic activity. Fortunately, none had reoccurred in the vicinity of Phoenix. As a precaution, Mika asked Tony to design a balancing station with steel lattice on the sides and a solid top for the precious sphere and its instrumentation to be done post haste. In the event of a severe quake, the globe would gently rock as the intricately designed floor balanced itself.

# Chapter Twenty-Two

"*Rise and shine, Phoenix residents.*

*It is I, Lasitor, wishing you a happy morning. It's now six a.m.*

*Of particular note, yours truly will be giving a historically significant seminar called* Live Your Happiest Life. *It's a two-part miniseries. The first part will teach you the art of pleasing a woman intimately, conversationally, and how best to keep her feeling like the queen she is. Opening a car door for her, pulling her chair out, etc. Part two is the art of flower bouquet design and examples of how to say,*

**I was wrong, you were right, I'm sorry.**

*It's a dark comedy written to not only amuse but inspire and give hope to those who are waiting for a woman to materialize. So please don't jam the internet by signing up. Yes, you've guessed right; it's available on our community news page.*

*Breakfast is served until eight a.m.*

*Good luck, it's going to be a busy day."*

# Best case scenario

**Dr. Mika Romanov**

Mika and Connor worked tirelessly, dissecting the information transmitted to Phoenix via the International Space Station. Mika had discovered a wide-angle shot of the former United States showed that California, Oregon, and part of Washington were not there, only an expanded Pacific Ocean appeared. When Connor found a signal calling for help and referring to themselves as a forgotten Environmental Project, emergency meetings were called, and they discussed response attempts. Sadly, a rescue mission wasn't an option. Messages of prayers and that no help was coming were sent into the sky without knowing if anyone received them. Not only was Phoenix amid the natural seasonal winter, which meant constant dark with extremely low temperatures and fierce storms but also, a worldwide storm was taking place outside of Antarctica.

While Mika evaluated the missing landmass from the United States, he came to a grim conclusion. He made several more calculations and then called for an emergency leadership meeting. When the men were assembled, they knew by his face that something cataclysmic was about to be shared.

"Gentleman, this may be the last time that we meet together," he began as he walked over and took a seat by Connor, and took his husband's hand in his. "A stretch of land approximately one thousand miles wide, from where the Baja Peninsula used to be up into the former state of Washington, is under the ocean. A gigantic wave of near extinction level will hit all of Asia over the next few hours. I suspect that somewhere in this area is or was a city of domes, like Phoenix. We may never know the answer to that."

"Good god, Mika. What's it mean for us?" Brad asked.

"I was coming to that, comrade. If my calculations are correct, I must caution you, I only have part of the facts, there will be a chain reaction of events caused by seafloor quakes, producing waves of unbelievable size. So, if I am correct, this wave will be wind-driven and given birth by the America-Asia wave. That wave will be typical, devastating, but typical. It will come across the Pacific floor and not show itself until it's ready to swell and rise as it nears land. In our case, it will be a visible sea top wave. Hitting the coast near McMurdo, they might grow higher as the waves travel inland toward Phoenix, but I doubt it. The speed of the tsunami waves may be as fast as jet planes. I considered the fact that we're in the middle of winter and that the ice stretches for miles, forming a protective ring around Antarctica. That and the fact that Phoenix was built deep into the shadows of a mountain range, Phoenix stands protected on three sides. It would help slow down the water and lessen the force of destruction. Our higher altitude and the blocks of ice forming natural water breakers may be our saving grace, but I don't think we'll escape untouched."

"What do you predict happening?" Brad asked.

"Best-case scenario is that it'll be diverted by the ice and the Victoria Sound mass. In which instance, we'll get a windstorm of cataclysmic proportions, which Phoenix may or may not survive."

"The worst-case scenario will be what?" Brad asked as Rick took his hand.

"The wave will head for and breach the glacial pass and flood this valley we are in. Which means we have a narrow window to a favorable survival statistic," Mika said softly.

"When will this event take place, and what are your recommendations, Mika?" Brad asked.

"If I were commander, I would make an overhead announcement activating the emergency response we practiced. There's no time to call a general assembly. We have sixteen hours at best, but it could hit in twelve. I would order the dome lids shut and secured by titanium bolts. I would have Tony's men activate the water breaker system. Also, flatten and place as many satellite dishes as possible face down to the valley floor. Just like we prepare for earthquakes, order all medical supplies and machinery possible to the caverns, and have anything that can be transported taken to the caverns. When this is done, Bryan and Tony, who know the lava tube system probably better than anyone, should guide everyone up the tubes to be as high in the mountain as possible. The water may not reach you, and it should recede in a matter of weeks, and if you're lucky, perhaps days. If we have done our jobs well and Phoenix is air and watertight, it just might survive with minimal structural damage. However, if we're breached, the water would freeze within hours. I see no way to save the airplane and other heavy equipment not stored in the machinery dome, which means leaving here will probably be out of the question.

"I hate to rush off the good company, but you best get started now. My and Connor's thoughts will be with you. Gentlemen." That said, Mika and Connor stood and started for Mika's lab.

"Where are you two going?" Brad asked.

"To be with our sons. It's impossible to move the sphere without endangering them, and we've chosen to sit by them."

"You are essential here! You must come with us," Brad insisted.

"Brad." Connor smiled at his friend and superior. "Would you leave Simon if he was confined to a bed, and moving him would kill him? I think you wouldn't. You can't expect Mika and I to do any differently. If we survived, we would never be able to forgive ourselves. Also, those alarms could sound any minute, indicating that the boys need to be extracted from the sphere. Who knows, we may get to hold them, if only for a while." Brad nodded in agreement and started making a general announcement even as Connor and Mika left for the lab.

Hours went by with a flurry of activity. Finally, nearing the twelve-hour mark, winds could be heard like thunderbolts assaulting the domes of Phoenix.

"Soldiers, you've done your job well. You best get to the cavern and tubes while there are still people to guide you up," Mika told the two young men who had been charged with guarding the unborn children.

"Thank you, sir, but we've talked about it and decided to stay on duty with you. If those alarms go off, you'll need help," Private Fritz told Mika.

Malcolm, the other private, agreed. "When I left home for here, my wife had given birth to our son, not a month before. I'd be overjoyed seeing a baby one last time."

"Thank you, but that's going above and beyond," Connor said to the men. "You should be with your friends in case they need help."

"You are our friends. And Malcolm is a little more than a friend to me, and we want to be here," Fritz explained.

About ten minutes later, as the storm picked up outside, the inhabitants of Mika's lab could hear the occasional crash of metal or possibly rocks hitting the lab pod. "Is it here?" Connor asked nervously.

"No, love, it's too soon. If I calculated correctly, this is going to go against the law of nature. The wind will not come with the wave but a few hours before. It'll be a while if the water comes at all," Mika replied, leaning over and kissing Connor lightly on the lips.

A noise was heard at the entrance to the lab then Peter and Rick entered. "What are you doing here?" Mika demanded, standing up.

"I'm here to help bring those boys into the world in a few hours," Peter responded like it was an absurd question.

"They need you. You must think of the men of Phoenix," Connor said, but selfishly feeling thankful to see his friends.

"Well, in a few hours, you're going to need me more than they do. Besides, if the water destroys the buildings and the labs, they'll have little need for a geneticist. I've spent a lot of time working for these boys to come into the world safely. So I'm not abandoning them or you and your husband now. Besides, I don't have anyone, just the occasional mouth at Quik-Fix Hall. So I won't discuss it any further," Peter explained while assessing the health status of the twins.

"Rick, are you sure Brad doesn't need you? Maybe Fritz and Malcolm can escort you down to the cavern? He'd be lost all over again if something happened to you," Connor pleaded with Rick, now worried about his friend being alone.

"I talked to Brad. He's a man of dedication and practicality, just as I am. His commitment is to save the men of Phoenix as best he can. My commitment and oath is to save lives. At the moment, I can best do that here. Brad agreed that realistically, if Phoenix is destroyed, every man in those tubes is doomed by drowning or freezing to death over the next several weeks or months. I would be able to do little about that. Besides, I'm an Apache. I'll walk with Brad always in my heart, even if my heart does not beat."

The men grew quiet, and all of them, even the soldiers, sat on chairs in a semi-circle behind the two fathers and waited. Occasionally, someone would share a pre-Doomsday memory of childhood and babies. Connor and Mika held hands and watched their boys kick and raise their tiny arms. Fritz and Malcolm shared a kiss and held hands. All the men had pools of water in their eyes, ready to spill over onto their cheeks, thinking of things that could have been.

# Epilogue

## Dr. Broderick Longarrow

The usual chaos and confusion accompanying emergencies and natural disasters were not present when Brad activated his well-chosen emergency preparedness team. No one panicked. The men of Phoenix knew what to do down to the last man. Brad had announced that it was not a drill but the imminent threat of a tsunami. Immediately, the titanium metal shutters closed, securing each dome and its connecting corridors. They had taken the steps diligently prepared over the past three years. The emergency management group comprised soldiers, medics, and other volunteers who managed the evacuation smoothly. The buffering system and water breakers were initiated to divert the water down the valley between the plateau and the foot of the mountain range.

Thus, hopefully, avoiding flooding Phoenix and the upward slope of the cave system in which Brad and the men had taken refuge.

After the first big earthquake, Phoenix had used that as a learning opportunity. The population was broken up into small groups; each had a task to complete before they made their way into the winding tubes of the vast cavern system. The smaller teams encouraged group cohesion and prevented splintering and unnecessary rescue missions. Right now, the group of most concern was the one deciding to stay with the unborn twins.

Brad had convinced himself that he'd been given a lifetime of happiness with Rick in the last several months. But like the soldier and scientist he was, he had told Rick that he had accepted the finiteness of existence. He and the men of Phoenix had waged an honorable battle for survival. The next several hours would determine the direction fate would take them. Would Phoenix be repairable, assuming it still stood, or if the water came and didn't recede as Mika thought, would they be sealed in a tunnel only to suffer a slow demise? Fortunately, they had an emergency preparedness plan in place, so they grabbed personalized emergency kits that included enough drinking water and food for each person to last several days. In addition, each man carried something that would contribute to the group's survival, including portable radios, batteries, chargers, oxygen tanks, blankets, axes, and a sundry of other useful items.

In the lab where Rick and the five men sat waiting, accepting, and hoping, a huge wrenching of steel twisting was heard, and a thunderous crash against the side of their pod shook the structure to its foundation; the precious sphere swayed gently, thanks to the ingenuity of Tony Bonillo. They couldn't see the outside since all windows had been placed in protection mode with quarter-inch titanium steel sheeting. Now only the steady rumble of the wind assaulted their ears. Connor leaned against Mika. "I have truly loved you above anyone else who has ever been in my life," he whispered.

"I know you have, and you are the first person I have ever loved. It has been enough," Mika replied, running his thumb along his husband's ivory, pale cheek and kissing his black hair.

The alarms sounded. Emitting an intense medical whine from several monitors. Rick, Peter, Mika, and Connor jumped from their chairs, some of them overturning.

"It is time!" Mika yelled. "They must be extracted." The lights in the room flickered but didn't fail. They flickered again and went out. Backup batteries kicked in at the same time Tony's turbine reactivated and sent a surge of electricity to the delicate machinery, causing some pops and cracks, but nothing that shouted fire.

Connor was the first to notice. "The sphere has stopped bubbling. Is it supposed to stop?"

"Fuck! The oxygen infusion system has failed! We've five minutes to do a fifteen-minute extraction!" Mika yelled and started manually undoing valves, afraid the auto-open would either fail or take too long. He was working from gut instinct—challenging for any scientist to do. Peter was on the opposite side, mimicking everything Mika was doing. Mika shouted to him in German, speeding up Peter's responses.

Rick and Connor were scrubbing up and trying to avoid being in the way. The two young soldiers, on Connor's orders, were retrieving a small table and linens. Hands now sterile, Connor could only stand back and pray.

A wave of leviathan proportions going six hundred miles per hour sped toward the Antarctica continent and the men of Phoenix. As Mika had predicted, it hit Antarctica near McMurdo Bay, the ice sheet surrounding Antarctica, which ran in a two-hundred-mile radius along the continent, and grew to maximum thickness and distance from the coastline during winter, and would help buffer against the wave's impact.

Ivan and Cian were born five minutes before the tsunami hit Antarctica. Mika and Peter hastily suctioned the babies' airways while they rubbed and stimulated the twins to take their first breath outside their artificial womb and cry. Peter clamped both umbilical cords. Rick cut the cords as there was no time for the dads to do the traditional cutting—there was simply no time for tradition. He gave each boy their vitamin K shot before wrapping them up in their pre-warmed baby blankets. The boys were screaming their little lungs out.

Mika and Connor had seconds to hug and congratulate each other as they both admired their newborns. They were pink and healthy-looking, indicating they were getting enough oxygen.

"Apgar score of ten out of ten," Rick told the new proud fathers. Mika and Connor nodded a thank you. Each held a baby swaddled in their safe cocoon when the whole of Phoenix rumbled, and the ground underneath their feet trembled. Just like the day the earthquake first hit Phoenix, but this time the rumbling never ceased, it continued, and it grew louder. Finally, explosive cracking noises startled them all into action.

"Come, we need to get to the highest point. We have minutes before the worst hits us. That was the wave hitting the coast," Mika said as they ran for the tubes.

Halfway there, clutching a baby to his chest, Mika stopped dead in his tracks. "I have an idea! We should climb into one of Peter's fridges, the empty fridge. Peter, your office? The temperatures are regulated, and it's supplied with oxygen. If the valley floods, we would be safely sealed inside until it recedes. I can't think of a safer place for the babies to be. We can feed them, keep them warm, and wait the worst out. What do you say, Connor?"

"If you think it's safer for the twins, we should go. What do you say, Peter?"

"Excellent idea, let's go!" Peter yelled, turning in the opposite direction from the cave system.

As they started to run, Rick halted. "I'm not going. I want to find Brad. You go on without me."

The two guards looked at each other and nodded in the affirmative to each other. "It's decided, we'll accompany him. Come, Doctor. We'll escort you. We know these tunnels. Come, Doctor Longarrow, follow us!"

\*\*\*

Connor looked at Mika and nodded in agreement.

"Be safe, my friends!" He called after the three men who were darting into the underground caves. Once again, the building shook, and anything that wasn't tied down was rattling, bouncing, and crashing to the floor.

"Come this way," Mika yelled, pressing his thumb and forefinger protectively over the baby's ears. It looked like they were walking at a steep incline as the building was undulating, stretching to maximum capacity. Just as they entered the Cryonics Laboratory, the steel door behind them swooshed closed. That was the automatic door locking system sealing the pod, just as Tony had designed it to do.

All corridors and domes had activated the double sealed vacuum locks. A safety mechanism designed only to unlock when the pressure on both sides stabilized and the sensors didn't detect H20 or outside climate. *The safest place we can be is inside a walk-in freezer*, Mika confirmed to himself.

"Come, friends." Peter pointed at a nondescript door. "This one I use as an office and to sleep in."

The walk-in refrigerator used as a room and office wasn't big by most standards, about fifteen feet by fifteen feet, but adequate enough for a desk, a chair, and a small cot. "Sit there on the cot, make yourselves at home. Have you decided on names?" Peter asked in an attempt to lessen the angst in the air.

"Cian," Mika said, looking down at the baby he held. "We're naming the baby after Connor's grandfather."

Connor got the little glass bottles filled with lab-created milk for the twins' first feeding.

Peter proceeded to close the massive steel door manually; it closed with a whoosh, sealing them inside.

The office desk lamp gave enough light, so Mika, who sat next to Connor, was able to adoringly watch the two baby boys. Connor said, "This one is definitely Ivan. I think I'm deaf in my right ear. He hasn't stopped screaming for his brother." Connor handed one milk bottle to Mika, and the two boys fed hungrily as a sudden silence fell over Phoenix.

\*\*\*

In the cave system, Rick and the two guards ran as fast as they safely could. Rick had to stop a few times to catch his breath. "Come, Doctor. It's not far now. Just around the next turn," Fritz shouted. The rumbling was deafening; loud snaps and cracks were heard coming from no identifiable direction. It sounded as if the mountains were breaking apart and was going to crash down on them.

"How will we know if the water has reached us? I keep thinking the rumbling can't continue this long. Something else must be going on!" Rick yelled above the roar.

"Come, Doctor! This is not the time to stop and ask questions." Just as the lead soldier was rushing Rick, a massive piece of rock fell from the cavern roof. "Fuck, we're going to die here. Run, Doctor!" his guard repeated.

They ran. Rick didn't stop to look back. Suddenly all the tube lights went out. Leaving the men running blindly into the dark.

"Stop! We can't run if we can't see."

"Wait, what's that?" In the distance, small lights glittered. "I think that's Brad and some of the men. Brad!" Rick shouted. "Brad!"

"Wait, I can hear someone calling back!"

"Rick, stay there, we're coming!"

Rick was short of breath. Hands on his knees, he waited in place. "Come, baby, lead us out of the darkness," Rick urged, frantic with adrenalin pumping through his system. "Here, here we are." Rick waved to the little light growing bigger and brighter. When Brad and his men reached them, Rick fell into his arms near sobbing. Glad to have Brad in his arms, he felt immediately safe.

"Where's Malcolm?"

"Who?" Brad asked.

"Malcolm and Fritz volunteered to bring me to you. I don't know where we could have lost him," Rick told Brad and Fritz.

"We have to find him!" Brad ordered.

Three men stepped forward to search the darkness with Fritz. "We'll go back for him, sir. We have light." Fritz and the three volunteers sprinted in the direction they came from, with Brad and Rick on their heels.

"No! Malcolm! No!" The inhuman wailing from Fritz echoed through the tunnels, signaling that the search party had found Malcolm.

"Here! We found him!" they called, as Brad and Rick ran another thirty yards into the dark tunnel. Fritz held Malcolm, but his body lay at an odd, unnatural angle.

The young soldier gave heart-wrenching cries and repeated, "No, no, no," as he sat on his knees with his best friend and lover's body draped over him. "Malcolm, what's wrong? Are you okay?" he asked as he turned him over and cradled his head in his arms. "No!" Fritz cried, traumatized by the sight of his lover.

The men were horrified by what they saw. Where the left eye should have been was a mushy hole filled with minced brain matter and bone fragments. The right eye had a dilated pupil. It was stiff in his head, staring into nothingness, all glazed over. Obviously, Malcolm was dead. His hair was drenched with blood dripping from the empty eye socket. Fritz sobbed his lover's nickname. "Mally, Mally," he cried over and over but got no response. Rick did a quick A-B-C assessment, uselessly checking for vitals. Finally, he looked up to Brad and shook his head. Brad moved over, putting his arm around Fritz, who was crying hysterically for his Mally.

"Must have been a projectile rock," Brad said softly to Rick.

"Or something," Rick said as he pointed as inconspicuously as possible to the back of Malcolm's head showing Brad an exit wound.

"Let's carry him to the light so I can do a thorough assessment."

"Sorry about your friend, my boy, come," Brad said, as he started to help Fritz carry Malcolm.

"He was more than a friend, sir. Please let me carry him."

Brad honored his soldier's request and backed away. After gently laying him down on higher ground, Fritz had again taken him into his arms. He held and rocked his lover, softly crying over his body. The men respected his time of sorrow, giving him space and support. The sound of despair was chilling and hair-raising.

They were high above the dry valley of the Phoenix domes. As if waiting for a tsunami to strike wasn't enough stress and drama, someone was shooting at his men. Brad could do nothing but wait. Rick watched as the men gathered around him as if drawing strength from him. Brad stood at the highest point they could reach while men encircled him and clinging onto one another, hoping and waiting. It was not cold; in fact, the warm mist was stifling.

Just as the roaring had stopped, they waited for whatever might be next.

Some prayed to a god that never seemed to respond but somehow eased their minds. Others spoke about the eternal black void and what it would feel like but could not grasp the concept. Some took the opportunity to find a hidden cove where they could grope, fondle, or suck another man in the darkness, not giving a damn if their sounds carried to others.

After comforting the men and offering help, Rick joined his new family. Simon and Paul were sitting on each of Brad's sides huddled over him. Rick sat between his knees so Brad could envelop him with his arms. Most had their hands linked together. They spoke of new allegiances and happiness they'd found since coming to Phoenix. But always, their conversations drifted back to the men watching the twins, hopefully safe inside Peter's Cryonics lab. The baby boys had given them all hope for a future.

*** 

The water reached Phoenix, but at a snail's pace. As Mika predicted, it reached a height of three feet and then froze in place. Most of the damage was due to earthquakes and wind. Somehow, they were all but one spared. Phoenix's total number of residents was now precisely two thousand and one souls.

Several hours later, Rick had performed an autopsy on Malcolm, confirming he had died from traumatic brain injury due to an unidentified projectile, typical of a gunshot wound. Malcolm was cremated the next day, after a remembrance ceremony. Phoenix was moving back into normalcy. They'd ensured that the water supply had been inspected and officially declared safe for use. Not a single area of Phoenix had been breached by the water.

The twins were visited by so many, and so often, as new uncles popped in daily with gifts and good wishes. Connor decided to break through to the empty apartment next door to them, so the boys had a bigger room to entertain their many visitors.

Brad, Rick, Mika, Connor, and Bryan decided to keep the information about Malcolm's death quiet so Bryan could investigate the shooting. Brad had pulled security feeds after the electricity was restored so Lasitor the AI program could search for suspicious behavior or any abnormal human traffic patterns in the cave system. The shooter's identity could not be determined, but shadows of a group of men, periodically moving in and out of the building, had raised suspicion. Bryan and Brad refused to close the case and informed Fritz that it would remain open until more answers to their questions surfaced.

Brad's lottery system was working. Couples wanting children were spaced with a realistic time frame so Mika and Peter could keep up with the demand. They decided on two families a year. Research and training continued to be provided to ensure growth and keep up with the need by balancing population growth. It made sense because Peter's anti-aging gel capsule implants—referred to as Peter Pan Drops by the general population—were made available to the population of Phoenix. Mika had developed a theory that the gel could possibly slow aging to one year for every twenty.

Enthusiasm and motivation to continue progress were overwhelming as the men of Phoenix believed more than ever in their own capabilities, their leadership, and the promise of hope and a future to survive and overcome any disruption to their magnificent community.

The End.

To be continued in; The Brawl King: We Are Not Alone.

# About the Author

Kashel Char

I/We write under the pseudonym Kashel Char. It means Castle Black. Chosen for the apparent reason that we are a Game Of Thrones fan.

"I found it surprisingly beautiful. In a brutal, horribly uncomfortable sort of way." ——Tyrion Lannister to Janos Slynt.

I/We write MM Sci-Fi Fantasy Mashups and love bubblegumming that with fantasy, folklore, and conspiracy theories featuring hot, powerful godly men. Our stories are unpredictable, sickly twisted with a dash of humor, centered around gay characters. We have a wild imagination and love to write stories that leave you with lots of contemplation and questions. We hope to transport you to worlds and make you wish you could escape to these places peppered with taboo subjects and foul-mouthed heroes who struggle and strive to save humankind.

Love to all Creatures.

Kashel Char

Website: www.kashelchar.com

9 798223 423249